Fall From Grace

Matthew Munson

Inspired Quill Publishing

Published by Inspired Quill: October 2011

First Paperback Edition

Fall From Grace © 2010 by Matthew Munson

Contact the author through his website:

http://www.matthewmunson.co.uk

Chief Editor: Peter Stewart

Typeset in Bookman Old Style

ISBN: 978-1-908600-00-4

Printed in the United Kingdom
1 2 3 4 5 6 7 8 9 10

Inspired Quill Publishing, UK
Social Enterprise Reg. No. 7592847

http://www.inspired-quill.com

Dedication

Mum and Dad ... thanks for always believing in me.

Acknowledgements

I'm over the moon to have my debut novel published; it's a feeling that I doubt I'll ever be able to entirely articulate. Writing can be a solitary exercise, but that doesn't mean a book is entirely created by one person – so many people have given me their thoughts and friendship.

My book's dedicated to my parents, but they deserve another mention. Sorry to both of you for the teenage years, and thanks for not drowning me in the sea during those years! You are my role models.

Kathleen, Charles, Irene and Walter; even now, you inspire me and I think of you all every day.

Fellow writers have given me guidance and advice as I've gone through a number of drafts, as well as the practical side of actually getting my book *out there*. Lucy, David, James and Richard; you are amazing friends as well as authors I respect and admire more than you know.

Chelby and Kirk took me through the process of hypnosis, and also gave me constructive advice on an earlier draft of my book; thank you, my friends.

Lynda, Christina, Kay, Hannah and Tristan; I'm very fortunate to have you as my friends. You always inspire me, make me laugh, and help to engage my brain with debates and discussion. Just don't talk to Lynda about Latin, whatever you do.

Sara-Jayne Slack, the living embodiment of Inspired Quill! I'm so excited to be part of something new. With conversations that usually involve diversion into the realms of science-fiction geekdom, I hope our relationship is long and fruitful.

Peter Stewart – I couldn't have asked for a better editor. Thank you for the honest opinions that helped Fall From Grace to improve.

Lauren; I *knew* your name would be perfect for one of the characters!

I live in terror of missing anyone out – or running out of space – but to all my friends and family I have, and haven't, mentioned here, I can say only this; I value you all beyond words. Thank you for your love and support.

Fall From Grace

The Celestial Observatory: 2,015 Years Ago

He stood at one of the large arched windows, his shoulders tense with frustration. His eyes were staring blankly out over the star-flecked darkness of the cosmos and his mind, usually absorbed by the awe-inspiring sight of entire galactic discs, was elsewhere; he was distracted by the almighty row he had just had with his Father.

The ever-changing view of the galaxies swirling slowly past usually helped calm him after one of their arguments - but it failed today. This row had been more intense, and the bubbling, underlying resentment between them had seemed far closer to the surface. The stars weren't doing anything to disperse the bubbling anger he felt inside. His ire was too great; the argument with his Father was still fresh in his mind, scattering any other thoughts.

"Brother?"

He looked round and saw Gabriel walking towards him, a look of concern on his youthful features.

"Gabriel," he said softly – more softly than he had spoken with his Father. After all, it wasn't Gabriel's fault that his older brother and Father couldn't last more than five minutes without arguing. "You shouldn't be here.

Return to the Chamber. They'll think you're allying yourself with me."

He couldn't keep the cynicism out of his voice, and immediately regretted not trying harder. He'd always suspected that their parents preferred Gabriel over him; he had learnt to accept it a long time ago, but that didn't mean he couldn't occasionally find it irritating.

Gabriel had always been the peacemaker between his older brother and their Father, trying to stop their arguments before they started – or at least soften the edges when they did, inevitably, erupt. It didn't usually work, but to his credit, he always tried anyway.

"I don't care if they think that," Gabriel retorted. "You're my brother. Why should I not stand with you? I agree with everything you said."

His elder brother blinked in surprise at the passion in Gabriel's voice – a passion that he didn't often hear coming from his mild-mannered sibling. Gabriel usually kept his own counsel, because the last thing his family needed was someone else shouting in the Ruling Chamber. He knew, however, that Gabriel was old enough to make his own choices now.

Wasn't that what my Father and I were just arguing about? *He thought.* Choice?

"Just ... be careful," he cautioned. "I'm the thorn in our Father's side; there's no reason for you to be tarred with the same brush. You know what Father and I are like. We argue. It will pass, as it always does."

Gabriel nodded. "I won't disagree with you on the first point," he conceded, and gave a wan smile. "Your arguments seem to be getting more frequent, though. They're always about the same thing, that tiny planet. Is there anything you two can find common ground over?"

His brother hesitated. It was true, there had always been a lot of heat between him and his Father, and their arguments had been increasing. He knew why, as well; he was no longer afraid to stand up to his Father, as he once had been. In his darker moments, he wondered if this was always a good thing, or whether he was picking a fight simply because he could.

He also wondered if he cared about the answer; he knew he liked to argue just for the sake of it. Shaking his head, he smiled back at Gabriel.

"Not much." He sighed. "I ... I dislike Father being so obsessive."

Gabriel interrupted with a nod of his head, and neither needed to say any more on the subject – they understood each other. He nodded back, and sighed again. He'd had the argument; he didn't want to go over it again with his brother. Gabriel was purely here as peacemaker - as he always was.

"I wish there was something I could do," Gabriel said. "Metatron is fuming, as you can imagine. Michael is taking the brunt of it so you don't have to, I suspect."

His brother laughed. "Metatron is always fuming. I think the heavens would fold in on themselves if she ever found peace. As for Michael ..." He hesitated. "I admire how he stands up to her. I think he's the only one that ever does. I can see why my Father made him commander of his armies; if he's not afraid of Metatron, there's not much he can be afraid of." He raised an eyebrow. "I wonder how much trouble she'd give me if it wasn't for Michael"

Gabriel laughed in agreement. He and his older brother fell into companionable silence; staring out of the window and watching the heavens float by.

"I need to fly," he said after a while. "I ... I need to centre myself, and I can't do it here."

Gabriel nodded, and watched his older brother go. Just as he was about to leave, a thought occurred to him and he called out his brother's name.

"Lucifer!"

His brother turned.

"You're my brother, and I love you," Gabriel said. "But sometimes I wonder if you argue with Father because you enjoy it or because you're convinced you're right."

Lucifer stared at Gabriel for a moment, then turned and silently left the Observatory. He didn't reply because he wasn't sure which statement he agreed with more.

Paul's Flat, Broadstairs:
Monday

P aul groaned as his alarm clock began to buzz, loudly, in his ear.

He'd only gone to bed - what was it? Four hours ago? A quick glance at the LCD display confirmed the worst - 06:55, just four short, stupid hours after falling asleep. Even then, the sleep he'd had been fitful and restless.

This is torture, he thought.

He couldn't remember what he'd been dreaming about, but knew it had made his heart pump with adrenaline. He had dreams like that far too often, and he hated them. Despite the dream and his exhaustion, he knew that he had been rudely awoken to go to work. And he needed this job, so he *had* to get up. Absolutely *had* to.

A fist slammed down on the "OFF" button.

Just five more minutes, he thought. *That'll do. I'll feel alright after that.*

A second later, he was snoring again – and having *the dream,* the one that he had been having for as long as he could remember. It didn't make any more sense this time than it did any other time, but he was used to that by now: his subconscious mind accepted it and just let it happen.

He's standing in a giant, high-ceilinged chamber. The sense of vastness is awe-inspiring, and he knows, instinctively, that this is no ordinary chamber - it's the ultimate one, *the chamber that ranks above all others. This is the court of final appeal, which his father presides over in cool, dispassionate judgement: or* had *done, until* she *had begun exerting more and more influence over him, making his judgements erratic and unpredictable.*

He looks up at the throne in the middle of the dais, where his father will soon be sitting, listening to his son's appeal, as well as watching him closely, studying him – trying to understand him, as he had spent so long doing.

And failing miserably at it, *he thought with a sigh.*

He had tried doing the reverse – understanding his father – but he had failed in just the same way. They had never been able to articulate any sense of common ground, and seemed to do nothing but antagonise each other.

How have we never managed to get it right? *he wonders.*

He glances left and right, and sees his friends standing around him. He draws strength from their presence, knowing that they would stand by him as he spoke, believing in him and his words. That meant more to him than he could ever say.

He lets another sigh go as he realises that whatever he says here, the outcome will remain the same. Nothing will truly change. A sudden wave of despondency floods over him, and he looks down at the floor, wondering if this is the right way to confront the injustices of his world ... and the material one, whose destiny had become intertwined with theirs.

A hand is placed in his, and he looks to his left at his friend and sees the look of understanding in her eyes. She smiles and, suddenly, everything is good within the realm, just for that look. He smiles back, his resolve quickly restored.

A susurration of noise from the assembled host made him look forward - it was time. He swallows, takes a breath and steps forward –

- and Paul sat bolt upright, breathing heavily in surprise at the sudden change of surroundings. The dream had invaded his sleep again, and it was still a shock, even after all these years.

You'd think I'd be used to it, he thought. *But it catches me off-guard, every time.*

"Idiot," he muttered. He ran a hand through his ruffled, jet-black hair, and forced a laugh. "You're too bloody old to be scared by a dream."

He checked that he hadn't woken up his girlfriend – thankfully, she was still fast asleep – then turned his head to check the time on his hated alarm clock. It read 07:45.

"Shit!" he exclaimed.

He was going to be late for work. *Again.*

Throwing back his bedcovers, he ran to the bathroom, cursing his oversleeping, his work and his dream, in that order. He was about to curse his girlfriend as well, but that would have been more out of habit than anything – and he felt a pang of guilt for even considering it.

What the hell does she still see in me? he wondered, not for the first time. One day, he'd get round to asking her ... when he wasn't running late.

Royal Mail Sorting Office, Ramsgate: Monday

P aul walked briskly through the main gates as his watch beeped 8.30am. He paused for a moment and glanced around the yard for anyone who might get him into trouble. Only a few posties were around, mostly having a cigarette break before their next delivery. Most didn't pay any attention to him, and the ones that did either looked at their watches and smiled (this was Paul, after all) or looked at their watches and scowled (it wasn't the first time, after all).

Paul resumed his quick walk and had almost reached the doors that led to the depot when –

"Morning, Paul! Good night was it?"

Paul grimaced, turned his head and quickly waved, all without breaking his stride. Roger was stood across the yard, smiling his sickly smile and waving back at him.

Paul couldn't bear talking to the guy, so he disappeared quickly inside the depot and began up the stairs to the locker room. Roger was one of those people that just naturally rubbed people - alright, rubbed *Paul* - up the wrong way. There wasn't even anything he could pin it on; the man was irritating, and Paul avoided him at all costs.

Entering the locker room, he quickly stowed his coat and bag and turned toward the exit, hoping he could get down to work before he saw –

"George," he said with a guilty start. He stopped in his tracks, swallowed nervously, and gave a weak, "Hi."

"Morning, Paul."

George was leaning against the door frame with his arms folded across his chest - or, rather, rested on his oversized stomach. He had an air of weary resignation and his annoyance was plainly written across his face.

"I ... uh ... morning," Paul replied, rather pathetically. "How's it going? Did you have a good weekend?"

"Yes, I had a lovely weekend, thanks, Paul. I just saw Roger, and he said you were in. How was your weekend? Sleep well?"

Paul flushed. He didn't even consider lying, or thinking up an excuse - after all, what would be the point? He had never been renowned for his punctuality: he'd even been late for his mother's second wedding, which was atrocious considering she'd asked him to walk her down the aisle. Over the last couple of weeks, however, he'd been outdoing himself, not making it on time to *any* of his shifts.

He had always struggled with timekeeping; Paul couldn't entirely explain it – it was just the way his mind seemed to be wired. It had become progressively worse over the past two years. A lot of the time, it hadn't mattered – he had been travelling the world, and having had various temporary jobs, from pub work to office jobs and a hell of a lot in between, to fund his travel to the next destination. If an employer disliked his laissez-faire attitude, Paul had just moved on to a different job – or a different city.

Before his travelling, of course, he'd had a job he'd believed in and been passionate about, so had been able to overcome his weakness. Of course, he would never go back to that career now. *Never*.

Of course, in this job – one he never imagined himself doing - being late meant letting down George, who had been responsible for hiring him in the first place. Despite his CV in the last two years being rather on the ... long side, George had seen something in the younger man that he liked, and hired him as a permanent member of staff, greatly alleviating Paul's rather pressing money worries. None of this helped alleviate Paul's sudden guilt.

"George, I ..." he began, but trailed off. All the lines that ran through his head just sounded too ... rehearsed: which, of course, they were, as he had been going over them since leaping out of bed half an hour ago. He stared at the floor instead, deciding against any of them; they would have seemed trite.

"Paul, what's going on?" George asked with a sigh.

He stepped into the locker room, his eyes never leaving Paul's face. Paul couldn't bring himself to raise his own eyes back up and see the disappointment across his boss' face.

Part of the problem, Paul knew, was that he couldn't commit wholeheartedly to a job he just didn't care about beyond the monthly payment into his bank account. He needed something that made him feel *alive*.

He found himself thinking back to his recurring dream. It was as if he were actually there, with emotions that were more genuine there than in real life. He always felt so confident and self-assured in his dream that it put his actual life to shame. If only he could understand what it meant; even now, after all this time, it didn't make any sense. The only way he could describe it was that it felt like a snapshot of something taken out of context; if he knew what the snapshot was *of*, he might finally understand its meaning.

"Paul?"

George's voice brought Paul back sharply to the present, and he realised he hadn't given his boss an answer.

"I -" He struggled to find the words, and flushed as he did so. *I haven't exactly been very coherent so far, have I?* "I haven't been sleeping well lately."

He held his hands up to forestall George's retort, which he could see was coming, and looked him in the eye for the first time. He saw the anger then, and was almost taken aback: George was *never* angry, and it made Paul's insides churn with guilt to think that *he* was the one to change that.

Shifting awkwardly from one foot to the other, he continued; "It's not just that, George, I've ... I don't know, I've just been struggling with - just with life. I can't explain. I -"

He cut himself off as he realised how lame it sounded. "If our situations were reversed," he conceded, "I'd probably feel as hacked off as you're feeling now."

George suddenly broke eye contact and looked away at the wall, expelling a breath as he did so. Running a hand over his rapidly-balding head, he shook his head.

"'Hacked off' doesn't quite cover it. Disappointed and let down is probably nearer the mark. You've been here, what – two and a half months now?"

Paul nodded, afraid to say anymore. He watched as George began to pace up and down. He had never seen the older man so full of pent-up frustration before.

"And in all that time," George went on, "you have never shown the slightest willingness to put some effort in. The fact is I put my neck on the line for you. I thought I saw something in you. Instead ..."

"George, I -"

But George waved away Paul's next words. To be fair, Paul wasn't entirely sure himself what to say, so he was glad of the interruption. He wasn't, however, quite so glad after George's next statement;

"Sorry Paul, but I don't want to hear it. I've had enough. I'm letting you go. Clear out your locker and leave. Now."

Lucifer's Private Office:
2,010 Years Ago

L ucifer smiled as the door to his office slammed shut. He'd been expecting this visitor for the past few minutes.

"What in the name of all that is holy are you thinking?"

Lucifer turned calmly round to see Satan stood by the door, shaking with anger.

"Good morning, my friend," he said. "Your day is going well, I hope?"

"Don't you dare!" Satan snapped. "Don't you dare try and calm me down!"

Satan was waving a finger angrily in Lucifer's direction. Lucifer, for his part, deliberately ignored it, and instead looked beyond it at his friend's face, flushed with uncharacteristic anger.

"I have just spent the past half hour on the Chamber floor," Satan went on, "arguing your case before your Father, Metatron and half a dozen others. Metatron would be quite content to see your head rolling past their feet and out into the cosmos right now. If it hadn't been for Michael and me, I rather suspect it would be."

Lucifer raised an eyebrow and glanced again at Satan's still-pointing finger. To his credit, Satan cleared his throat and carefully lowered the digit. He began to pace up and down the office.

"What in heaven's name possessed you to challenge your Father's policy towards Earth on the floor of the Chamber? There are angels who disagree with it, of course, but there are ways of making your disagreement known, my friend ... and at the top of your voice in your Father's Chamber isn't it."

Lucifer shrugged in an attempt to mask his frustration; he'd thought that his friend would have supported his actions, given how close their opinions were.

"He needs to see that he can't have complete dominion over heaven and earth by continuing his autocratic rule."

"You just criticised your Father, the Almighty, on the Debating Floor! You've barely got any supporters, my friend, and how do you ever expect to get any when Metatron is glaring daggers at you and looking ready to strike you down at any minute? You need to learn that you can't be impetuous and thoughtless without there being consequences to your actions!"

"I think you've confused me with my brother," Lucifer said sharply.

"I don't think I have. Gabriel's grown up. What have you been done in the meantime?"

Anger welled up inside Lucifer. He and Satan had been friends, compatriots, for more centuries than he could count, and he didn't like being on the wrong end of his friend's tongue.

"Why are you so angry?" he snapped. "Do you wish that it had been you on the Floor, making the argument, instead of me?"

Satan blinked and looked hurt. Lucifer felt instantly terrible at speaking so rudely. His friend had, in reality, always been there for him; advising him, helping to refine *his arguments, as he imagined Michael was there for his Father. And yet, while Michael's cool, tempered advice had allowed the Almighty to be – for the most part - a magnanimous leader, Lucifer was still as hot-headed as ever; he often wished he knew how to be as level-headed as Michael or Satan.*

"Forgive me," he said, waving his thoughts off. "I didn't think."

"You never do, do you?" Satan quietly replied. "After all we've been through, you think I'm jealous? I'm not, Lucifer, in the least: I'm tired. I'm tired of constantly defending your thoughtless outbursts. Your father has become autocratic, yes, and we need to change this realm ... but not like this. We require allies. We won't secure them by appearing arrogant."

Lucifer chewed at his lip as he listened to his friend. He saw the logic in Satan's argument; he was right, of course. He was always right. He didn't have the hang-up of his Father being the Almighty, like Lucifer did, and so was far more grounded.

In return, Satan watched his friend's face as he became lost in thought, and wondered what he was thinking. Truth be told, Satan did envy Lucifer in a way; his dynamic nature was one that Satan didn't have. He was a thinker, a planner; he could argue, yes, and the Chamber floor held no fear for him, but he sometimes wished that he could be more like Lucifer and just act on his feelings.

Thoughtful and emotional, *he thought wryly.* I wonder if there's a middle ground we should be aiming for ... or do we take each other there anyway?

Lucifer and his Father had argued for so long that it had almost become traditional; Satan struggled to remember when they had ever been united on a subject.

Certainly never one as contentious as Earth, and an absurd desire to see the two realms united under a divine leadership.

The Almighty's eldest son loathed that idea, out of an instinctive desire to see free will mean *something somewhere. He felt that his own free will was minimal, trapped as he was under the weight of his Father's expectations; he didn't want that same lack of freedom to be felt by the mortals on Earth.*

"What would you do?" Lucifer asked his friend. "If you were me?"

Satan sighed. "I thank all the elements every day that I'm not *you, my friend."*

Lucifer laughed and after a moment, Satan joined in, immediately diffusing the tension between them.

"I'm sorry for my words," Lucifer said again. "They were thoughtless."

"Apology accepted," Satan replied. "In answer to your earlier question ... if you are serious, then you must start making alliances. Your Father is furious with you for arguing with him in the Ruling Chamber, and is sending Metatron down here, right now, to discipline you. Metatron can get away with it because her power is increasing by the day, and she has the support of the Almighty. Imagine-" Satan stopped as he saw the flash of inspiration in Lucifer's eyes.

"Yes," he said. "Imagine what I could do with angels standing behind me.*"*

Satan smiled. Perhaps there was *hope for his friend after all – and for me as well, he thought with a private smile.* Passion and logic united. Perhaps there's hope for both of us.

Christ Church University, Canterbury: Monday; Two Weeks Later

S he was in the antechamber, pacing the floor and scowling as if the room itself had somehow offended her. It was a cramped and airless space that had no chairs, no windows - no small comforts of any kind. Its austerity helped to remind visitors that they weren't there on a social visit.

Nerves began to flutter in her stomach, and she took a breath. Why was she feeling nervous? It had been her that had requested the meeting in the first place, to argue her case in front of the woman who was expanding her power base. It had made sense at the time, talking with Lucifer and Satan in the privacy of Lucifer's private office, to approach Metatron directly and try to reason with her. The Almighty took her advice, so gaining her sympathy had seemed crucial to their cause.

You've got nothing to feel nervous about, she chided herself.

That was the logical part of herself talking – the emotional part, however, couldn't suppress the nerves deep inside her. The person on the other side of that door had the ability to wrong-foot visitors almost from the start of any conversation, just by her attitude.

The door to the office opened, and she knew it was time. She exhaled, took a step forward and –

- Lauren blinked a couple of times. She shook away the light spots that had appeared before her eyes and sighed.

Another bloody fit, she thought in annoyance. *They're getting worse.*

She'd had the absence seizures for years now and, despite their increased frequency, had become used to them. They weren't *physical* seizures; instead, they involved her mentally "disappearing" for a few moments. To anyone who didn't realise, it would look as if she were daydreaming – instead, her brain was going off like a firecracker and she was having bizarre hallucinations that she only ever partly remembered.

At least I get over them quickly, she thought in relief.

She mentally shook away the last vestiges of the fit – which she had become expert in doing – and clicked open her emails. She laughed at the first one; it was from Dr Harrison, her GP, reminding her of her appointment this afternoon.

Perfect timing, Doc.

The fact that she'd been given an appointment so quickly meant that her test results were back, and the outcome wasn't that brilliant. If everything was normal, she'd probably have been slotted in sometime next week.

She glanced at her watch. It had just gone 8am, so she doubted that her supervisor, Dr Tempest, was in yet. After replying to the email, and forwarding it onto Tempest, she leaned back in her chair and rubbed her face, conscious of a sudden headache behind her right temple.

As a 24-year old, Lauren was the most junior psychotherapist on her team, but she was already being spoken of as a future leader in her field – hence already having her own office.

"It's a broom cupboard!" Lauren had protested to her mother; that fact hadn't stopped her mother from telling *everyone* that her daughter was important enough to get her own office.

Lauren laughed at the random memory, but quickly sobered as she glanced again at the email. She'd only agreed to the tests under duress; her brother had nagged at her until she had given in, just to shut him up. Now she wasn't sure she wanted to hear the answer.

She looked up as someone knocked on her door. Who would be visiting this early?

"Come in," she said.

The frown was replaced with a smile as Paul Finn opened the door.

"Paul!" she exclaimed. She stood and kissed him on the cheek. "Where have you been hiding yourself?"

"I could say the same about you," Paul replied with a grin.

He sat down in the chair opposite Lauren and put his feet up on the desk. Lauren gave him a withering glance, and he quickly pulled a face and put them on the floor.

"*I* haven't been hiding myself anyway," she said. "I'm still in the same place, which is more than I could say for you. Has job hunting really taken up *all* of your time?"

Instead of answering her question, Paul picked up the name plate that was on her desk - an affectation picked up by the university's vice-chancellor during a visit to America.

"Lauren Crabtree-Tempur," Paul read out. "Nice calligraphy, but they haven't left room to put your PhD on there. I'd speak to Human Resources ... or your union. Hey, do psychologists have a union?"

Louse snatched it out of his hand and placed it back on her desk.

"Displacement activities," she said. "They're very common when people want to avoid talking about a subject."

"Don't try psychoanalysing me, Mrs Crabtree-Tempur," Paul laughed. "I want to get out of here without having to pay you for therapy."

She smiled at him and rolled her eyes, in much the same way that a mother would do with a recalcitrant child. "So you've lost the post office job?" she said. "I assume it was your timekeeping again?"

Paul shifted awkwardly. "Yeah," he replied, then added rhetorically, "I wonder who told you that?"

Lauren didn't reply – she didn't need to – and Paul carried on; "It wasn't what I wanted to do, anyway. At least this gives me the chance to try something new."

"So what are you doing now?"

"Uh ..." Paul finally looked up and caught her eye. "Temping," he said. "Admin. At Lloyd's bank, right here in Canterbury. It's my first day today, actually."

"Ah. Of course. Just what you've always wanted to do."

"Hey, don't knock it," Paul retorted. "It's a job that pays the rent. Until I ..."

"Figure out what you want to do," Lauren finished for him. She sighed and raised a querying eyebrow.

Paul sighed. "Yeah, whatever," he replied. "I'm not going down that road with you this early in the morning."

Lauren frowned. "You never do," she challenged. "Perhaps we should, one day. Talk about what exactly you do want. Do you know?"

Paul stopped. Lauren had never openly confronted him about his apparent inability to discover a new career path before, and he found it slightly discomforting. Shrugging, he said, "I don't know. But I'll know it when I see it."

He found himself fixed with a steely glare, as if Lauren suspected him of lying, which he wasn't: he genuinely didn't know what he wanted; ever since he had left a job he'd once thought he'd do forever. Paul had drifted across three continents and who-knows-how-many time zones in the two years since, running away from the shame and embarrassment, and hoping that along the way, he would find something that gave him the same drive, the same ambition.

He hadn't.

Paul was frustrated with himself, because it was more than just a vague feeling, this conviction that he would find something. He had always had a nagging itch at the back of his brain, trying to attract his attention and convince him of his purpose, but he could never quite ... grasp it. He knew it was important, he just couldn't say *why*.

He never told anyone about the feeling, not even Joseph or Lauren, because he knew they would look at him as if he was crazy. Instead, he kept it to himself and hoped that he would figure it out before it drove him mad.

Paul decided to change the subject. He leaned forward and –

- caught the ruffle of a wing, the flutter of wind against his face, and a sudden, gnawing anger –

"Paul?"

And it was gone.

He blinked a couple of times, tried to get it back, but it wouldn't come - instead, it drifted away, like a mist on the wind.

"Paul?"

He turned and looked at Lauren. She seemed concerned – but also had a smile on her face, as if she wasn't entirely sure this wasn't an elaborate practical joke.

"You were away with the fairies there," she said. "You okay?"

"Nothing," he said, then forced a smile onto his face and a tone of jollity into his voice. "Sorry, I was just ... Sorry, ignore me."

Lauren raised her eyebrows, but said nothing. She clearly didn't believe him, and was likely to pursue it if he gave her half a chance.

"Anyway," Paul went on, desperate to change the subject, "I just wondered if you wanted to meet for lunch today? So I can make it up to you, as I haven't been around much these last couple of weeks."

Lauren shook her head regretfully. "Sorry Paul. I wish I could, but I've got a doctor's appointment at two."

Paul suddenly felt guilty; the tests had completely slipped his mind. When he had first seen Lauren have a seizure many years before, he had freaked out. He felt a brotherly affection towards the woman, and even now, he always tried to keep an eye on her, even though she was probably more in control of her life than he was of his.

"Want me to come with you?" he asked. "I can easily blow off work for the afternoon."

Lauren shook her head. "No!" she exclaimed. "Paul, you need to keep this job, at least for a while. I'll be okay, honestly. Now, sod off to work."

Paul thought about protesting, but caught the look in his friend's eyes, and decided against it. He gave in with good grace, kissed her on her cheek and left her to work.

As he walked through the campus towards the exit, he found himself still worrying about Lauren. Her epilepsy had never been overly serious, and always been controllable by medication. However, ever since she had been married and widowed in the space of 18 months, the seizures had increased, now occurring every two or three days.

Lauren had refused to see doctors about it in the past, assuming it was just stress-related. Paul and Joseph had never been convinced, thinking there was something deeper to it, but she would never listen to them. Thankfully, when she began working for the university, she had agreed to undergo tests and write about it as part of her final thesis.

Paul was glad: he had seen her go through the slow death of her husband as well as put up with these fits, and he was relieved she would soon get an answer. The fact that it was so quick had to be a good sign, he was sure of it.

Lauren and Paul had known each other since secondary school, where he had first befriended her brother, Joseph. Because she was younger – by two years – their parents would often make Joseph look after her, and so she would resentfully hang around them. After a while, she came to enjoy it, and saw them both as friends, and so did they – although Joseph wouldn't always admit it at the time. It wasn't the done thing, spending time with your younger sister.

However, when her brother and Paul left school, Lauren would socialise with them because she wanted to. Joseph lost his self-consciousness, and they found they actually enjoyed each other's company. As a result, she got to know Paul, and was glad of that – and they now enjoyed a firm friendship.

Almost without realising it, Paul had walked into the city centre. He paused and glanced up; suddenly conscious that he was stood by the magnificent Cathedral. Paul peered in through the gates, up at the awe-inspiring building. He had always admired its design; it was a truly breathtaking construction. In the past he had found a spiritual comfort in it – now, however, he admired it for purely architectural reasons.

Shaking his head, Paul laughed quietly to himself. How could all of that be only two years ago?

It feels like a lifetime.

Despite that, he knew it would define him for the rest of his life.

Ramsgate:
Monday Evening

"So, this new job of yours, mate. Is it everything you hoped it would be?"

Paul gave his best friend his most withering stare and took the glass of wine from him. Joseph sniggered and sat down.

"Yes, Joseph, it's perfect," he replied, sarcasm dripping from every word. "In fact, I'm already hoping for a promotion. There's a job coming up as a senior data input assistant. It could be a good start on the career ladder."

"Yeah, I'll bet," Joseph Tempur said with a smirk.

Paul laughed, and so did Joseph. Their long friendship – they had been known as the "Terrible Twins" at school, as they were inseparable – meant that they could get away with teasing one other mercilessly.

Joseph put his cider on the table. He and Paul were at their regular haunt, the Belgium Bar. They had been coming to the pub since before they were legally allowed to; they had a fondness for it for different reasons. Joseph found the bar staff were, more often than not, attractive enough for him to stare at all evening, and

Paul loved the wine; he considered himself a connoisseur of alcohol.

"Paul, Paul, Paul," Joseph said in the big brotherly tone he often found himself adopting around his friend. "What are we going to do about you?"

"First off," Paul retorted, wagging a warning finger, "you are precisely five months older than me, so I don't know where you're getting that tone from. Secondly, what do you mean 'we'? Since when did you want to get more involved in my career plan?"

Joseph shrugged. "I don't," he replied, a resigned tone pervading his voice. "I'm just … annoyed with you. Mate, it's been two years, and you haven't done anything with your life since you threw away the collar, except travel to different countries and get a succession of dead-end jobs."

"They weren't all dead-end," Paul half-heartedly protested. He was stung by his friend's words, but couldn't dispute them.

Joseph looked at him witheringly; Paul didn't meet his gaze, and his friend sighed.

"I just wish you'd *do* something with your life," Joseph went on. "You're intelligent enough to do anything you put your mind to."

"I am putting my mind to something!"

"You're a temp at Lloyds! Before that, you were a sorting clerk for the Post Office. Where's the success in that? Sure, it suits some people … but not you."

Paul snorted a laugh, took a sip of wine, and then turned back to the view. In the summer, on sunny evenings like this one, they often took to sitting outside and watching the world go by. Paul found himself engrossed by the ships in the harbour for a moment, before becoming aware of an intense silence to his right.

He looked, and saw Joseph still looking at him with a frown on his face.

"Paul, seriously," Joseph said, "what's going on? You've always been laid back, that's just you, but ... you don't seem to care any more."

Paul was surprised: he had thought his friend had been semi-joking, but the look on Joseph's face told him otherwise. It surprised him because Joseph had never confronted him before about his lack of drive. He'd sometimes sensed his friend's disappointment, but they'd never actually discussed it. Now, all of a sudden, he could hear the anger in Joseph's voice.

"Joseph, what the hell -?" Paul said, but it was a fairly weak retort. In truth, he knew all this; in the back of his mind, he felt the same way.

Joseph, in turn, had to admit that he hadn't intended to confront Paul quite so directly, but the words had tumbled out before he realised the strength of them. Now they were said, he knew he had to stand by them.

"I just ..." Joseph ran his fingers through his hair, taking the chance to think about what he wanted to say. "I remember when you had ambition ... and you *cared*. In the last two years, you've accomplished what? You made the choice to leave the church, but you haven't done anything since to make me think that was the right decision."

Paul felt a sudden rush of anger.

"Are you suggesting that *I'm* to blame as well as Kerry?" he said hotly.

Joseph shrugged. "Did she force you to have sex with her?"

"I -" Paul spluttered over his words, unable to think of a single clever reply.

"I'll accept that you were young and naive," Joseph said. "You were raised a Catholic, for god's sakes. That's enough to mess up anyone's sexual experiences. But you've got to accept responsibility for what happened. You felt ashamed for breaking up a marriage and your own vows, so you walked away – and you've been walking ever since. You had a *choice*, Paul – you could have stayed, if you had felt strongly enough about it. But you didn't ... I just don't think you've found anything since to match up to that."

"I had to leave," Paul mumbled. "I *had* to. The bishop was against me, Father John and I had that blazing row –"

"And yet you *still* could have stayed," Joseph interrupted. "You could have fought. But you'd lost your conviction; that was just your excuse to leave."

Paul suddenly felt his eyes well up, and he rubbed them with the back of his hand, feeling stupid. Deep in his heart, he couldn't disagree. His friend had said what a part of him had been thinking for a long time.

Joseph released a breath, trying to diffuse the sudden tension.

"I'm sorry, Paul," he said. "You're my best friend, and you've always been there for me. I'd hate myself if I wasn't there for you as well. You're meant for great things, even if you can't see it."

For a moment, they sat in a silence which suddenly felt a lot more companionable. Joseph placed a comforting hand on his friend's shoulder: Paul gripped it for a moment and then took a deep breath.

"I was so scared when I quit," he confessed. "But she ... she was everything I wasn't. Focussed, liberated ... experienced. I was so ... flattered by the attention."

"Most men would be."

Paul caught Joseph's eye and they both smiled. Joseph had come out as gay years ago, and his interest in woman could be written on the back of a postage stamp.

"When Father John found out, I was ..." Paul cleared his throat. "Well, stubborn, I guess. But then, why shouldn't I have been?"

Joseph sat back in his chair and lifted his head to take in the evening's last few rays of sunlight. "In the same circumstance, who knows – maybe Father John would have done something similar."

Paul laughed. "I couldn't ever imagine Father John being young."

"Up until two minutes ago, I couldn't imagine you ever talking about this."

Joseph let Paul think about that for a couple of minutes, then opened his eyes and used a hand to shield them from the sun.

Unconsciously echoing his sister, he pointed a finger at Paul and said, "Okay, so all that crap's happened, and you've made your choice ... for better or for worse. But you've spent the last two years skirting the issues. You need to start looking at your life and deciding what you actually want from it."

Paul heard the challenge in his friend's voice and felt a sudden, intense desire to step up and accept it. He thought back over his life so far – his faith, his shattered desire to serve God, and an unfocussed and aimless two years – and he wondered he *did* want.

And then he knew. "I want to feel alive again."

"You want to go back to the church?"

Paul shook his head. "No," he said. "No way. They rejected me when I made a stupid mistake. When I -"

He looked down at his now-empty glass, embarrassed.

"What?" Joseph asked, curious.

"When I needed them. They were my family, like you and Lauren, after my parents died. Then they went and turned their backs on me. That ... that hurt."

Joseph was silent for a moment. Paul often found it difficult to talk about his emotions and didn't want to break the spell. He felt honoured that he had been included in the family circle; Paul was like a brother to him.

"If not the church, then what?"

"I ... I don't know," he confessed. "The answer's out there, I just need to find it. I'll tell you one thing though."

"What?"

"I'm not going for the senior data input assistant job."

Joseph laughed. "Good man. I'll get another round in."

In the Other Realm, Michael watched the men.

"You've found courage," he whispered. "I knew you would, one day. Your friends would always push you in the right direction."

He shifted on the stone seat, and wondered how long it would take before the fireworks began.

Paul walked home that night. He often liked to do that in the summer, because it was a nice view along the clifftops. Today, though, he did it because he wanted to think.

He needed to find out what it was he wanted to do; see what that nagging itch was at the back of his brain. There was something out there for him, he knew it.

His girlfriend, Marie, was asleep by the time he got home, and Paul was secretly glad. They hadn't been getting on well lately, and seemed to argue every time they spoke. They'd met in Cambodia, about a year into

Paul's journey, and gave each other a form of emotional support: both were damaged goods. Since they returned to the UK three months ago, they had stayed together, thinking that they were destined to be that way or, at the very least, because they couldn't be bothered to think of anywhere else to be.

Lately, they had fallen into a trap of constantly bating each other with stupid comments, bickering, making up, then starting all over again. Marie especially seemed to be bouncing off the walls of their shared flat, as if constrained by them. It was clear, at least to Paul, that she was missing the nomadic lifestyle that they had lived, whereas Paul was glad to settle.

With an abruptness that surprised him, he got hit by a wave of exhaustion, and collapsed into bed without even undressing; then dreamt of wings, fighting ... and flying.

St Mary's Church:
Two Years Earlier

"**P**aul!"
Paul quickened his pace, his shoes clacking staccato on the floor.

Click click click click.

"Paul! Stay and talk to me!"

Click click click click.

"What's there to say, John?" Paul shot back. "We've both said enough!"

"Come on, Paul, don't be stupid!"

Click –

Paul turned on his heels, calm suddenly diffusing the anger as he looked at Father John who was stood at the altar.

"What did you just say?" he said in a whisper that still managed to reverberate down the entire transept.

Father John stepped down and walked towards Paul.

"Paul," he said in a softer tone, "this is absurd. I'm sorry I reacted the way I did. Come into my office and we'll talk."

Paul paused for a moment as his mind raced. They had both said some stupid things in the past fifteen minutes, after Kerry had left the church in tears. He should have gone after her, he knew, but wanted to stay and argue his point with Father John, the man who had walked in on them.

"No," he said. "Contact the bishop if you want, but I know what he'll say."

Father John stopped, still a distance from Paul, and watched as a small piece of white, crumpled cardboard fell to the floor.

Click click click click.

St Mary's Church: Tuesday

A dam Wild, Verger of St Mary's Church, looked out over the pews. It was 7.45am and Wild felt calm, although he knew that wouldn't last forever. He always savoured this time of day, before Father Simon arrived. It was as if the church was his, and he could fantasise that he was in charge.

He shook his head and laughed. "Humility is a virtue, Adam," he reminded himself.

Pushing his daydreams away, he stepped down from the pulpit. He had about half an hour before Simon arrived - just enough time to have a cup of tea, read the morning paper, then –

"Adam?"

Inwardly, Wild sighed. The church was, of course, open - it was open from the moment a member of the local clergy or the lay team arrived, but it was incredibly rare for anyone to come in at this time of day. He put on a smile and turned: and then the smile became a genuine one.

"Paul!" he yelled.

An overjoyed laugh escaped his lips. He was in a jog before he knew it, practically running down the main aisle. Paul was laughing, too: at Wild's reaction and the spontaneous joy on his face. It was flattering to see that someone was still pleased to see him here. They embraced, Wild heartily slapping Paul on the back.

"Good to see you, old friend," Paul said - and he meant it.

It had been two years since he had seen anyone who was connected with the church, and he suddenly realised how much he'd missed Adam, who'd been a true friend to him for years.

Wild released Paul from the embrace, but still held Paul's arms firmly; it was almost if he didn't believe his friend was really there. He laughed as he realised what he was doing, and then let go.

"Come on," the verger said, "let's go into the office."

A couple of minutes later, Paul gratefully accepted the offer of tea and sipped from the mug. His dreams the previous night had included half-forgotten memories of his time in the church. It was as if his brain had gone into overdrive after his conversation with Joseph yesterday, so caffeine in any form was very welcome.

He'd woken up at 6.30 and gone for a walk to clear his head, but returned to his flat with as many questions as he'd left with. To top it off, Marie had already left for work, leaving behind a note saying, 'We need to talk. Tonight.'

That's not good, he thought.

He realised afterwards that he didn't feel very worried about what the note could mean.

Sounds like I've already made my mind up, he thought.

He didn't know whether that was bad or not.

In truth, he didn't know why he was here, especially as he hadn't set foot inside the church for two years. But now he knew he wanted to find a purpose in life, he had reasoned that he might as well start in the last place he'd had that same feeling.

Or am I just looking for some sort of closure? he wondered.

Wild sat down next to him on a small two-seater couch that had been crammed into the room. Kicking off his shoes, he folded his feet up under himself.

"So," he said, "what's been going on? Found your new calling yet?"

Paul snorted, and his friend winced.

"Sorry," he said, "I didn't mean that as harsh as it sounded."

"It's alright," Paul replied with a shrug. "I deserved it."

Wild smiled, but didn't quite make eye contact. There was only a year and a half between the two men; they shared a similar sense of humour and a devout nature – or had done once.

Things had certainly changed since then.

"No," Paul replied, "I haven't found my place yet, although I'm still looking."

Wild looked down into his tea mug.

"So do you still see ... *her*?" he asked. There was a forced note of casualness in his voice that didn't quite convince Paul.

"You mean Kerry?"

Wild nodded, still not looking at him.

Paul shifted in his seat, feeling slightly awkward. As close as he and Wild had been over the years, they were straying into territory that they'd never had the opportunity – or, more likely, the inclination – to discuss. Paul's departure had been so abrupt that they hadn't even said a proper goodbye.

"No," he replied slowly, "no, I don't. She refused to see me again after ..." He cleared his throat. "After Father John found us. She felt humiliated, and I don't blame her." He shrugged. "I felt humiliated too, but then it's always worse for a woman, isn't it?"

"I'm a Catholic priest, remember."

Paul flushed with embarrassment. "Sorry," he muttered.

Wild continued staring intently at his friend. "You just ... went, Paul. You disappeared, and you didn't even say goodbye."

Ah, Paul realised. *I think I see where we're going with this. And I don't blame him.*

"I know," he replied, "and you have every right to be angry with me. But -"

Wild looked surprised.

"I'm not angry, not anymore," he said. "I was in the beginning. I thought you'd just abandoned everything we'd worked for in order to ... what's the word? Scratch an itch? I think I'm more confused now than anything."

He gave Paul a piercing glare. "You always had more faith than me. You were more - well, passionate. And that's what I respected about you ... then you just chucked it away for *her*."

Paul set down his mug, trying to suppress a bolt of anger. "She had a name, Adam, and she wasn't just some random *itch*. She -"

He stopped himself and took a breath. The feelings had sprung up almost from nowhere; talking to Adam was bringing it all back. All the anger and the shame welled up inside his chest.

"I thought I loved her," he said quietly. "She opened my eyes ... and I saw that there was so much in the world beyond this stupid, hypocritical church. Then ..."

He drew a breath and then slowly released it, but it did very little to calm him. "Then Father John found out, and it turns out she didn't feel anything near as much toward me as I did toward her. Because she could just walk away from me. But I couldn't come back, not after that. Not ... when Father John and I said all those stupid, *stupid* things to each other. I started to *hate* the church – just when I needed it the most, it turned its back on me."

Adam had reacted better to the insult against his church better than Paul had expected, and he was grateful for that – he genuinely hadn't come here to start an argument.

"How about now?" Adam asked. "Do you still hate the church?"

Paul shook his head. Abruptly, he stood up and grabbed his coat.

"This was a mistake," he said. "I shouldn't have come back."

"Paul, wait."

Paul's hand was on the door handle, but he didn't turn it. He glanced back, and saw Adam was standing too.

"I shouldn't have come," Paul said again. "I don't even know why I did."

"Because you wanted answers," Wild replied.

Paul laughed - more to himself than anything, as Wild had unwittingly hit the nail on the head. "Answers to what, though?"

Wild shrugged. "Life," he replied. "Like everyone does. But you want to know if your life has got meaning any more, and so you started your journey in the last place you ever felt that you had that meaning."

Paul smiled, fleetingly. "Since when did you become so old and wise?"

Wild shrugged, but didn't return the smile. "You don't have to be old to be wise. And if our situations were reversed, I know that's what I'd want to do about now." A thought suddenly struck him. "Come with me, I want to show you something."

Wild led Paul down the length of the church to a small anteroom near the main entrance. The room itself was like a cupboard, cut out of the wall, and contained three lockers, a bike and just enough room for two people to step into.

Grinning with infectious humour, Wild spread his arms to encompass the tiny room.

"Welcome to my office," he said. "I'm the only one who uses it now since you and Rick left."

"You're still cycling in?" Paul asked incredulously, pointing to the worn-out bike. "I can't believe you do that all the way from Minster."

"Don't knock it, mate - means I'll always be fitter than you."

Paul rolled his eyes; he couldn't disagree. Adam had always been a fitness fanatic, while Paul's idea of hard exercise was lifting the remote control. Curiosity got the better of him. "What was it you were going to show me?"

Opening his locker, Wild pulled a photo off the inside of the door and handed it to Paul.

"Oh my ..." he gasped.

There were four people in the picture. It had been taken just outside the main doors, in the church gardens, on a bright and sunny day. Father John Goodman, who had been parish priest at St Mary's when Paul joined - and left - was standing in the centre.

Around him were his three junior priests – Paul and Wild being two of them.

"That was taken three years ago," Wild said, smiling as he saw nostalgia race across Paul's face, "about ten months after the three of us took holy orders, and just after Father John made you assistant priest."

"I remember," Paul whispered. "I remember this being taken, but I'd forgotten all about it."

He, Adam and Rick - the third trainee priest in the picture - had been through ecumenical training together. They had been fortunate enough to be assigned to the same diocese and been placed under the tutelage of John Goodman, who lived up to his name by being a genuinely decent and kind man.

Paul's eyes were drawn to Father John, the man who had made Paul his assistant and had been almost a father figure in his eyes - until they had fallen out. He swallowed, not wanting to remember that painful memory. He'd respected Father John a great deal and their argument would never change that, even though they had both been stubborn enough to not want to make the first move towards reconciliation. He looked up as he felt a hand on his shoulder. Adam was smiling at him.

"I knew you'd want to see it," he said.

Paul nodded. "Thank you."

Paul needed some air after the flood of memories that had come back to taunt him, so excused himself and stepped outside into the warm morning air. He looked up towards the bright sunlight, savouring the moment.

He heard the solid, timber doors closing behind him with a powerful *slam*: Wild walked up beside him but remained tactfully quiet.

"I came back for Father John's funeral," Paul said quietly.

"I know. I saw you."

Paul blinked in surprise; he turned round to face his friend.

"You saw me?" he said in surprise. "I thought you'd have chucked me out."

Wild shrugged. He didn't meet his friend's eyes; instead, he was looking out over the church grounds.

"Why would I chuck you out? I knew how much you thought of Father John, and how much he thought of you. Despite how you both left it." He finally looked at his friend. "Before you say anything, I know it was both of you being as stubborn as each other. Neither one of you wanted to be the first one to apologise."

Paul opened his mouth to argue, but stopped himself. He had admitted it to himself just a minute or so ago, so knew it was indefensible.

"I flew out again the next day, back to New Zealand. But there was no way I was going to miss it."

His brief visit home, however, had been the beginning of the end for his travelling. Although Paul had only been home for twenty six hours, it had been enough to remind him that there were things for him here. He only went back to New Zealand to convince his girlfriend to join him.

Half of me wishes I hadn't bothered now.

"Anyway," Wild went on, "Father John always held the door open for you, even after you left. It wouldn't have been right to shut you out at his funeral."

"What?" Paul said. His eyebrows knitted together in a frown. "Father John would have had me back? After everything that happened?" He laughed. "I don't think so. You didn't hear the argument."

Wild shook his head. "Father John would have had you back like a shot. He left the assistant priest position vacant, even though he knew Rick was desperate for the promotion. He thought you might rediscover your faith and come back to us."

Paul shuddered. "Don't, Adam. Just don't."

"You didn't answer my question earlier, you know."

"What question?"

Wild raised an eyebrow. "Do you *still* hate the church?"

Paul didn't answer straight away, but gave the question some thought: Adam was a good enough friend to warrant that.

"I can never forgive it," he finally replied. "I ... was confused and didn't think about the consequences. I needed help, and instead I was made to feel wrong. I lost the woman I loved and the only job that's ever given me meaning. The bishop came round to see me after he found out, and asked if I wanted to renounce my sins."

He rubbed his forehead. "Hate is a strong word ... but I do hate what it did to me. It's left me confused, and I know that I can't ever go back to it."

Wild didn't answer: there was nothing he could say - and both of them knew it. Paul walked a little, down the path towards the crematorium, and Wild followed.

"Rick was pretty pissed off when I got promoted over him, wasn't he?" Paul said, more for the change of subject than anything else.

Wild gave a snort of laughter. "Yeah, you could say that. I always wondered about him, you know. I always considered him a friend, but he had huge personal ambitions for someone who wanted to serve God."

"Isn't that kind of the point?" Paul mused.

Wild shrugged, obviously not convinced, but didn't say anything; he clearly didn't want to get into an argument over it.

"Still ..." Paul went on, "I see your point. He must have been *doubly* pissed off when John passed him over a second time, still for me."

"Yeah. It's why he left, in the end."

Paul sat down on a bench, which was shaded from the sun by some large trees. Wild sat down next to him, and they sat in companionable silence for a few moments.

"I miss those days, sometimes," Paul confessed. "I miss ... the simplicity of the life. The structure of our days."

Wild laughed. "If you remember our days as being simple, my friend, then you really *have* forgotten the job. There's far more to it than just order and structure."

Paul sighed. "Yeah, perhaps you're right." A thought suddenly occurred to him. "Do you ever wonder what you'd be doing right now, if you weren't in the priesthood?"

"No," said Wild without hesitation. "I never wonder. Because this is what I want to be doing. I couldn't ever imagine doing anything else."

Paul nodded. "Not the answer I was hoping for, to be honest."

They exchanged a glance and laughed.

"I should be going," Paul went on, and stood. "I need to get to work."

He realised that he was still holding his friend's photo and went to hand it back, but Wild waved it off.

"Keep it," he said. "It might bring back some more happy memories."

Paul and smiled his gratitude. He looked down at the photo again, and frowned. "Whatever happened to Rick? Did he stay in touch?"

"No," Wild said, shaking his head as he, too, stood up from the bench. "He left before Father John's funeral - didn't even come back for that. He left a note for me, pinned to my locker, saying that St Mary's wasn't right for him anymore ... that the church wasn't right for him, and he needed to find his place in the world. Sounded familiar, but I can't think why ..."

Paul laughed, and punched him in the arm. "Shut up." He paused again, then carried on; "He and I never really saw eye to eye on ... well, virtually anything, did we?"

"No," Wild replied soberly.

"I'm surprised," Paul said. "Rick, leaving the church? He was always so ... so committed, even more so than you. No offence."

"None taken. I can't take offence at the truth, can I? I wish I could tell you more, but he vanished off the face of the earth. I tried to find him, but didn't have any joy." He sighed. "And then there was one."

Paul shook his head; he'd come here to try and get some answers, but it hadn't worked. He was flattered that Father John had continued to think well of him. He just wished he had overcome his stubbornness and made amends while he had still had the chance. He said as much to Wild, who frowned.

"Hindsight's a wonderful thing," the verger said. "Don't let it torment you. He was incredibly fond of you. If you're going to take anything away with you, take that. You've got enough to be thinking about without going on a guilt trip as well."

Paul hugged Wild tightly and thanked him for the photo.

"That's what friends are for," he said, then added, "Don't be a stranger, Paul."

"I won't, Adam. You have my word."

Lauren Crabtree-Tempur's Home: Tuesday

L auren had wept all of yesterday afternoon, and woke up that morning feeling as if her emotions had been pushed through a wringer.

She was sitting in her flat, in the window seat that gave her a beautiful view over the river and park. On a normal day, when she had no other plans, she would be in the park reading a book and watching the world go by.

Today, however, wasn't a normal day, and she had no inclination to leave her flat. For one, it felt as if her head was stuffed with cotton wool. Her eyes were red and puffy; she had no make-up on and had ignored the phone when it rang.

Inside her brain, a tumour was eating away.

Even now, she could still see the look on her doctor's face as he had given her the news; it was a combination of guilt and sadness. Dr Harrison had been her GP for over a decade and had seen her through a lot of trauma.

She had suffered with fits since puberty hit at twelve and had learnt to live with them. James, the man who would eventually become her husband, had known all about them from the start, and still loved her – making her feel almost normal.

Then, after five years together, and one year of marriage, she lost him. He had died from a horrendously painful cancer that had moved swiftly throughout his body ... and she had watched it kill him.

It had taken her a long time, but she had begun to feel ... if not fully normal again, then at least on an even keel. Her job and her family were giving her huge amounts of self-worth, and she was beginning to enjoy life again.

Then Dr Harrison had unleashed his news, and she felt as if she had taken five steps backwards.

It was a different sort of tumour than her husband's; hers was far more localised, for one thing. She didn't even know if it was benign or not - or if it was definitely the cause of her seizures or completely unrelated, although she suspected that there was a connection. She had had so many questions running round her head, it felt fit to explode.

One thing she was desperate to know was if this tumour was also responsible for the visions she experienced whenever she had an absence seizure - visions of tall-ceilinged rooms, with hosts of people, looking down in judgement upon her. There were also visions of flying, of wings - and of war. She just wished she knew what the hell they meant.

She jumped as the entry buzzer gave its low-pitched alert. She checked her watch; 12.30pm. She wasn't expecting anyone all day. Deciding to ignore it, she leaned back in her chair and looked out the window again.

The buzzer then went a second time – and a third.

"For God's sakes," she muttered.

Her mind raced as she picked up the intercom phone; she couldn't think of a decent excuse.

"It's me."

Just hearing her brother's voice made her feel a tiny bit better. A small smile creased her face as she said, "Shouldn't you be at work, big brother?"

"The beauty of being a freelance journalist," he replied. *"Come on, let me in."*

She pressed the release button door and headed into the kitchen to compose herself. Joseph bounded up the stairs and let himself in with his spare key. He quickly found his sister in the kitchen; she was facing the sink and he couldn't see her face.

"Why didn't you answer your phone earlier?"

Lauren didn't reply: her brother frowned in confusion. "Sis?"

She turned round and Joseph saw the tears falling from her eyes. He stepped forward and she allowed herself to be swallowed up into his unquestioning arms.

Five minutes later, they were sat on one of the sofas in the front room, Lauren lying with her head on her brother's lap. She felt embarrassed at having cried again, after having spent so long yesterday sobbing from the shock, but was glad it was only her brother that had seen her.

"Sis?"

"Yeah?"

"How big is it? This ... thing?"

"You can say it, Joe, it's okay. The tumour."

Joseph winced. He'd hated using that word when James suffered from it, believing - stupidly, he knew - that by giving it a name, people were giving it legitimacy. He had refused to use the word then and, he decided, he would refuse to use it now.

"The *thing*," he repeated with more emphasis. "How big is it?"

Lauren shrugged and pushed herself up. She pulled her legs up under her and folded her arms around her stomach, as if to defend herself from the invisible attacker.

"About the size of a walnut," she said, in a quiet voice. "They reckon it might be the cause of my seizures, but that it was too small to notice before. I'm going in next week for a biopsy, to see if it's ..." She trailed off, unable to finish the sentence.

"Yeah," Joseph said in grim agreement.

Lauren had a sudden desire to change the subject. "Did you and Paul go out last night?"

Joseph nodded. "Course we did," he replied. "Otherwise the world might implode."

Lauren laughed. For Joseph, that sound alone made the self-deprecation worthwhile. He and Paul had gone out every Monday evening for as long as he could remember. It was sacrosanct - only utter emergencies ever got in the way of their Monday Evening Drinks.

"Mind you," he said, his smile fading, "I did have a bit of a go at Paul."

Lauren raised her eyebrows. "Really?" she said. "Wow. Why did you have a ... No, wait, let me guess. Did you finally tell him what you really thought about his career choices?"

Joseph nodded. He hated giving his sister the satisfaction of being right, even in her current situation. Lauren had told her brother on several occasions that he should confront Paul over his lack of ambition.

"What happened?" Lauren asked. "What was so different about yesterday that made you suddenly decide to say something?"

Joseph shrugged. "Dunno," he said.

This earned him a smack in the arm from his sister.

"That hurt!"

"Tough. Now *tell* me what happened."

"I don't -" Joseph caught his sister's eye. "Sorry. I was just getting tired of hearing him talking about each new job as if it was going to be *the* job, when it was one dead-end job after another."

"Joe, that's *good*," she conceded.

Lauren was fond of Paul; they had very differing views, but he was like a second brother to her. Resolving to call him in the morning, she found her thoughts suddenly – and without warning - being drawn back to the ... thing in her head.

Tumour, she thought to herself. *Stop turning into your brother.*

She shuddered at the mere thought.

Joseph saw the change in his sister's face, leaned forward, and kissed her forehead. "I can take the afternoon off if you want," he said.

Lauren thought about it for a moment, then shook her head.

"No thanks. I'll be okay."

She appreciated him offering, but knew that he had a couple of deadlines brewing. Besides, she was sure now that there was literally nothing inside of her to cry out.

"Okay," her brother said reluctantly. "In that case, you can walk me back to the office."

Lauren frowned. "Joe, look at me. I'm a wreck. I'm not leaving the flat."

Joseph looked at her, and shrugged. Sure, her eyes were red, and she was wearing old, baggy clothes, but she looked otherwise okay to him. He didn't pretend to be an expert on matters pertaining to his sister's level of attractiveness, but she seemed alright. He checked his watch distractedly.

"Come on, sis," he said, "it'll do you good to get out for a bit. You can't just sit around here all afternoon. A bit of fresh air will do you good."

"No, Joe, I don't really feel like it."

"I'll give you some money to buy yourself a top."

"Get my red shoes. They're in the cupboard over there. I need five minutes to put some eyeliner on."

Paul's Flat:
Tuesday Evening

"I'm home!"

"I'm in the lounge!"

Paul closed the front door to his flat and chucked his keys down on the small table. It was black and iron-wrought, with elephant heads and trunks for legs - and went with nothing else in his flat. He wasn't bothered; he'd inherited it from an aunt and had an instant, eccentric liking to it. That, and Marie hated it - for some stupid reason, that made Paul want it even more.

Is this what we're reduced to? he thought. *Bickering over furniture?*

The flat itself wasn't a large one - certainly smaller than the ones Joseph and Lauren lived in - but it had served Paul well in the past two years. A place to sleep, eat and watch TV - that was all he needed.

Part of him wanted to put off the talk with Marie, but he couldn't think of a good enough reason. Work had been crappy; it was as mundane and boring as he had expected from the life of a temporary data input assistant.

He had spent a large portion of the day with nostalgic memories flooding over him, both happy and sad. He remembered the joy at being ordained, his happiness whenever he presided over a wedding or baptism. He could still feel the sadness when he gave the last rites to a dying man, or oversaw a funeral, but took comfort from the fact that he was doing God's work.

When he had left the church, he had felt as if he had been stripped of all that – that the church he had trusted to be strong was in fact the opposite; it was weak and unable to accept that its members were only human. It was demanding too much from him, and he had walked away.

Stepping into the living room, he saw Marie sitting in the recliner, waiting for him. She didn't rise to greet him, just offered a tired smile. He returned the smile, and sat opposite her, on the sofa.

"You okay?" he asked.

For the first time in a while, he noticed how tired she looked. Marie opened her mouth, hesitated, and closed it again. Paul chuckled.

"Bit of a loaded question, I guess," he said.

"Yeah," she replied in a whisper. She didn't even smile, let alone laugh at Paul's attempt to lighten the moment.

Paul sighed; this clearly wasn't to go well. "You wanted to talk?"

He cringed at how that had come out: truth be told, he did as well, he just wasn't as good at it as she was.

Damnit, he thought. *Wish I'd got Joseph's advice last night.*

He felt a stab of guilt when he realised that he hadn't actually thought about Marie at all last night. *Did she spend any time thinking about me?*

"Yeah ..." Marie said, giving him an unfathomable look. "I need you to tell me something."

"What?"

"Do you love me?"

Paul opened and closed his mouth for a moment. He certainly hadn't expected Marie to be so ... blunt.

Shows how much thought I've been giving this, he grimly thought. *How stupid am I?*

"I ..." he began, then trailed off as his mind went blank – as if it had suddenly switched off, unable to process the question.

What do *I feel?* he thought, knowing that she deserved an honest answer – more honest that he'd been with her for some time.

They'd had an instant connection when they met in that out-of-the-way Westener's bar in Cambodia. They had ended up talking all night. Paul had been out of the priesthood for a year and he found her intoxicating.

Suddenly, a flash hit him: he couldn't actually remember a time when they had ever sat down and discussed moving in together. It had just been an assumption they returned to the UK. It just seemed to happen, and that pretty much indicated the state of their entire relationship - things "just happened."

But I don't want things to "just happen" anymore, he realised. *I need to take my life back. I've been letting it coast for too long. I need to* do *something with it.*

"I don't know," he said.

He hated himself for saying it, but knew he needed to carry on, before he lost the courage altogether. "I don't know whether or not I want to make this work."

Marie surprised him - he had expected a deeper, more ... hurt reaction. Instead, she barely flinched. She nodded, almost as if she understood ... and perhaps felt the same way.

"Okay," she said, her voice no more than a whisper. "Okay."

Paul watched her carefully. "Do you love *me*?"

There was silence in the room for a moment, then Marie chuckled. "I don't know anymore. I ... I alternate between thinking you're wonderful and an annoying idiot. I don't know if there's a reason for that either – I think we just grate on each other."

Paul couldn't argue with that. "Probably a shorter conversation than either of us were expecting, huh?" he said.

The corners of Marie's mouth creased up for a second, but it couldn't charitably be called a smile. "Something like that."

She stood. "I'll ... I think I'll go and stay with my sister."

Marie hesitated, as if expecting him to speak up, but he didn't know what he could say. He couldn't look her in the eye as he came to a realisation - he *didn't* love her anymore. It didn't come as a crashing truth from on high – it was just what he had felt for a while, and now knew how to express.

"Kerry, I -"

He stopped, realising what he had said. He looked up at Marie, and saw a tear fall down her cheek. He looked away, feeling ashamed, and didn't stop her as she headed for the bedroom. He didn't stop the tears falling down his own cheeks either.

When Paul needed to think, he walked. It didn't always give him a solution, but at least it helped him sort out his head.

On this occasion, he just wanted to get out of the flat while Marie packed her stuff. Any thinking would just be an optional extra.

He *did* like her. She was witty and clever. She worked in local government, always had interesting things to talk about, and enjoyed her job. However, after the initial 'honeymoon' period, she and Paul had just lost the ability to talk and enjoy each others' company. Instead, they had just ... existed, moving from one day to the next, like a metaphor for the last two years of Paul's life.

He hadn't realised how much Kerry still weighed on his mind. To call your current girlfriend by a previous ... liaison's name was unforgivable, which was why he hadn't even tried to apologise for it.

Some things are way beyond an apology.

Paul had followed his holy orders to the letter, including the one prohibiting him from sexual relations. Adam had, too, and didn't seem overly concerned by the prohibition. Rick, the third member of their unofficial triumvirate, had always been the most rebellious out of the three of them, and had refused to obey that regulation – and the church seemed happy to turn a blind eye.

Which was why it had been even more galling for Paul when he'd had his own ... dalliance and the church had, in his eyes, cast him out.

He cut through Pierremont Park, wanting to get back home and sleep the rest of this stupid evening away.

Paul would never forget the shame he felt at being found out, and at not going after Kerry ... and for the angry exchange between him and John. That hadn't been necessary. He could never forgive the Bishop, though, who had made an unannounced visit to Paul's house the day after, and told Paul how disgusted he had been at the assistant priest's actions.

Where's the compassion? Paul had thought. *Where's the church's infamous forgiveness when I need it?*

The final straw had been when Kerry had written him a letter, telling him that she was going back to her husband and never wanted to see him again.

The crushing sorrow inside him had been too much, and he had run away.

He got back to his flat just after eight, having walked solidly for an hour, to find it empty. There was no note; Marie was just gone.

What to do next was the big question floating round his head; now that he and Marie were as good as finished, he needed to focus on his mind on what *was* working in his life.

Not much, he thought. *Except my friends. I don't know where I'd be without them.*

A thought suddenly occurred to him; a name that sent his mind off in a new direction.

Rick.

That was something he could do – try and track down his old friend. Perhaps he could help Paul come to terms with his past. After all, Rick had managed to reconcile his human desires with his religious beliefs for quite some time before leaving, unlike Paul. If anyone was going to be able to guide him, Rick could.

The Celestial Observatory: Present Day

G abriel entered the Celestial Observatory quietly and respectfully, as befitted such an important place.

It never ceased to fill him with joy when he walked into the Observatory: partly because of the sheer beauty and size of it, but mostly because it meant that he could make sure They were safe.

They were represented on both all the walls by small screens depicting each of Them going about their lives, unaware that They were being monitored, catalogued and processed, to ensure nothing untoward occurred. The images were overseen by a small circle of appointees, who ensured that any issues could be quickly reported. Thankfully, there never had been a problem – but it always paid to be careful.

Gabriel looked further into the Observatory, and saw today's observer sat on one of the stone benches, his eyes closed as if in meditation.

"Michael."

The older angel opened his eyes and smiled as he saw his friend.

"Gabriel," he replied. "Come, sit with me."

In his private moments, Gabriel still found it strange that Michael treated him as an equal, given their... chequered past. From Michael's days as the Almighty's chief-of-staff, to the present when he lived out his enforced retirement as Chief Observer of Them, and the Civil War that had split those two periods in two, they had somehow managed to come together in a most unexpected friendship. Gabriel had even been able to forgive Michael.

"Who are you watching today?" Gabriel asked as he sat down.

Michael pointed to the giant arched window in front of him. "See for yourself," he replied.

The image magnified and split into three segments, each showing a sleeping form.

"What are their names again?" Gabriel asked.

"Paul, Joseph and Lauren," Michael replied, pointing them out as he said their names. "They change so often, it's difficult to keep track."

"From our point of view, they change," Gabriel replied. "To them, this is the only life they'll ever have. Metatron made sure of that."

"I played my part in that," Michael added quietly. "We can't put the entire blame on her. It was my suggestion that led to this."

"Because you had to!" Gabriel protested. "You found a compromise, to keep them alive. If it wasn't for you, Metatron would have killed them. She's still frightened of you, even now."

"You should be more careful, my friend," Michael cautioned. "Such talk could be seen as seditious."

Gabriel swallowed. "She won't do anything, not with you around. You'll protect me, I know it."

Michael hesitated, then nodded.

"I was thinking of the Almighty as well," he admitted. "He can hear anything, no matter how quietly it's spoken."

"I know," said Gabriel. "But does he care?"

Michael couldn't answer that one. He sighed, and turned back to the screens, lost in thought. He sometimes envied Them their freedom, although he doubted they would ever see it in the same way.

St Mary's Church:
Wednesday Morning

A dam skidded to a halt outside St Mary's, his bike kicking up the gravel as the brakes forced him to a sudden stop. He was embarrassed to admit, even to himself, that he had overslept. He had spent the evening looking over old photos from his days at the seminary and completely lost track of time. It had been two in the morning before he had finally gone to bed – and forgot to set his alarm.

He wheeled his bike into the locker room and paused for a moment to catch his breath. He pulled a picture out of his backpack and looked at it again, causing him to smile; he'd brought it in to replace the picture he had given Paul.

One weekend when they'd been given some time off, the three trainees had decided to go camping. They found a deserted and wild corner of the New Forest that was perfect; a return to nature. It was near a river, there was a canopy of trees allowing dappled sunlight to speckle through and there were no human disturbances to make it artificial.

They had spent the first evening sat round a campfire; telling jokes, swapping stories - just talking. The following morning, they awoke to find a Scout group pitching up in the clearing. Even Rick had laughed at the irony of the supposedly "deserted" spot.

The picture Adam had in his hand was of him, Rick and Paul with the Scout Leader and some of the scouts, taken by Rick's camera on a timer.

As it turned out, they'd still had a good weekend - helping with fishing, making firewood, things that the Scouts had wanted to learn. As much as the three of them hadn't wanted to admit it at the time, they'd still enjoyed it.

For Adam, it just showed that God moved in mysterious ways.

I wonder what Paul and Rick would make of it now, he speculated.

With a final glance at the picture, he put his collar on over his black shirt, closed his locker, and left his 'office.'

Paul approached St Mary's Church for the second time in two days.

Bloody hell, he thought. *I avoid this place for two years and now I can't stay away.*

The surge of nerves he'd felt at coming back here told him that he was still right in thinking his life lay away from the church. However, he knew he had to come back today; he wanted to find Rick, and this was the best place to start his search.

As he approached the nave doors he paused and looked out over the grounds. A wave of memories suddenly flooded over him; there was where he had performed his first burial, there was where he had once carried a de-consecration so that the police could exhume a body. Right here was where the groom had been physically sick with pre-wedding nerves, and the bride had walked in ten minutes late, cool as a cucumber.

"Memories everywhere," he muttered. "Can't bloody escape them."

He then felt guilty for swearing on consecrated ground, and had to stop himself from bending at the knee to ask forgiveness. It was an automatic reflex had never left him.

Paul sighed. He turned his back on the past and pushed open the doors. The first thing he noticed was the sound of running feet. It wasn't entirely unknown to run inside a church, but people usually had more decorum.

Stepping inside, his eyes tracked the sound to a source - a man, dressed head-to-foot in red and black, with a blue balaclava, running towards the doors at the back of the church.

He was about to shout something out, but something made him stop; almost like a sense of self-preservation.

Why's he wearing a balaclava in this weather?

The man reached the back doors and yanked them open. Paul moved forward, to try and track the man's movements, but he had already gone out of view.

"What was that about?" he muttered.

Then, as he turned to face the altar, something caught his eye. His knees gave way as he saw the footprints. It wasn't the footprints themselves that bothered him, it was the fact that they were in blood.

Paul stumbled back, his mind reeling in shock. He knew it was blood, he just knew it. When he was seventeen, he had been visiting friends in London and witnessed a stabbing in Hyde Park. The blood had been everywhere - on the man, on the concrete path, on Paul, who had tried to staunch the wound. It was a physical effort to stop himself shaking.

"Hello?" he said weakly. Clearing his throat, he tried again, stronger this time, "Hello, who's there?"

Finding that his legs had regained their strength, Paul moved forward, careful not to step on the fresh footprints. He followed them up the pews, approaching the altar. Paul was afraid to consider what was at the other end of them, but he wanted - no, he *needed* - to know.

The footprints turned left after the very end pew, and Paul swallowed hard before looking. His knees finally gave way, and he found himself doing the kneeling action that he had resisted not five minutes before.

"Oh, no," he gasped. "Please, please, *no.*"

There were two bodies, crumpled on the floor. One, an older man in his mid-forties, Paul didn't know. But the other one he recognised instantly - it was Adam, lying in a pool of blood.

QEQM Hospital:
Wednesday Morning

"Paul? What the hell's going on?"

Paul looked up from his untouched coffee and felt a wave of relief as he saw Joseph and Lauren. He stood and hugged them both, but didn't trust himself to speak.

The three sat down round the table; Lauren peered closely at her friend. He looked tired and drawn, and she instinctively reached out and squeezed his hand. Paul gave her a wan smile and squeezed back.

They were in the hospital's restaurant; Paul had gone there to get five minutes' peace after a flurry of ambulances, police cars and wailing sirens. He was glad that Joseph and Lauren were there to give him a semblance of normality.

"What happened, mate?" Joseph asked. "You weren't making much sense on the phone."

Lauren stared at her brother. "His friend's just been attacked and left for dead," she said incredulously, "and you don't think he wasn't making much sense on the phone?"

Joseph ignored his sister and nodded encouragingly at his friend. Paul hesitated, then started talking. He worked backwards, first relating the story of how he had discovered the bodies at the church, and had planned to stop there – but, before he knew it, he was spilling it all out; his first visit to the church, his split with Marie, everything.

He eventually stopped, and there was a thoughtful silence around the Formica-topped table. Paul looked from one face to the other, and laughed.

"I don't know what's more amazing," Lauren said thoughtfully. "The fact that you found Adam and Father Simon so quickly after it happened, or that you were inside a church and didn't burst into flames."

Joseph looked round at his sister in shock. Suddenly, he saw the funny side, and sniggered before he could control himself. Paul looked up and a snigger erupted from him as well. Suddenly, all three were trying desperately to stop themselves from laughing any harder. They covered their mouths and averted their gaze.

Paul's laughter died away; suddenly feeling guilty, he swallowed a mouthful of the tepid coffee, flinched at the terrible taste and pushed the cup away. Joseph became serious and he rested his elbows on the table.

"How's Adam?" he asked.

Paul rubbed his face as a sudden wave of tiredness flooded over him.

"Critical," he replied. "They said Father Simon didn't stand a chance, but Adam's still fighting."

"What caused the wounds?"

"A knife." Paul shook his head; he'd been tormenting himself with the images since the doctor had told him about it. "Father Simon was attacked first, according to the police forensics guys; something to do with the pattern of blood and how it leaked out onto the floor."

Joseph and Lauren remained quiet; there was nothing to say.

"Adam must have heard something," Paul went on, "and interrupted the attacker. The surgeons are operating on -"

Paul stopped talking, and lowered his head. Lauren held onto his hand as he sobbed.

Ten minutes later, Detective Sergeant Kirby walked up to the table and asked to speak to Paul alone. Joseph and Lauren protested, but Kirby was quietly insistent. Reluctantly, the Tempur siblings left the table, assuring Paul that they would only be across the room.

"Thank you for speaking with me," said Kirby. He pulled and notebook and pen out of his breast pocket and set them carefully on the table. If he had seen Paul's red eyes and tear-stained tissues – donated by Lauren – then he didn't let on.

Paul shrugged. "I figured you'd need to at some point."

"Did you know Father Simon?"

"No. I worked under his predecessor, Father John. Er, John Goodman, that is."

"That's right," Kirby said, "you were a priest at St Mary's once, weren't you?"

"Assistant priest," Paul corrected him. "I was confirmed in my holy orders, but never became a full priest. How's Adam doing?"

"He's still in surgery," Kirby said distractedly. "The surgeons haven't told me anything."

He blinked, as if he realised he was being rude. Folding up his notebook and putting it away in his jacket pocket, he made a promise to check in with the nurses.

"You two were good friends," he went on.

It was more a statement of fact than a question, but Paul found himself nodding anyway.

"Yes," he replied. "We did our training together."

"Yet you didn't stay in touch with him after you left the church?"

Paul shook his head. "No, I -" he began, then frowned. "How did you know that?"

Kirby was nonplussed at being caught out. "Mr Wild keeps a diary. We found it at the church, in his locker. It detailed your meeting yesterday."

"What the hell are you doing reading Adam's diary?" Paul could hear his voice rising, but he didn't give a damn – his anger had flared and he wasn't inclined to suppress it. "What possible reason could you have for invading his privacy?"

A flash of annoyance flashed across Kirby's placid features.

"Because he was attacked and left for dead by an unknown assailant, Mr Finn, and we need to find out who did it. Diaries often give experts a clue as to leads."

Paul quickly checked his own anger and took a deep breath. Leaning back in his hard, plastic chair, he took another sip of coffee - and winced when he realised it was now stone cold ... and foul.

"You're right, Detective. I ... apologise."

Kirby shook his head. "No apology necessary, Father. This is a trying time for you."

"Call me Paul," he said with a laugh. "I haven't been 'Father' in two years."

"Would you like another coffee?" Kirby asked, the softer tone back in his own voice.

"Thank you, but no," Paul replied. "I wouldn't drink that one either."

"At least you're honest." Kirby hesitated, then went on; "Look, how about I come back later? When I know more about Adam?"

"That might be better," Paul conceded. "I'm more on edge than I realised."

"Mind if I ask you one thing, though?"

"Sure."

"Do you know of anyone who might want Adam dead?"

"Adam?" Paul snorted. "Detective, no-one could want Adam dead. He was a decent, honourable human being."

"You're wrong about one thing."

Paul frowned. "What?"

"Someone could want Adam dead; even if it was to stop him talking about Father Simon's murder. There's at least one person who's going to want to get to him, if he pulls through."

With that, Kirby walked away.

Paul felt an icy grip take hold of his heart; it terrified him to think that anyone would want to harm his friend. He looked round at Joseph and Lauren - then cried out in sudden, overwhelming pain and collapsed to the floor.

The Celestial Observatory:
Present Day

P aul was lost – and confused.

The sharp, stabbing pain in his head had vanished; he was no longer in the hospital restaurant. Instead, he was in a large, domed room where two figures were sat, side-by-side, on a stone bench, looking at a moving wall.

As Paul focussed, he realised what the images on the wall were; people.

"My god," he muttered.

They were people, all of them - and there was a thousand, possibly tens of thousands of screens. He gaped at the enormity of what he was seeing - he couldn't begin take in the sheer magnitude of it all.

What is going on? he thought. *Am I hallucinating? All these people are being watched.*

He looked to the two men sat on the stone bench. They were facing away from him, watching one of the giant walls of images. They were utterly engrossed, and Paul wondered for a moment how they could possibly decipher what they were looking at. They hadn't seemed to notice him at all.

Paul's brain suddenly caught up with his eyes. He blinked hard – and then again, but it still didn't change what he was seeing. They each had -

"You!"

One of the observers, shock evident on his face, was now looking directly at him. The other, a fraction slower, now turned, and his reaction was identical. As they stepped forward, the first one asked, "How did you get here?"

"What do you mean?" Paul replied, feeling as if he was about three paces behind the conversation. "The last thing I remember was being in the cafeteria. I passed out, I think, and now I'm here." He looked round. "Where am I? Am I still in the hospital?"

"Michael," said the second observer, placing a lightly restraining hand on the first one's arm. "He could just be here accidentally."

"He shouldn't be here at all," Michael said. "If Metatron discovers him here, we'll be blamed, regardless of how it happened. I'm sending him back where he belongs. He's safer on Earth."

"No, Michael, we could ask -"

Before the observer could finish his sentence, Michael raised his free arm and pointed it at Paul. The observer's eyes widened and, as Paul felt a sudden jerk in his stomach, he pushed Michael's hand off-centre. The drag in Paul's stomach went sideways for a moment, then –

Everything was white, pure white, with no depth or shadow to define anything.

What the hell? he thought.

Not quite, said a voice.

He shook his head, twice. The voice had appeared directly inside his head, as if it hadn't travelled the intervening distance and entered through his ears.

Turning, he saw the source of the voice ... and frowned. A ... person of indeterminate gender stood there. Not androgynous exactly, just - otherworldly, different. If he had to close his eyes and then been asked to describe the person, he very much doubted he would be able to. A luminescence emanated from the being, and he felt strangely unworthy.

A sudden anger bubbled up inside him. How dare anyone make him feel inferior? No-one could rightly claim to be better than anyone else.

Wrong again, the being said, a faint tone of amusement tingeing its voice. *We are all, in some way, inferior to him, if no-one else.*

Paul was confused, but finally found his voice.

"Who?" he asked. "Who are we inferior to?"

The person smiled a sad smile, but didn't reply.

"Who?" Paul persisted.

The figure pointed: Paul turned his head to follow –

QEQM Hospital:
Wednesday Morning

−**a** nd he woke up with a gasp, pushing himself up on the bed.

"What -" he said, but stopped as he felt a hand rest on his shoulder.

Paul turned and gripped the hand tightly, desperate to hold onto something real before the scene shifted again. His eyes focused on a young woman dressed in nurse's blues, who had a mixture of amusement and concern on her face.

"Glad to have you back with us, Mr Finn," she said, a South African twang accenting her voice. "You had us worried."

"Worried?" Paul repeated. He paused, but his brain just didn't seem to be assimilating the information, so he repeated his initial enquiry; "What?"

He then realised that he was still holding onto the nurse's hand, and quickly let go just as his cheeks flushed red.

"I don't know even know your name," he said with a stupid smile spreading across his face.

The nurse laughed. "It's Christina. Now, just lie back, Mr Finn. You're going to be fine, but I just want to take your blood pressure."

Paul's brain had slowly started catching up with the events of the real world.

"What just happened?" he asked. "One minute I was in the cafeteria, the next, I was -"

He hesitated. Where *had* he been? It felt like a dream, but one where he had felt awake and tingling with an energy he had never experienced before.

"You passed out," Christina said. "It's probably the stress of everything you've been through. You've been unconscious for about fifteen minutes."

"That's impossible."

Paul pushed his bed covers off him, and was pleased to see that he was still in his clothes.

"Mr Finn, stay where you are, please," Christina said. "I need to take your blood pressure."

"No, I need to ... er, I don't know, I need to find my friends."

Paul spun his legs off the edge of the bed, resolutely ignoring Christina's firm and instant hand on his shoulder.

"Your friends are fine," Christina said. "They've just gone to get a drink. Just wait -"

She increased the pressure on his shoulder, but he resisted. He pushed against Christina's hand until she sighed and released him.

"Fine," she said. "Up you get then."

"Thank you," Paul said with relief.

He placed his feet on the floor, pushed off the bed ... and began to sway.

"Whoa."

Colour spots suddenly started to appear before his eyes and his knees began to buckle. Christina laughed, and caught him as he started to collapse. She gently navigated him back to the bed. As soon as Paul was settled, she set up the blood pressure machine.

"Your BP's low," she said. "Hence you need to listen to your nurse's advice."

She was looking intently at the reading and had the faintest trace of a smirk on her mouth.

"From now on, I will listen to whatever the nurse says, without question," Paul replied.

He smiled as she glanced at him. She smiled back, then flushed slightly and began putting away the machinery.

Paul realised he was staring, and stopped. She was attractive, he couldn't deny it - auburn hair held up by a clip, a stunning smile ... and the nurse's uniform certainly didn't hurt.

He swallowed. Two years ago, he would never, ever have thought like this; it just wouldn't have been in his nature. He had been too committed to the priesthood for anything to get in the way of his work.

Then Kerry had come along and changed all that. She had been the first woman to turn his head, but certainly had not been the last. After leaving the clergy, but before meeting Marie, he had been something of a ... user. He hated himself every time he thought about it; his wild days, where he had been unleashed on an unsuspecting female population. Now, whenever he found a woman attractive, he found himself drawn back to those few months and he shivered in shame.

He realised the silence between him and Christina had become slightly uncomfortable, so quickly found something to break the tension.

"Sorry I didn't listen to you before, Christina. I'm stubborn at the best of times."

"Wow, you *do* surprise me."

Paul laughed. "When do you reckon I'll be able to leave?"

Christina shrugged. "I'm not sure," she admitted, "although I doubt it'll be too long. The doctor will want your blood pressure to go up slightly, and they may just want to run a few minor tests." She smiled reassuringly. "It's just a reaction to everything you've been through in the last few hours – it's completely understandable."

"Thank you."

"I'll be back in a little while, Mr Finn," she said. "Make sure you drink something."

Nodding to Joseph and Lauren, who had arrived by Paul's bedside, she left for the nurse's station.

"Bloody hell, mate," Joseph said, sitting on the end of the bed, "you need to stop scaring me like that. I'll have a heart attack soon."

Lauren laughed. "You won't have far to go if you do."

Walking round to the bedside table, she poured out some water into a cup, and offered it to Paul. He waved it away, and began to say something to Joseph … but realised Lauren's hand hadn't moved. He looked back up at her, and saw a glint in her eye that told him he shouldn't argue. Meekly, he sipped from the cup. Lauren went and sat in the visitor's chair, not saying a word. Joseph started laughing, but quickly turned it into a cough after a glare from Paul.

"What's the latest with Adam?" Paul asked.

He pretended not to notice the look Joseph and Lauren exchanged, and took another sip of water. His stomach churned as he thought again about what he had found that morning - the blood, the angle of Father Simon's limbs ... Adam, his friend, lying there.

It was Joseph who answered. "He's still critical. He was stabbed twice - one in the neck, missing the jugular by inches. He was then stabbed in the chest, and the blade nicked his left lung. He's been in surgery all morning."

"But he's out now?"

"Yeah," Joseph replied, "but he's in intensive care. I'm sorry, mate, but he's only got a thirty percent chance of pulling through."

It had taken another twenty minutes before Christina and the doctor had allowed him to get up - and Paul hadn't argued once. When he'd had his blood pressure checked for what felt like the twentieth time, he got out of bed, relished the feeling of *not* having a head rush, and walked up and down the ward twice to prove to Christina that he could do it without fainting.

He left Joseph and Lauren in the restaurant and followed the signs to the ICU. As he was walking, he found himself thinking back to the dream. It had felt so *real*. It had been like he knew that place, as if he had been there before. But that wasn't possible.

Was it?

He arrived at ICU and hesitated ... there was a long corridor of rooms, and he had no idea where Adam would be.

Much easier to get directions, he thought.

It ended up taking him five minutes to find a nurse who, in turn, wanted to run it by the matron before letting Paul in, given the nature of Adam's admittance. Once the matron had been found, and the paperwork had been checked and double-checked and signed, Paul was beginning to lose the will to live.

Finally, he was ushered into Adam's side room which, ironically, was only just a couple of doors from where he had started. As Paul saw his friend, he gasped in shock.

I should have expected this, he chastised himself. *I should have - oh, god, you bastard, look at him.*

Adam was being kept in a coma to help his body recuperate faster. He was hooked up to various monitors, with electronic beeps and chirps filling the air. A respirator was helping him breathe though his good lung, and his chest was wrapped tightly in bandages.

As Paul got closer, he saw that more bandages had been wrapped around thick padding on Adam's neck, covering where the knife had first entered. An involuntary shudder ran through Paul's body, which surprised him; he didn't usually feel so squeamish around things like this.

He took a breath. *Okay, come on, Paul, stop being so stupid. You're a grown man – stop acting like a five year old. He's your friend.*

He pulled up a seat and sat down close to Adam's head. Putting his hand over Adam's - being careful not to dislodge the needle stuck into one of the veins - he said quietly, "Hey, Adam, it's me."

He suppressed his awkwardness at talking to someone who was unconscious; *I just want to talk to my friend.*

"Adam, I ..."

Suddenly, he didn't know what to say; his mind had gone blank. Sighing, he envied Adam his untroubled sleep. Paul himself would have liked some sleep like that - for weeks now, he hadn't had one uninterrupted night.

"What the hell's going on, Adam?" he whispered "I've felt so ... so alone in the last couple of years. I've not known what to do, where to go. I've had crappy, second-rate jobs that just go nowhere. I can't ... no, I *won't* go back to the church, but I don't know where else to go. Who else will take me?"

He leaned back in his chair and looked up at the ceiling, watching the shadows from the lamp light dancing on the plain white surface.

"I just feel so *angry*," he confessed. "I'm angry at the world for not having a place for me. I'm angry at me ... for not finding my place."

Shaking his head, he let go of Adam's hand and clenched and unclenched his fists as he went on; "I want to know why I'm here. There's got to be a reason for it. I can feel it. There's something more out there, but I just ... I can't work it out, and I don't know where to start looking."

"How about an anger management course?"

Paul jumped. He instantly recognised the voice; it was impossible not to. "Rick!"

He heard a disapproving tutting from a passing nurse, and realised how loud he had said his friend's name. Ignoring the critical look, Paul stood and looked round at his friend. His mind was reeling.

"Rick Walton. Bloody ..." His voice tailed off as he realised what he had been about to say, then smiled a stupid grin. "Bloody *hell*."

"And you, a man of god," Rick replied, a half-smile on his face.

Paul rolled his eyes. "Not any more."

Rick had been leaning against the doorframe but, now that Paul was walking towards him, he pushed himself upright and extended a hand. Paul took it.

Out of the three of them, Rick had been the most ambitious, the one everyone expected to make full priest first. When Paul had been promoted ahead of him, Rick seemed to harbour some unspoken resentment for quite some time, until Paul had grown tired of it and confronted him.

They had eventually cleared the air, and Rick seemed to accept the situation as a result of their conversation. It did, however, leave the friendship somewhat strained for a while. Paul believed that it had never fully recovered, and was the main source of all their continuous bickering and disagreements over the years.

Paul clapped his friend warmly on the shoulder – whatever had happened between them in the past, today wasn't the day for recriminations. They were both here for Adam.

"It's good to see you," Paul said. "I'm glad you came."

"Of course I came," Walton replied. He looked over at Wild. "I saw the story on the news this morning. As soon as I realised it was St Mary's … well, I couldn't *not* come."

Without realising it, they were now stood side by side, watching Adam sleep. Rick breathed out heavily, and then laughed.

"Adam was always the peacemaker, wasn't he?" he said abruptly. "Between us, I mean, and Father John."

Paul just nodded. Rick pulled over a second chair to the bedside, and Paul went back to his own seat. They said nothing for a while, as Rick stared at his friend lying unconscious in the bed, surrounded by all the machinery needed to keep him alive.

"Rick?"

Walton gave a start; Paul half-regretted interrupting his train of thought.

"Yeah?" he replied.

"Where did you go?" Paul asked. "Adam said you just upped and left one day."

"Yeah. I did."

He sat in silence for a moment, as if gathering his thoughts, and Paul let him. He was surprised to see that Rick didn't seem to look any different than he had done when they last spoke, the morning before Paul's departure from the church. Rick still had his tanned, intense features, his strong, dark eyes, and the same crew cut hair style he'd always sported. Paul's ruddy-ginger hair was striking by comparison.

"I spent time travelling," Rick went on. "Went to Europe, the Middle East, places like that. Just by myself, no dog collar or anything. Didn't want to preach, I guess, I was just there to learn."

Paul was surprised: Rick's faith always burnt bright, and he loved debating matters of faith with believers and non-believers alike. For him not to want to spread the Word, or even just let people know he was a priest by means of his dog collar, was unlike him.

He must have been going through a tough time as well, Paul realised, *to go off like that. I wish he'd said something when I was there. We could have talked about it.*

"Adam said he didn't hear from you after Father John died?"

Walton shook his head. "I ... couldn't face it," he confessed. "You know, Father John was always convinced you were coming back. I ... I knew you wouldn't. You were determined to forge a new path." He laughed. "Temping at a bank isn't the path I expected you to take, though."

Paul laughed as well. "I know," he replied. "Hey - this is the first time all three of us have been in the same room in two years."

"And Adam would've been the one to get most excited about it."

Paul looked up as another figure appeared at the door - it was Joseph.

"Sorry," he said, "I didn't mean to interrupt."

"No, it's okay," Paul replied. "Joseph, do you remember Rick Walton? We studied at ecumenical school together. You met him at my -"

"Graduation," Joseph finished with a smile, rolling his eyes at Rick over Paul's apparent lack of memory. "Yeah, I remember. Good to see you again, Rick."

"You too," Rick replied, shaking his hand.

"Paul," Joseph said, "Lauren needs to go. She's got a couple of meetings at work she has to be there for. I'll understand if you want to stay here, but you can get a lift if you come now. I could always drop you back later if you wanted."

Paul hesitated; he wasn't sure about leaving Adam, especially as he had been the one to find him, and hated making Joseph his personal taxi service. Rick seemed to sense his hesitation.

"You go," he said. "I'll stay here for a while. I'd like to anyway."

Paul slowly nodded, and looked at Adam, before turning back to Joseph. "Give me one minute, would you?"

"No problem," Joseph replied. He said goodbye to Walton, and stepped outside.

Paul and Rick looked at each other for a moment, and smiled.

"We used to argue about some stupid crap, didn't we?" Rick said.

"Yeah," Paul replied. He shrugged. "It was all stupid."

Rick looked at Adam, then back up at Paul.

"I'll be gone by the time you get back tonight, Paul. I've got some stuff to do, but do you want to meet up tomorrow? Catch up on the old times?"

Paul was mildly surprised. He wasn't entirely sure why, but he hadn't expected Rick to be quite so keen on meeting up again, especially because of their often fractious relationship. He was glad, though; it was a strange way to find Rick again, when he had been expecting a long, drawn-out process. He made a decision.

"Sure," he said. "I'd like that."

"Good," Rick replied. "How about Beaches at nine? We could have breakfast."

That suited Paul - it was an extremely short walk from his flat to Beaches café just off the high street. He agreed the time and location, and they parted, with Paul squeezing Adam's hand and then leaving Rick alone in the room.

Joseph was stood a bit further down the corridor by the nurse's station. He gave his friend a supportive hug, and they left the ward. It wasn't until well after they dropped Lauren off and were on their way to Paul's flat, that he realised Rick had known about his temp work at the bank without Paul actually talking about it - and Rick hadn't actually told him what he was doing now.

I'm going mad, Paul thought, resting his head against the passenger seat headrest. *No, I'm just getting distracted in my middle age. Ah, well, I'll just ask him tomorrow.*

Almost as soon as he was home, Paul fell asleep. He wouldn't have thought he needed any more, not after his enforced sleep at the hospital, but then again, his dreams had been rather ... overactive.

Thankfully, for the first time in a long while, his sleep was dreamless.

The Celestial Observatory: Present Day

Michael and Gabriel had spent some time watching events unfold, making sure no lasting effects had occurred as a result of their brief meeting with Paul.

"I think everything is back to normal," Gabriel said with relief.

"I hope so," Michael replied, a far-away expression in his eyes. "He's not ready."

Gabriel looked round at Michael, but he didn't seem aware of what he had said. Michael wasn't often worried or nervous, but now he seemed both.

"What do you mean?" Gabriel asked. "He's not ready for what?"

Michael opened his mouth, but didn't say anything. A strange expression, which Gabriel couldn't read, flittered across his face.

"I -" He stopped and waved off his thoughts with a hand. "Ignore me," he said instead. "Forgive me. Ignore an old, tired angel. I think I need to stretch my wings."

Gabriel swallowed as he watched Michael go. The only time that he had seen Michael so perturbed was two thousand years ago, at the end of Civil War.

Why was that discomfort showing itself again today, on the same day that Paul Finn had shown some latent power he should, by rights, not even have?

Christ Church University: Wednesday Afternoon

L auren firmly closed the door to her office behind her and sat in her chair. She sat in quiet reflection for a while, listening to the sounds of the students chatting outside at the Union. Some of the staff hadn't been too pleased to learn that their brand-new psychology building was being built right next to the Student Union, but Lauren was glad - she had been assigned some classes as part of her studies, and it meant the students had no excuses for being late.

Suddenly, she was jerked into alertness by a noise, which she quickly realised was her name being called out. She sat up in her chair, feeling quite disorientated.

"Lauren, are you okay?"

She blinked a couple of times, rubbed her eyes, and focused. Realising that she was no longer alone, she cleared her throat to hide her surprise.

"Jim!" she exclaimed. "Sorry, I didn't hear you come in."

"No, I think you were having one of your moments."

Tempest was one of the few people on campus who would recognise the symptoms of Lauren's absence seizure epilepsy; his daughter suffered from the same problem.

Dr Jim Tempest was the deputy director of the psychology department, and her supervisor in the doctoral programme. She liked Jim a lot - he was a kind man with vast amounts of patience who was genuinely liked by both staff and students. Physically, he and Lauren were chalk and cheese - she was tall and slim, with a bob of blonde hair, and he was shorter and a lot rounder, with thinning grey hair and a salt and pepper beard. Lauren always joked that, when the two of them stood side by side, they looked like the number ten. Thankfully, Jim took it in good humour.

"I had a fit?" she mumbled.

She pulled open a drawer in her desk and began rooting around, but continued talking; "They're getting more frequent. I had one first thing this morning, and three yesterday. I can't remember the last day when I didn't have a single one."

Finally, she found the glucose tablets she was looking for and popped one in her mouth.

"Well," Tempest said, "I hope you haven't forgotten our first hypnotherapy session today."

Lauren gave a guilty start - she *had* forgotten.

"Therapy sessions are an essential part of any doctoral programme," her supervisor gently chastised. "You can't progress without them."

"I know," Lauren protested. "Honestly, I'm not trying to get out of it. My mind's just somewhere else at the moment."

Tempest nodded. "I've just come from the director's office - I've heard the news. I'm sorry, Lauren. Incredibly sorry."

Lauren smiled her thanks, but didn't trust herself to speak for just a minute. Tempest told her to take ten minutes, and quietly left her office.

Ten minutes later, on the dot, Lauren knocked on Tempest's door and entered his office. The deputy director welcomed her in, and ushered her away from the formality of the desk to the two leather chairs by the large double windows.

Looking around, Lauren couldn't help but laugh. "This office is at least four times as big as mine," she said. "When this building was being designed, you'd think the architects could have divided the space up a little more evenly."

"Ah," Tempest replied, "one of the bonuses of being deputy director is having the bigger office."

Lauren chuckled, but didn't reply; they weren't here to talk about architecture, after all.

Tempest had been correct earlier; during a doctoral student's training, he or she had to undergo therapy sessions themselves, to help them better understand the process and see it from the patient's point of view. The student could choose how they take their sessions, and Lauren had elected to go for hypnotherapy. She had chosen this as she thought it would help keep her honest and not give any half-truths in her answers. She was also glad that Dr Tempest had agreed to lead on her sessions - she was comfortable with him.

As she laid back on the couch, Tempest came back over with his materials; pocket watch, notebook and pen, and video camera – so Lauren could watch the session back afterwards. After setting everything up, he moved one of the leather chairs into position next to her head, and gave her a smile.

"Ready?" he said.

"You're really going to be using that?" she asked, nodding towards Jim's pocket watch.

Tempest laughed. A trained hypnotherapist could use almost anything to hypnotise someone; as he had once pointed out, it wasn't what a person *used* that was important, it was the tone of the person's voice. He boasted that he had once hypnotised someone with nothing more than a copy of the *Sunday Times*.

However, he did prefer to always use this silver pocket watch he was currently holding. It had belonged to his grandfather, and been passed down to him many years before.

"Yes," he said mock-haughtily, "I will. Any problem with that?"

Lauren laughed. "None whatsoever," she replied. "I'm ready."

Tempest knew that people reacted differently to hypnosis; everyone could be hypnotised, but how deeply depended on the individual's personality. The only people who couldn't be hypnotised were people who didn't *want* to be. As Lauren was a willing participant, he was confident of its success.

Very soon, Lauren was under, in that deep, sleep-like state that people often appeared to be in. Her breathing remained constant, her eyes were half-open, and she seemed very relaxed. Tempest was happy with her reactions, so began the session.

"Lauren," he said, "do you know where you are?"

"Yes."

"Could you tell me, please?"

"Christ Church University, in the psychology department."

"Thank you. And can you tell me your full name and date of birth, please?"

"Lauren Samantha Crabtree-Tempur. Tenth January nineteen eighty-seven."

"Excellent. Thank you, Lauren. Now, I'd like to talk to you today about your past."

Tempest didn't bother making notes; the video camera would do that for him. He relaxed back into his chair.

"So," he went on, "let's go back to your childhood. Can you remember much about your very early childhood?"

"I remember it vividly."

Tempest was surprised by that. "Vividly?" he asked. "I don't think I've ever heard anyone call their childhood memories vivid before."

Lauren nodded. "I remember it all vividly," she replied. "I remember that when I scraped my knee when I was five, I remember the first time I ate broccoli, and the first time I fell from the tree at the bottom of our garden."

Tempest relaxed, and chuckled. Lauren's use of "vividly" was obviously a liberal interpretation of the word. This was normal memory territory. He opened his mouth to follow up on the tree-climbing, but was stopped as Lauren cut in.

"I remember my first word," she went on. "I was 11 months, two weeks and three days old. It was 'cat'. I remember the first time I ate fish fingers without them being cut up for me. I was four years, three months, one week and six days old. I remember -"

"Okay, okay!" Tempest exclaimed.

He held up a hand to stop the sudden flow of information, although he knew that she couldn't see what he was doing. He was stunned – *This can't be right*, he thought. *And even if by some fluke it is, I've got absolutely no way of checking. Would any parent have such exact records?*

But then again ... she was under hypnosis. He considered himself to be an expert in the field, and could tell when someone was faking the semi-conscious state that came with being put under - and Lauren was *not* faking it. Tempest shook his head; in all the years he had been working with patients, never had they been so ... exact in their recollection. They could remember big events in their life - younger siblings coming home, deaths, etc, but never fish fingers being cut up and their own first words.

"Lauren ..." he began, then hesitated. He wasn't entirely sure how to continue, and paused as he tried to frame a question.

"My parents named me Lauren after my father's sister, who died in a fire," Lauren said suddenly. "Before that, I was known as Elizabeth."

Tempest blinked.

"Did your aunt die before you were ... Before? Do you mean your parents had originally planned to call you Elizabeth?"

"No. My aunt died before I was conceived. In my life before this one, I was known as Elizabeth ... after my grandmother."

Lauren was conscious and back in the red leather chair, nervously tapping a foot against one of the chair legs. Her mind was whirring; she had just watched the session back and seen herself recite a history of names, dates and facts ... the overwhelming majority of which weren't even from her lifetime.

"Jim," she said, "I know the theories behind past lives ... I just don't think it's got any merit." She shrugged. "I don't believe in it."

Tempest gave a wan smile; "Maybe not," he replied, "but past life theory sure as hell believes in you."

Jim realised he was sinking down into his chair, which had moulded to his shape over the years. To stop himself going down any further into the plush leather, he pushed himself forward in a rather ungainly fashion so that he was now perched on the edge of the seat.

"You spent an hour listing your previous lives," he went on. "Right back to ... err, AD 1004." He frowned in thought. "I wonder why you stopped there."

Lauren laughed. "Why not?" she retorted, a tinge of hysteria now in her voice. "I had to stop somewhere, didn't I? Someone had to be my first life!"

Tempest gave her a sharp look. "Come on, Lauren," he replied, "let's talk about this properly. Cynicism doesn't befit you."

Lauren's hands fell to her lap as she stared at Tempest in open amazement.

"You're not seriously telling me you believe in all this ... crap that I've just spouted, are you? Seriously, Jim, you're a man of science. So am I."

She blinked as she realised what she had said, and shook her head. "You know what I mean. All this past life stuff - it's not ... well, it's not exactly scientific, is it?"

"Well, there have been scientific studies on past life regression," he said. "I wrote a paper on it. It's an interesting subject."

"I know, I've read it. It came down very heavily *against* past lives, if I remember."

"Indeed," he replied. The doctor was always comfortable about people challenging him - he actually rather enjoyed it; because it helped him refine his own arguments and opinions. "But," he went on, "it's rare to find someone who goes into as much detail as you.

"In 1492, you were living in Bath as an artist. You listed the names of your husband, children and business partner, as well as the street you lived in. In 1701, you were a serving girl to the court of King William of Orange, and go into details about your life there."

"Jim ..."

Lauren didn't know what else to say. She had seen the videotape, and was stunned at the amount of nonsense that had come out of her mouth. Never having been overly interested in history, she hadn't realised she had that knowledge locked away inside her mind.

"You can't be honestly telling me that my consciousness has existed before!" she exclaimed. "That's ... crazy!"

Lauren realised she was raising her voice, and quickly decided that that wasn't the best thing to do; no matter how much of a friend she considered him, Tempest was still her superior. She mumbled an apology, which Tempest accepted with a nod.

"Why do you disqualify the previous existence of your consciousness?" he asked.

Tempest was genuinely intrigued. He felt that this would be a good entry in Lauren's portfolio, and would certainly shape the direction of her own research – he just wondered how open she would be to it, given her initial reaction.

"Because it ... well, I ..." Lauren was struggling to verbalise the arguments that were floating round inside her head. She took a deep breath and tried again.

"Because some people know the human consciousness by another name," she went on. "The soul. And if the soul lived again, and again, and again, then many people could use that as an argument in favour of a god."

"Very true."

Lauren stood up, suddenly wanting to stretch her legs. She paced the length of the office, pausing to look out the window. Students were sat on the outside tables and chairs at the Union, relaxing between classes, unaware of the discussion raised in the office above them.

"This is starting to stray more into the realm of the philosophical," she muttered.

"What's your faith?" Tempest asked. "I notice you wearing a cross around your neck."

Lauren's hand automatically reached for the cross. It had been a gift from her mother on her sixteenth birthday; she had worn it every day since.

"This was a present," she said. "I haven't considered the religious connotations for years."

With a sigh, she moved away from the window. Not feeling ready to sit back down yet, she perched on the edge of Tempest's desk.

"I was raised a Catholic," she went on. "Joseph and I both were. But, of course, we inherited a lot of Catholic guilt as well." She laughed. "I could say it came with the territory, but it was just us, I think. We were naturally inclined to … feel guilt about things that we wanted to change, but couldn't."

"And now?"

Lauren shrugged. "I'm a … lapsed Catholic," she confessed. "I still think of myself as spiritual, but … not a religious person. Not since Joseph came out. He struggled with his own self-image, and shed-loads of self-doubt, before he realised religion was just holding him back, so he just ... well, just stopped believing, I guess. He's an atheist now," she added, "and extremely rational. He needs evidence ... cold hard evidence before he'll accept anything as true." She smiled. "Actually, he always *was* contrary, so I think he was just looking for an excuse not to believe."

Tempest smiled back. "The majority of people challenge their faith at some point in their life. Some return to it, many don't. Most religions discuss reincarnation at some point. Many don't believe in it, per se - they believe that the soul exists once on Earth and then goes on to eternal heaven or eternal hell. Many spiritualists, however, believe the soul is part of a larger consciousness that comes down to Earth, and comes down time and time again, as there's always something to learn."

Lauren shook her head, and stood up again. This time, she began pacing the room.

"This is absurd," she muttered, half to herself. She abruptly stopped and spun on her heel. "Jim, if this is some trick to get me talking about ... I don't know, but something, just tell me now, because this is starting to freak me out."

"You're the one who brought it up," he said. "I'm just going with the flow."

Lauren had no answer for that one, so she just gave him a glare and slumped back down in her chair.

"I'm not comfortable talking about this," she said. "It just doesn't seem ... I don't know ... real." She laughed. "Probably because it's not. I'm kidding myself if I even consider it for a second."

Looking up at him, she went on; "Can we finish there? I want to read up on this - try and make some sense of it."

"Sure," Jim said in agreement, glancing at his watch. "Our two hours is over anyway. Give me ten minutes and I'll have a copy of the recording made up for you."

Paul's Flat:
Wednesday Evening

Paul was finding it hard to hide his emotions. He looked very uncomfortable about what he had just seen. Lauren glanced at Joseph; he was sat with his mouth open in shock.

Lauren had wanted to get their opinions on her session, so arranged for the three to meet at Paul's to watch the DVD. However, judging by their reactions, she was beginning to regret her decision.

"So ...?" she asked. "What do you think?"

"I ... well, sis ..." Joseph said, trying – but failing - to keep the disbelief out of his voice, "come on. I mean - reincarnation? Seriously - you're saying you've been how many other people over the last thousand years? Your brain did ... I don't know, some clever trick that made up some different lives. You were always really creative as a kid. You must remember those stories you used to make up and then force me to act in for mum and dad?"

"Yeah," Lauren said. She relaxed – she'd forgotten that and was glad Joseph remembered them so well. She'd always had a very active imagination, and it was entirely possible that her adult subconscious had continued with these types of ... fantasies.

Her brain was suddenly alive with possibilities. She had, as a child, considered careers in acting or writing, but had found such interest in understanding how people thought; how they justified their actions and reactions, so psychology made perfect sense to her. That hadn't stopped her active imagination, even into adulthood, and she often found herself jotting ideas down in a notebook in case she ever wanted to start up writing again.

"I used to enjoy our playacting," she recalled, a smile spreading across her face.

"I didn't," Joseph said grumpily. "I used to get bossed around by my younger sister, being made to act out these stories, when I wanted to be out down the park with my mates."

Lauren ignored her brother – his complaints had become mere background noise to her over the years - and looked over at Paul, who was clearly deep in thought.

"Paul?" she said.

When he didn't reply, Joseph gave him a dig in the ribs, making Paul jump.

"What?" he asked in surprise.

"You were doing a Lauren on us, mate," Joseph said.

Joseph's eyes widened in shock as he realised what he had said. Paul just glared at him, appalled that their secret nickname for a vacant expression had suddenly come out.

"Did a *what*, Joseph?" Lauren demanded.

While Joseph was usually insistent that everyone call him by his full name, his sister was resistant to that, and usually called him "Joe" - mostly to wind him up. Joseph had learnt to live with it; she now only used his full name when she was angry with him.

"Nothing," he said weakly.

"'Do a Lauren'?"

Joseph realised he had well and truly dropped himself in it; it had been a private saying just between him and Paul, and he had been stupid for letting it slip.

"You know I love you, sis, yeah?"

Lauren just glared at him, and Joseph couldn't think of a response that wouldn't dig himself even deeper into a hole ... so he decided to shut up.

"I want to meet Dr Tempest."

Lauren blinked in surprise; that was the *last* response she been expected from her friend.

"Why do you want to meet him? You've seen the video. There's nothing else."

"Yeah," Paul replied, "and I think I'd like to try it."

Paul sat up late that night in bed, thinking about what Lauren had shown him. There was something about the regression therapy that was striking home with him. He sighed, just wishing that he knew why.

His eyes started to droop, and strange dreams started to flutter along the insides of his eyelids; Dr Tempest flying around the countryside with wings, and Lauren in dungarees, painting a landscape image. Joseph was standing to one side, his arms folded across his chest and a frown creasing his face. The Dream-Joseph finally turned in Paul's direction and nodded at him.

"Typical, isn't it?" he said. "First time we're free in two thousand years, and Lauren starts painting. Still, at least we're enjoying the air."

Before Paul could reply, he felt a jerk in the pit of his stomach - or was it just the dream equivalent of his stomach? - *and he found himself in a strange, airless* room. The difference was immediate, and shocking; the change in air pressure hit him, and he almost gagged.

Like his earlier hallucination, the pure whiteness was everywhere - but, this time, there was depth to the space, a feeling that there was an ending to it. It was a room, certainly - almost like an office, but Paul couldn't quite make it … settle.

He turned his head and jumped. The same, anonymous figure as before was stood there, his or her white luminescence still as stunning - but, as with the brightness of the office, slightly dimmed. This meant that Paul could see an outline of a figure, certainly more than before. The figure was just as tall as him, in what looked like a suit, with short hair. Paul still couldn't tell the person's sex.

"You again," its voice said with an audible sigh. "This is beyond a mere annoyance now. We do not allow mortals into our inner sanctum. You certainly shouldn't have the ability to do so without one of us guiding you."

"What are you talking about?" Paul demanded. "Am I dreaming?"

There was no response. Paul got the impression that the figure was staring intently at him - he didn't know for sure, as he couldn't see their face, but it was just a gut feeling.

"Where am I?" he repeated. "And who the hell are you?"

"Do you not know?" the person asked.

Paul frowned. "No," he replied. "Why should I? Have we met before?"

This brought a laugh from the white, shining person, and more confusion from Paul. "Oh, yes. We've met many, many times. You just don't remember."

The being paused; when it spoke again, it sounded almost amused. "Shall we see if one of your friends remembers me any better?"

The figure brought up their left hand and clicked their fingers.

Paul looked round at a change in the air, and jumped as he saw Lauren abruptly stood beside him.

"Paul?" she said, shocked. "What …?"

She looked round, taking in the room as Paul had done. "I'm dreaming," she whispered. "I must be dreaming."

"You're not dreaming," the androgynous person said. "This is more real than you can imagine."

Lauren frowned. "Who are you?"

"You do not remember me either!" the figure said, sounding slightly disappointed, yet maintaining the amused tone at the same time. "It's proof that Michael's system works, if nothing else. Now, perhaps you should both go back to where you came from … and try to not find your way back again. The system's worked well for so long, it would be disappointing to have to revert to the back-up plan now."

And, like that, Paul was back in his bedroom. Sitting up, he quickly calmed his breathing, and looked round at his bedroom clock. It read 04:32.

"Damn," he whispered, running his fingers through his hair. "This is messed up."

Beaches Café:
Thursday Morning

Paul hadn't been able to get back to sleep after his dream; adrenaline had been pumping through his veins at the sheer *reality* of it. He briefly considered calling Lauren, but decided against it when he realised how stupid he would sound.

Without realising it, he then dozed off; when he opened his eyes again, it was 8.30am – *and I promised to meet Rick at nine*, Paul realised in a panic.

As he rushed to get ready, he had a sudden flashback to a couple of weeks before, when he was rushing to get ready for what was to be his final day at the Post Office.

I had a dream the night before that as well, he remembered. *Still, it's only breakfast. I know I can't get sacked here.*

He walked into *Beaches* five minutes late, smiled at one of the waiters and took a look round the half-full cafe. His attention was caught by a waving hand; Rick was sat at a table near the back.

Paul smiled, and waved back, but his smile wavered as he saw someone else sitting at the table as well. He didn't recognise her – she was, however, beautiful, and not in an unhealthy, stick-thin way, either. She had bobbed, blonde hair and deep blue eyes, which were focussed intently on him.

He couldn't suppress a twinge of irritation towards Rick. The ex-priest hadn't mentioned bringing anyone else along to breakfast, and Paul had been quite looking forward to catching up with his old friend - especially after their apparent détente yesterday.

"Hi," he said as he approached the table. "Rick, it's good to see you again."

"And you, old friend," Rick replied. "Let me introduce a friend of mine, Lucy Golding."

Paul turned to Golding. "Hello," he said, "pleased to meet you. I apologise - I hadn't expected to meet anyone else, but it's always a pleasure to meet a friend of Rick's."

Paul knew the hint wasn't that subtle, but didn't really care - he just wanted to get his point across. Rick should have let him know if he was bringing someone else along.

Rick leaned forward, looking uncomfortable. "Golding and I are old friends," he said. "We ... knew each other during school, and just ... well, stayed in touch."

Paul blinked at Rick's rather lame explanation. He resolved to question Rick about it if they had a moment alone. In the meantime, he slipped into the seat opposite Lucy and, with an easy smile he didn't entirely mean, asked, "You call all your female friends by their last name?"

Golding laughed. "There were three Lucy's in our form," she said, "so everyone got into the habit of calling us by our last names. Rick has trouble with change, so I leave him be."

Paul nodded in mock seriousness. "I understand," he replied.

The waiter quickly took the drinks order and then left, leaving the friends free to talk.

"How was Adam yesterday?" Paul asked. "Was there any change?"

Rick shook his head. "No, nothing. He was still the same. I called them this morning; he survived the night. In the doctors' eyes, I think that's what they call a miracle."

"It's what you'd call a divine miracle," Golding added, a smile on her face.

Rick laughed. "Yeah, I suppose so."

Paul shifted in his seat; Golding's piercing blue eyes were still focussed intently on him. He didn't know what she was thinking, but she seemed overly interested in him.

He inwardly sighed. This breakfast wasn't going to be what he had planned, and he had to resign himself to that. After the waiter had taken their orders, Paul suddenly realised that he had been meaning to ask Rick a question.

"Rick," he said, "how did you know I was temping at Lloyds?"

Walton paused, his cappuccino half-way to his lips. "Sorry?" he replied, surprise registering in his voice.

Paul laughed; he realised how accusatory he had sounded, when he was actually just intrigued.

"Sorry," he smiled. "I didn't mean to sound so forceful." He shrugged, suddenly self-conscious that Lucy was again watching him closely. "I was just curious."

"Oh, I see," Walton replied. He sounded relieved, and put down his cup without taking a sip. He laughed, and the sudden tension dissipated. "Yeah, I ... Well, that is -

Adam and I used to stay in touch occasionally, by letter or email. He told me."

Paul nodded. "Okay," he replied, and decided to leave it there ... because he had caught Rick out in a lie, and didn't know how to react.

How would Adam have known he was temping? They hadn't spoken since he had left the church, and so Adam would not have had the slightest idea of what his friend had been up to. Paul then remembered something Adam had said - that he hadn't stayed in touch with Rick since he left.

And Adam just wouldn't lie, he thought. *I know it.*

Those lies, along with Walton's weak explanation of where he and Golding had first met, were all adding up to something suspicious. Paul's mind was reeling, but he kept it hidden behind a neutral mask. He knew that Walton and he had had their differences over the years, but he would never have suspected his one-time friend would have lied to his face.

He managed to maintain a genial chit-chat throughout breakfast, but was struggling with Rick's deception. Paul also noted, out of the corner of his eye, that Golding was continuing to stare at him, with a mixture of curiosity and that same familiarity ... as well as a sense that she was trying to size him up.

They chatted about this and that; memories were exchanged about their early days in the seminary and at the church; neither Golding nor Walton referred again to their school days together, which made Paul doubly curious.

At the back of his mind, Paul was still wondering what Walton had actually been *doing* since he left the church. He blurted out the question before he could stop himself.

His friend looked briefly surprised, then recovered himself – but not before glancing briefly at Golding.

I'm asking you *the question,* he thought, *not her, so you don't need to get her approval before you answer it.*

Walton sighed, not raising his eyes to look at Paul. He began fiddling awkwardly with his fork. Paul watched the fork twirling in between his friend's fingers, and couldn't hide a frown – his friend was clearly uncomfortable with the question. Paul leaned back in his chair - something was obviously going on, and he damn well wanted to know what.

"Well," Walton said slowly, "mostly travelling. Some research as well." He hesitated, cleared his throat, and finally looked up at his friend. "Paul, I'm still in holy orders."

Paul raised his eyebrows. "Wow," he said, surprised. "I didn't see that one coming."

Walton was silent, giving Paul the chance to work out what to say.

"I didn't realise," he said after a moment. "I just ... I assumed you'd left. Your note was fairly vague, but I took it to mean you wanted to find a new path. Something away from the church."

Walton was silent, again averting his eyes. He carried on playing with his fork, obviously unsure what to say. Golding leaned forward, resting her elbows on the table.

"You know," she said, "I considered being a nun once."

"Really," Paul replied flatly.

He wasn't in the least bit interested about Golding's religious leanings. He was angry now; a low, bubbling anger, at Rick - for being evasive and a liar; for not going to Father John's funeral; for running away when things got tough, and for forcing him to see the same things in himself. Paul was also annoyed at Golding, who hadn't even given them a modicum of privacy so they could delve into their shared past. He was also angry at himself for not staying in touch with his friends, even Walton, who was still a friend despite their mutual ability to wind each other up.

"In the end, I decided against it," Golding went on, "because I couldn't find a religion that fully represented my beliefs. I admire all those people who could follow a religion not of their own making no matter what. It all seemed too ... splintered to me, too fractured."

"Do you have a point?" Paul asked with a sigh.

"Yes, I do," Golding replied. Her tone suddenly changed and became harder. "My point is that religion ... oh, religion is so amusing when you look at it. All your little rituals and attempts to touch the hand of God, and hear his words. You're angry because you thought Rick had seen sense like you had and left behind that precious slice of the cake of religion, when in fact he stayed true to his beliefs. Unlike you."

Paul's voice was equally as hard as he responded; "I don't think you know me well enough to be quite so critical. You know *nothing* about my life!"

He wasn't going to give her the satisfaction of being right, after all – he couldn't deny what she was saying, but wouldn't agree with this arrogant woman, purely on principle.

"I know enough about you to know I'm right!"

Paul shot a glance over at Walton, who was suddenly staring daggers at Golding, as if she had said too much. She realised what she had said, and wisely shut up: instead, she sat back in her chair with her arms folded angrily across his chest.

"I think it's time for me to go," Paul said angrily. He pulled some money out of his wallet and threw it on the table. "We never could stay civil for long, could we? I'll see you around."

Paul walked for over three quarters of an hour, trying to clear his head and make some sense of that ...bizarre meeting.

He knew that he wasn't entirely blameless, but he was angry with Walton for lying and misleading him. Walton might not have actually *said* he had left his holy orders behind, but had lied by omission. To Paul, that was just as bad.

This week couldn't get any worse, he thought.

Walton and Golding sat in Beaches for a while longer, a strained silence filling the air.

"Well," he finally said, "I think you fouled that one up, don't you, Golding?"

"Don't call me that," she snapped.

Like I care, Rick thought. He didn't say that aloud, though, because his fear of her was greater than his desire to wind her up too much. Golding was dangerous when she was angry – and he had no desire to rouse that anger again.

"You've spent all this time searching for him, and now you let him walk out." Walton was confused, and made no move to disguise it. "I don't understand. You should have let me deal with it. Despite our ... differences, he would have trusted me. He does that - trusts people."

"Then he's an idiot," Golding said. "There are still options. Now I've got his scent, I should be able to track him more easily."

"His *scent?* I don't understand -"

Golding cut him off. "You don't have to, Father."

She knew Walton would never truly understand. Perhaps he didn't have to – as long as he did what he was told, that was all that was mattered. She was glad she had finally met the infamous Paul Finn in the flesh.

I'm glad I did, she thought. *Especially here, on his terms for a change. It's given me an opportunity to truly study him.*

She glanced at Walton again. Her irritation at him momentarily faded. He'd finally fulfilled his promise – he'd helped her find Paul. He seemed a lot less committed to their mission lately, though.

I wonder if he will outlive his usefulness very soon. If he does, then he's no use to me alive.

The Ruling Chamber:
2,000 Years Ago

F ear swept over Beelzebub as she watched Satan take the floor. He had always been a consummate public speaker, far better than her, but if she could take his place right now, she would.

She looked out over the Chamber floor; the Almighty was there, of course, sat on his throne. He looked distracted, as if a weight was pressing down on his mind. Beelzebub knew why; his eldest son had finally found his calling in life, but it wasn't the one his Father had wanted for him. He was fighting for free will – and that didn't suit his father ... or Metatron.

Michael was stood behind the throne, looking thoughtful as he watched Satan walk forward. Beelzebub had always thought that the commander of the Almighty's armies was a decent and honourable person who always tried to guide the Almighty down the right path. Despite his position, he never sought out war unnecessarily, and was considered to be a wise and calm influence. Beelzebub respected him, and could only imagine his frustration at seeing Metatron's influence rise over the years, slowly warping the Almighty's regime.

How long will he stand by and just let that happen? *she wondered.* Will he ever stand up and say "No"?

Metatron herself was sat to the right of the Almighty, looking out over the assembled masses. For a moment, her eyes locked with Beelzebub's, and narrowed. Beelzebub refused to look away.

Not anymore, *she thought.* I won't be frightened of you. We're too strong for you now.

Eventually, Metatron looked away; and Beelzebub breathed out in relief. Lucifer was sat near her, but his focus was entirely on Satan. The last ten years had moved in the blink of an eye for the heavenly realm, but Lucifer and his friends had used the time wisely. Many here were still undecided about the wisdom of the Almighty's actions, but many more had already been swayed by the arguments Lucifer, Satan and Beelzebub had made.

Even Gabriel was here, sat in a pew further back. His Father had put pressure on him to remain completely neutral, and stay away from today's debate, but Gabriel wouldn't – he was determined to be with his brother and his friends. He had been looking over Beelzebub, but flushed as she made eye contact with him, and turned his eyes away. She smiled – she had caught the mixture of passion and curiosity in his eyes.

Lucifer has the same look in his eye, she thought with a touch of pride. I think he's even learned to temper it with wisdom ... at last.

Beelzebub turned as Satan began talking, directing his comments to the Almighty.

"Almighty," he begun, "thank you for allowing me to speak before you and the Chamber. It is, I assure you, a great honour."

He paused for effect, and the Almighty inclined his head as if Satan was a supplicant making a petition.

"*I Am Always Pleased To Speak With My Angels*" the Almighty replied.

As always, his voice boomed out across the Chamber, richer and deeper than any of the other angels. It was a voice that people would listen to, without question, and could carry to any part of their realm.

Metatron glared at him, clearly unable to hide her anger.

You don't believe the Almighty should be doing this, *Beelzebub* realised. You think it's beneath him. You think it's beneath *you*.

She glanced over at Michael; his face was carefully neutral, but she could see his eyes flicking from one face to the next, judging the mood of the crowd.

Satan smiled; it was his politician's smile, neutral and yet full of hidden meaning. "I am here today because of your decision to unite the angelic and physical realms. We wish to protest against this in the strongest possible terms; we feel it to be both unjust as well as unfair."

The Almighty remained unmoved, his holy presence stock still in his throne.

"*Strong Words From Someone So Young,*" he pronounced. "*I Was Already Old When You Were First Formed. What Makes You Feel You Can Speak On Such Matters?*"

"Free will dictates that I must speak on such matters, Almighty. You yourself guaranteed me that right." He glanced over his shoulder, as if to draw strength from his friends. "I speak with the full authority of Lucifer."

There was a low susurration of noise from the assembled hosts of angels. With interest, Beelzebub noted how many of them were swayed by such a simple statement. Satan had strengthened his argument by invoking the Almighty's eldest son; Lucifer, through the guidance of Satan and Beelzebub, had become a thoughtful and passionate angel.

The Almighty said nothing, merely continued to stare carefully at Satan; to his credit, Satan stared calmly back, keeping his body still and calm. Metatron, however, suffered no such compulsion. She sprung from her seat and whispered in the Almighty's ear. Michael glared at her, clearly irritated by her interruption, and Beelzebub was surprised to see him step forward and square up to her. He said something no-one else could make out; with great reluctance, she sat back down.

"My Son Is A Leader Of Your ⋯ Group," the Almighty said. *"It Is Sad Your Fellow Leaders Do Not Stand With You Whilst You Speak."*

"It's not that they do not wish to, Almighty," Satan replied, "it is that they are forbidden. We are merely following the rules of the Chamber – that only one person may stand upon it. As I understand, Metatron herself introduced these rules."

Michael leaned forward to whisper in the Almighty's ear. He nodded, and his eyes flicked to Metatron for the first time, as if defying her to argue with what he was about to say.

"Bring Your Friends Forward. Let My Son And His Friends Stand Before Me And Speak."

Beelzebub and Lucifer exchanged a surprised glance, but decided not to argue. They rose, met in the aisle and began the walk down towards the floor of the Chamber. Lucifer gave Beezlebub's hand a friendly squeeze.

"What's your Father thinking?" she whispered.

"I don't know," Lucifer replied. "Metatron's furious. Look at her."

Beelzebub looked, and knew Lucifer was right. Her face had taken on an angry, ruddy complexion; an involuntary shudder went through Beelzebub's body. She knew that Metatron would never dare take her anger out on the Almighty directly, and wondered who would get the lash of her tongue instead.

Michael should be careful, *she thought urgently.* There will come a day when she will challenge him for sole access to the Almighty ... and I honestly don't know who will win.

The two angels stepped onto the Chamber floor and stood next to Satan. Lucifer turned and, assiduously ignoring Metatron, focussed all his attention on the Almighty.

"Father."

"My Son·"

Father and son studied each other carefully for a moment, and the assembled host of angels seemed to hold their breath. Lucifer saw a ruler whose time had now passed and whose increasingly autocratic rule needed to end. The Almighty saw a young usurper who wanted to make his mark on the cosmos.

"Thank you for allowing me this opportunity," Lucifer said.

"You Are My Son," the Almighty replied matter-of-factly. *"While We Do Not Agree On Many Things, I Will*

Always Allow You To Speak Your Mind ⋯ As I Am Sure You Would Do me."

Satan smiled, immediately understanding *what the Almighty was trying to do.* He wants the sympathy of the assembled host, *he thought.* I don't know if that will sway them – especially if Metatron remains here, scowling at everyone.

His thoughts were interrupted as Lucifer spoke again. "Of course, Father. There should never be any secrets between Father and son."

The Almighty didn't respond. His eyes were full of intelligence and wisdom, and he was looking at his son carefully, intrigued at where their conversation would lead.

Metatron rose again from her seat. Instead of turning to the Almighty this time, her eyes were fixed on Lucifer.

"Whatever secrets you think you might have," she said, *"should remain just that. At least until you have spoken to your Father about it in private."*

"I disagree," Lucifer said sharply.

"As do I," Michael intoned *for the first time in the proceedings.*

"Tough!"

That single word was spat from Metatron's mouth, but bounced around the Chamber and the assembled host like a ball, bouncing from wall from wall, ear to ear. The host, by now, were deathly silent, hanging on every word.

The Almighty, too, was silent, as he turned to face Metatron. Michael's face briefly clouded over and he stepped forward, clearly ready to speak his mind, but the Almighty held up a hand. Michael bowed slightly and stepped back. He did not take his eyes off Metatron, though. Beelzebub opened her mouth to speak, but was quickly interrupted.

"We have a right to hear what Lucifer has to say."

"Gabriel," Lucifer whispered. He swallowed. Stay out of this, *he thought.* I want to preserve your innocence for a while longer.

Lucifer's brother, who he had always tried to protect from the worst of his Father's – and Metatron's – anger, made his way down to the Chamber floor. Once there, he stood proudly next to his brother.

"Free will, brother," he whispered. "I'm not afraid to be standing with you."

"Lucifer," Beelzebub whispered. "It's time."

Lucifer expelled a breath, closed his eyes for a moment to prepare himself for the onslaught still to come, and turned back to his Father – who was oddly calm at the sight of his two sons standing against him.

"Father," he said, "I know of your plans. You want to merge the physical plane of Earth with our world by mating with a human. I will stand against you if you refuse my terms."

The Almighty raised an eyebrow. "Which are?"

"Agree that Earth must be left alone, forgo your plan to unite the realms ... and then stand down as ruler of our kingdom. Your position as Almighty over all of us has become untenable. I will take your place as regent until a new leader can be elected."

Lucifer's statement was finished, which was fortunate; he wouldn't have been heard anyway. The uproar from the assembled host was loud and riotous – and it remained that way for quite some time.

Thanet Star Offices, Margate: Thursday Morning

J oseph Tempur loved being a writer. He had wanted to write for almost as long as he could remember, and had indeed completed his first book at the tender age of nine; a rip-roaring masterpiece of a book about a cowboy who flew into space which ran to nine whole pages, with colour illustrations done by him. Thinking back, and judging by his current lack of any drawing ability, the illustrations might not have been all that good, but his teacher - Mrs Cooper, bless her – had still raved about all of them.

In the intervening eighteen years, he'd not had much success with novel writing (although he still tried when he had the motivation), but was still earning a living in the world of writing; as a columnist for his local paper and as an investigative journalist. He sometimes had to pinch himself, because he was doing what he had always wanted to do; he had come to appreciate that even more since Paul's job-hopping over the past two years.

Joseph was now sat in the offices of the Thanet Star, the local newspaper. He was only contracted to work one day a week; however, the editor was old school – a proper investigate hack, as Joseph described it, rather than the new breed of journalist that was actually just a sociology graduate - and didn't mind him using the office during the week to work on other projects.

Lauren had made him promise not to tell anyone, even Paul, about her tumour until she had been for the biopsy. She especially didn't want their parents to know, because she knew - and Joseph found himself agreeing with her - that they would both insist on coming down to "help out". In the long run, she reasoned, that would cause her more stress than just not telling them and then dealing with the consequences after the biopsy.

As for Paul not knowing, Joseph understood - he and Joseph had been best friends for years, and he had an almost brotherly connection with Lauren. Whereas Joseph was level-headed, Paul was prone to deep and passionate emotions. Joseph had learned to deal with them over the years, but Lauren occasionally found it wearing - and didn't want to have to deal with his constant fretting, especially when she was doing enough of it herself.

Sighing, he picked up a notepad full of his hand-written notes - and frowned.

"Bloody hell," he muttered. "What in god's name does that say?"

"Joseph! How's it going?"

Joseph looked up, and then smiled. Gabriel Wilson, the Gazette's editor, had stopped at Joseph's desk and was perched on the edge. In his early fifties, with a salt-and-pepper black moustache and thinning hair, a permanently-furrowed brow - from years of battling against a deadline - and a slight paunch that had been carefully developed from years of expert whisky-drinking, Wilson was someone who gave off a permanent air of affability and wisdom, but who was also not afraid to show his temper on the rare occasion it was needed.

Joseph had never experienced the anger first-hand, but seen one person be on the receiving end of it, when Wilson had found out that the journalist in question had invented a story out of thin air, without any attempt to check or correlate his facts.

Joseph handed the editor his notebook. "Can you read that?"

Wilson studied the handwriting carefully before handing it back.

"Looks something like, 'Green is the new black, and we must save the children.'"

Joseph frowned, and took back the notebook. "It looks nothing like that."

"You caught me. You know I can't read your handwriting; it's like a dyslexic spider with only three legs trying to dance."

"I need a Dictaphone," Joseph retorted. "I also need a secretary. Can I have a secretary?"

"Sod off," Wilson retorted. "Even I haven't got a secretary. What makes you so special?"

Joseph shrugged. "My column is extremely well-read, and I'll have you arrested on trumped-up charges of homophobia if you refuse."

A roar of laughter escaped from Wilson, causing several other people in the office to turn and look. Joseph didn't care; he was just glad that his editor had got a good sense of humour.

"Actually, as you're here, do you mind if I ask you something?"

Wilson looked intrigued. He pulled up a chair. "Do tell."

Joseph thought about his question for a moment, trying to decide how to phrase it without sounding like a complete madman.

"Do you know anything about hypnosis?" he asked. "Specifically, hypnosis used in psychology and past life regression?"

"Only what I've read in the papers," Wilson replied thoughtfully. "My daughter's a psychology student at university, so there's usually one of her magazines lying around. I remember seeing an article in one of them." He hesitated. "The two aren't necessarily always linked, if I remember. You can have one without the other, can't you?"

Joseph nodded. He had been doing some research of his own on the internet, but it hadn't really helped - if anything, it had made him more confused.

"Yeah. But whole process interests me - how a person can conjure up ... imagines from their subconscious, I guess, and weave it into what they believe is an actual previous life."

Wilson smiled. "Sounds like you've already made your mind up already," he noted. "I don't think you need me."

Joseph laughed. He riffled through his papers for a minute, then looked back up at his editor, who hadn't moved, and hadn't interrupted his train of thought. *The mark of a true journalist*, Joseph thought.

"What's this for?" Wilson asked slowly. "A story?"

Joseph shook his head. "No," he replied, "just some ...personal research."

He hesitated for a moment; he needed some advice and, if he couldn't go to Paul, then he needed someone else that he knew he could confide in - and Wilson definitely fitted into that category.

"My sister, Lauren ... she's doing her PhD in psychology and had to do some therapy sessions as a part of it."

Wilson nodded. "My daughter's only at the undergrad stage, but doing something similar. I always worry that she's going to spend the entire sessions talking about me."

"Same here."

Joseph went on to relate the story of Lauren's session the previous day. When he had finished, Wilson looked genuinely interested.

Joseph scratched his head. "I thought you'd be laughing at me by now."

"Not at all," he replied. "I find it interesting, all the past life stuff." He caught a doubtful look on his friend's face. "Surprised?"

"Yeah, slightly," Joseph said with a smile. "I'm incredibly sceptical. I assumed you would be as well."

Wilson sighed, and looked thoughtful. "*There are more things in heaven and earth, Joseph, than are dreamt of in your philosophy.*"

"Hamlet, Act One, Scene Five. And it's 'Horatio', not 'Joseph'."

"How the hell do you remember that?"

Joseph shrugged. "What good does quoting Shakespeare do me?"

"Here was me thinking you were an educated man," Wilson replied. "Lauren went back in her mind over 1,000 years of history. You're convinced that it's all invented from her subconscious. Why?"

Joseph hesitated, as he struggled to find the words. It just felt *wrong*, with every fibre of his being. "Ockham's Razor, Gabriel. '*Entities should not be multiplied unnecessarily.*' More simply, the simplest explanation is usually the right one. In this case, that her subconscious is creating these lives out of its own imagination."

"Ninety-nine percent of the time, agreed," Wilson countered. "What about the one time out of a hundred, though? What if Lauren is that one percent?"

"What are you saying?" Joseph asked incredulously. "That her subconscious is telling the truth? That ... that she was once a knight following Joan of Arc?"

Wilson shrugged. "Just following the argument through to its conclusion," he said as he stood up. "Like I already said, it sounds like you've already made your mind up."

Joseph watched the editor walk away from his desk, heading purposefully back to his office.

It's not true, he though. *I'm an atheist, and I don't believe in all this ... reincarnation stuff. It allows for the existence of a higher power, and I* know *there isn't one of those.*

He rubbed his forehead as a sudden tension headache began throbbing in his head, and decided that some fresh air would do him some good.

As Wilson closed the door to his office, he watched Joseph go - and smiled. He didn't entirely disagree with the younger man – but he loved being Devil's Advocate every now and now, especially if it took people out of their comfort zone.

Christ Church University, Canterbury: Thursday Lunchtime

L auren hadn't been focussed on her job all morning. She'd sent some emails, met with a student who was having anxiety issues, and done some research for her final dissertation, but it had all been in a distracted, half-hearted way; the contents of her therapy session were still at the forefront of her mind.

Despite that, she found herself avoiding Dr Tempest and she wasn't entirely sure why. After all, he hadn't made her say those things. It had been her subconscious that had created the stories; Tempest had just helped her express them. The session had made her think about her beliefs more since that two hour session than in many years before.

Lauren had been ambivalent towards religion for a long time. It had proved itself to be intolerant towards her brother, and no great comfort to her when she was a kid with typical teenager angst. As Joseph had discovered atheism, Lauren had discovered something else; agnosticism. The Catholicism she had grown up with suddenly felt like it a habit more than anything, and she no longer felt committed enough to be an active believer.

Lauren had never gone as far as Joseph in becoming an atheist, with passionate anti-religious views; she just didn't care enough to debate religion. Even Paul and Joseph had tactfully worked out a verbal tap-dance around the subject, so they wouldn't have a repeat of the terrible row they once had when they were both undergraduates.

She looked up at a sudden knock on the door. "Come in."

Her smile faltered as Tempest walked into her office; his eyebrow quirked in amusement as he caught the look on his student's face.

"Thought you'd got away with it, hmm?" he asked.

Lauren didn't even bothering denying it - he wasn't stupid and could see straight through her. She had known him long enough to develop a lot of respect for the man, and wouldn't have him lose respect for *her* by lying.

"Something like that," she replied. She motioned him to the seat opposite her on the other side of the desk. "Sorry I can't offer you a comfier chair, perhaps something in red leather."

Tempest laughed as he sat down. "You'd have to put it in the hall, with an office this size."

Lauren glanced around the office - a full third of the space was taken up by the desk and hard backed chairs. Most of the remainder was taken up by the bookcases, window and patient's reclining chair.

"I thought you might want to follow up on yesterday's session," Tempest said, his round face suddenly turning serious and thoughtful. "I think it left you with a lot of questions."

Lauren nodded. "Yeah, I'd say," she admitted with a sigh.

Tempest crossed his arms across his huge belly as he shifted, slightly uncomfortably, in the hard backed visitor's seat.

"Have you discussed this with anyone? Got anyone else's opinions?"

"Yeah, my brother, Joseph, and his best friend ... well, one of my closest friends too. I wanted ... other opinions." She felt awkward saying it. "Sorry, I didn't hope that doesn't offend you."

"Not at all!" Tempest said, laughing. "I hoped you'd say that. It's always healthy to get opinions. Anyone who tries to stop you getting other opinions ... well, they're not worth much cop." He looked thoughtful. "Your brother ... he's an atheist?" When Lauren nodded, he went on; "Hmm, I think I can imagine what he might have said. This friend of yours, though - what's his name?"

"Paul."

"What did he think?"

Lauren laughed. "Well, I think he managed to completely surprise me," she confessed. "Joseph, as you guessed, was very dismissive of the whole idea, very sceptical. Typical Joseph, really. Paul ... well, he's usually very outspoken about things he can't explain, but from a different perspective. He's an ex-priest, you see."

Tempest's eyebrows shot up with interest. "Really?" he asked. "An ex-priest? What does he believe if he's left his orders?"

Lauren opened her mouth to reply - and stopped.

"I ..." she began, paused, then began again; "I don't actually know. I never thought to ask."

"Okay," Tempest replied with a smile. "What was his take on the session?"

"That's what surprised me," Lauren said. "He didn't completely dismiss it out of hand. When he was a priest, he completely disliked any sort of non-Christian spiritual activity - it made him feel very uncomfortable. He'd actually like to meet you. To perhaps have his own session, experience it for himself."

Tempest shrugged. "I have no objection to that," he said. "How do you feel about having your friend go through the same regression?"

"I'd welcome it," Lauren replied. "It would be good to have someone else experience the same thing."

"You need to understand, though, Lauren, that everyone's hypnosis session is different. What I will do with Paul is ask him exactly the same questions as I asked you, in exactly the same context, and see where it leads. He may not even experience any regressions."

"But I want to see what happens," she said. "It'll … help, I think. I'd be more comfortable if I could see someone else going through it. It might help me understand the process."

"Or," Tempest added, laughing, "it might give you even more questions."

Lauren fixed him with a glare. "Shut up."

Broadstairs:
Thursday Lunchtime

After his breakfast with Walton, Paul had managed to walk off his annoyance at his old friend before going to a meeting at his recruitment agency. The bank position had ended, and he needed something else to pay his rent. His heart really wasn't really in the search, and he could tell the agent knew that too.

All credit to her, though, he thought. *She's not giving up on me. Who knows, she could be the one to find me the job of a lifetime.*

He chuckled to himself; it was a vain hope, because he still didn't know what it was he wanted to do himself. He'd briefly considered retraining and becoming a teacher – after all, with his life experience, geography or religious studies would be a breeze. He dismissed the idea when he remembered that he didn't like children.

Perhaps I could be a writer like Joseph? he thought. *Nah, I haven't got any ideas ... or the patience.*

As he left the agency, he looked up at the clear, blue sky. Not a cloud was in sight and the sun was beating down on his face. He released a breath and frowned as he felt a sudden tension in his stomach. For a moment, it felt as if he were being watched by someone.

He looked around, up and down the high street, but no-one *was* watching him. The usual mix of people were going about their business, but none of them seemed in the least bit interested in *him*.

He looked up at the sky again, squinting his eyes against the sun. There was no earthly reason for his sudden discomfort, but he felt … *something*.

Suddenly, his mobile rang. It brought him out of his reverie and instantly made him forget the discomfort. The phone call was from Lauren, wanting to know if he was able to see Dr Tempest for a hypnosis session at 5pm. He pretended to check his "busy" diary; she swore at him and he laughed, promising to be there.

That would've been weird if that had been Joseph just as I was thinking about him.

His phone rung again; it was Joseph. He quickly agreed to lunch, and was soon on his way to Ramsgate. He didn't think about his discomfort again for the rest of the day.

In the Celestial Observatory, Michael watched the screen carefully. Paul seemed to have forgotten about his momentary feeling that there was something outside his consciousness looking down at him.

For which I am eternally grateful, *Michael thought. He was relieved – when he had put his plan into action all those centuries ago, he hadn't been sure if he was doing the right thing … or if he was being exceptionally cruel.*

If he were truly honest with himself, he still didn't know.

Soon after, Paul and Joseph were sat outside the

Belgium Bar. It was a sunny day and both had wanted to make the most of it while it lasted.

As per tradition, Joseph had got the first round in, and they watched the world go by. It was mostly office workers out for lunch, young kids out on their bikes with their mums (thankfully, it was a school day, or else Paul would have insisted on sitting inside, given his intense dislike of nearly everyone under the age of eighteen).

"So what do you think of Lauren's hypnotic revelations yesterday?" Paul asked as he took a sip of his wine. "Good choice with the wine, by the way."

"Thank you," Joseph replied. "It came recommended by one of the bar staff."

"Which one?" Paul asked, peering inside the pub. "The blonde Polish girl? What's her name again?"

"Unpronounceable, and no, she's not working," Joseph replied with a shake of his head. "It was the ginger-haired English one."

Paul frowned. "Which one was that?"

"Rob."

"Oh." Paul shrugged. "More your type then?"

"I would hope."

"Anyway, what do you think – about Lauren's hypnosis?"

"You know what I'm thinking," Joseph replied. "I'm an atheist, so I'm fairly predictable."

"Heathen more like."

"If I'm going to hell, then at least I'll go there defending my beliefs to the last."

He sipped at his Jack Daniels and shielded his eyes against the sun. "Lauren's my sister and I love her, but I can't square what she said with anything I believe."

Paul didn't reply. He wanted his friend's opinion to help him form his own; at the moment, he was wavering.

"I know Dr Tempest didn't lead her on," Joseph went on, "but I'm curious to know where this all came from. It's not as if Lauren has *ever* been interested in history – I doubt she's ever read a history book outside of school, and she wouldn't ever use the internet to look something like that up. It just wouldn't interest her."

Paul laughed. "They didn't have the internet when we were growing up."

"Fair point," Joseph replied with a smile. "The Encyclopaedia Britannica then. But isn't it just human arrogance to assume that there's a life beyond this one, purely set up for the human soul to go to, and then be given the chance to come back to Earth and live more lives, time after time?"

"Hmm," Paul replied neutrally.

Joseph glanced over at him. "Mate," he said, "if you were still a priest, you'd be right there, agreeing with me. You were never a believer in all the man-made religious conventions either, but all this spiritualist stuff ... well, that was totally off your radar. You felt it was dangerous ground to go into. Don't tell me you're a closet spiritualist now."

"No," said Paul quickly ... then hesitated again. "Well ... I don't know any more. I mean, I don't think so. When I was travelling, I came across loads of different belief systems that I'd never encountered before. I can't say I believed in them, but it definitely opened my mind. I mean, I'm not a full-blown psychic or spiritualist or anything. It's just ..."

Joseph jumped in; "Do you still believe in God?"

"Yes."

The answer was out of Paul's mouth before he had a chance to process the question - he just knew the answer, the same way he knew his own name or that Joseph was his best friend.

"Wow," Joseph said.

Paul bit his lip. "Yeah."

"I'd never even thought to ask you that before," Joseph confessed. "Don't know why - just didn't seem the right time, I guess. I kind of assumed you left all that behind when you left the church."

Paul didn't meet his friend's eyes. Instead, he stared into the murky depths of his red wine.

"I don't pray or anything," he said, a bit defensively. "It's not as if I follow any of the rites. To tell you the truth, I was glad to be rid of them. You don't need all that to believe in a god."

Joseph nodded. "I'm with you on that one."

"I never lost my faith, though," Paul went on, quietly. "It's like a ... a feeling I've got, just a kind of knowledge of someone looking over me."

"We all have that. It's called your conscience."

Paul looked up at his friend and shook his head. "It's not that. It's something more."

Joseph didn't even try to argue; instead, he finished off his Jack Daniel's.

"I don't think we'll ever agree on this, will we?" Paul said with a wry smile on his face.

"*That's* something I can agree with you on."

After a moment, Joseph smiled too, and they both laughed, diffusing the tension.

"Anyway," Joseph went on, "what do *you* think about Lauren's regressions. Do you believe she did it, or do you agree with me that she's just a complete loony?"

"Well, I don't believe she's a loony," he replied.

"So you believe her then?"

Paul stared inside the bar again, and smiled - the barmaid with the unpronounceable name had just started work.

"Anything's possible, mate," he said simply. "Anything's possible."

Christ Church University, Canterbury: Thursday Evening

Tempest's chat had done Lauren good; a weight seemed to have lifted off her mind and she was felt able to focus on her work.

As she sipped her coffee, she reflected on how bad she felt at not talking to Paul about his feelings after he had left the priesthood; she had assumed that he would talk about it when he was ready and would have loads people badgering him about the whys and wherefores. She knew from her studies that sometimes, people just needed friends around them that were completely hassle-free. The problem was that Paul seemed to internalise everything, and she and Joseph had never thought to follow it up.

She was still in her office at just gone five o'clock when Joseph and Paul arrived.

"I was expecting Tweedledum," she said, "but not Tweedledee as well. You here as a professional sceptic, big brother?"

"I'm here as a friend," Joseph replied calmly, knowing not to rise to his sister's bait.

True enough. Lauren's hackles, which had irrationally risen at her brother's presence, immediately went back down; she immediately realised how stupid she was being. Just because her brother was sceptical about other-worldly things didn't mean he couldn't be here to watch the session if Paul wanted.

Paul sat automatically in the one visitor's chair, leaving Joseph to perch, with bad grace, on the edge of the desk.

"Don't worry, I'll be comfortable here," he grumbled.

"Okay," said Paul distractedly. He turned to Lauren and asked; "How's it going to work? I mean, is it the traditional couch and a pocket watch?"

Lauren frowned in mock-confusion. "Well, yeah, there's a couch, Paul, but why do you want a stopwatch? It's not as if you'll be telling the time when you're under."

"No, I mean to hypnotise me. Don't people use pocket watches or something?"

Lauren laughed as she remembered her own surprise at Tempest's pocket watch the previous day.

"Jim uses a pocket watch, yes," she conceded. "It's not compulsory to use one, though."

Paul and Joseph exchanged a glance, and smiled at each other.

"What?" Lauren asked, confused.

"'Jim'?" Paul asked. "First name terms, are we?"

Lauren's face clouded over, suddenly as dark as thunder. *How dare they insinuate anything?* Had they suddenly become so obtuse that they had forgotten how recent her husband's death had been? She remembered the slow, devastating decline she had witnessed, until she had lost him, two years ago. He had only been twenty two.

Both Paul and Joseph saw the emotions running past her delicate features; Paul shifted awkwardly in his chair, and Joseph was suddenly glad he wasn't sat directly opposite her.

"What are you saying, Paul?" she demanded. There was an edge to her voice that warned Paul he needed to be very careful.

"I ... uh, well ..."

Paul cleared his throat, crossed and uncrossed his legs, and quickly looked to Joseph for support. Joseph, however, was determined to stay as far out of this as humanly possible; he may have been the older sibling, but was absolutely unwilling to get involved when his sister was angry. Even his best friend was immune. He was just glad the attention wasn't on him - and it served Paul right for stealing the only visitor's chair.

Lauren coolly arched her eyebrow. "You were saying?"

Joseph heard a tinge of humour in her voice; she was clearly enjoying making him squirm.

"I'm sorry, Lauren, I really am," Paul said quickly. "I didn't think. Too soon, huh?"

"More than you could possibly realise," Lauren said quietly.

In reality, she couldn't ever be angry with Paul for too long; she knew he hadn't meant anything by it. He, James and Joseph had been friends, and wouldn't ever do anything to besmirch his friend's memory. Paul just wanted Lauren to be happy, and had tried to gently broach the subject of dating with her over the past couple of months, with Lauren brushing the comments off every time. Hearing her mention her supervisor by his first name must have briefly excited him, making him think that there was a man she was interested in.

"Jim is my boss," she explained, "and the man who will be hypnotising you. I've known him long enough to be able to use his first name. So don't read any more into it than there is. That goes for both of you."

"I didn't say anything!" Joseph protested.

"Coward," Paul retorted.

Lauren decided to bring the subject back to why they were all here.

"Paul, just … be open-minded in the session, okay? I know your subconscious mind will be in control, but I'd hate to think any part of you is saying something because it's similar to what you heard me saying on the DVD."

"Is there anything you want me to do, little sister?" Joseph asked

"Yes," Lauren replied. "Stay out of the way. I don't want to hear you tutting."

"I don't -"

Joseph stopped himself, closed his mouth and nodded in passive agreement.

It wasn't long before Tempest called them all into his office. Joseph and Lauren had agreed to remain outside and wait for the end of the session – given the apparent ease with which Lauren had been hypnotised the first time, Tempest didn't want to risk her going under again.

As he laid back on the couch, Paul was suddenly hit by a wave of apprehension.

What am I doing? he thought to himself. *I don't even know if I believe in this stuff. It just seemed like a good idea at the time.* He took a deep breath and closed his eyes. *At least it might help Lauren put her session in some kind of context.*

He abruptly remembered the weird dream he'd had the previous night, where he'd been in the light-filled room with that … person, and Lauren had appeared. He'd meant to mention it to her earlier, and cursed his bad memory.

Before he knew it, he was in a hypnotic state. Never having been in one before, he'd been worried what it would feel like; thankfully it wasn't unpleasant. Instead, it felt like he was gently floating on a cloud, high above all of his worries and concerns; as if by casting them off, he could do anything.

There was nothing behind his eyelids except the darkness that he always saw when he closed his eyes. As the seconds ticked away, however, he became aware, for the first time, that the darkness had different shades to it - almost shadow-like. It was as if there were movement across his vision, and he was seeing their reflected shadows on his eyelids. Frowning, he stretched his arms out in front of him, but there was no-one there.

So where are the shadows coming from? he thought. *And what are they?*

He vaguely heard Tempest asking him some questions - the same ones he'd asked Lauren, in the same order - and some answers came out of his mouth. He wasn't that interested in the responses - they were mostly banal and uninteresting. Paul had the vague sensation that he wasn't quite saying the right things. However, his conscious mind, on that peaceful cloud, wasn't entirely sure what those things were - the cloud was helping him float above all everyday worries, and things suddenly didn't seem important.

Outside of Paul's mind, Tempest was being careful to keep his voice light and neutral, as he had done during Lauren's session, but things weren't progressing in the same way. Ninety-nine percent of his brain had fully expected this - after all, everyone reacted differently under hypnosis, and he couldn't have expected Paul to suddenly go into full regression just because he had asked the same questions as he had asked Lauren.

However, it was just that one percent of his brain that was disappointing him. He refrained from sighing, not wanting to give Paul an indication as to his frustrations, even in his hypnotic state.

Where do I go from here? he wondered. *Any more than what I'm doing, and I'll easily be leading Paul into saying what I want him to say.*

Before he could decide on a plan of action, Paul's head jerked awkwardly to his left and he began muttering under his breath. Tempest leaned in closer, but he couldn't quite make out what the young man was saying.

"Paul?" he said quietly. "Can you speak a little louder?"

Inside Paul's head - or wherever his subconscious was floating - his mind was struggling to keep on an even keel. It felt like it was being pulled in a hundred different directions from an unknown force that was suddenly all around him, yet invisible to all his senses. It was as if something deep inside him was trying to pull him apart into a thousand pieces.

Stop, came a voice suddenly out of nowhere. The voice came from everywhere and nowhere at once, shaking his mind.

"Who are you?" he said - or at least, tried to say. He knew that the words he wanted to say had presented themselves, but had they come out through his mouth? He couldn't tell.

You know who I am, Paul. The voice seemed to hesitate for a moment. *Your name changes so frequently; I am ... surprised I remember it.*

"I don't understand. What do you mean?"

I don't expect you to. You're so small, so ... human. It's pathetic ... and so unappealing. I dislike what you have become.

Paul suddenly realised where he recognised the voice from. He had met the androgynous figure twice now, although never actually seen his or her face – he had gone there, wherever *there* was, and met the figure on its turf. Now, however, the figure had come to him.

"I'm the same person as I was the last time we met," he said. "I'm Paul Finn."

You remember our meetings? I thought I'd removed all memory of them from you. Perhaps part of your previous existence survived after all.

Paul was struggling to understand what the voice was talking about, so he decided to take charge of the conversation.

"You didn't answer me," he said firmly. "Who are you?"

There was a sigh. *Maybe you will remember ... one day. You shouldn't be here, Paul. You're getting near to unlocking secrets you will never understand. Go home.*

"Who are you?!" Paul demanded, furious at the voice.

Someone who loved you – and hated you at the same time!

Paul suddenly sat up, gasping for breath. His hands were shaking, he felt sick, and his breathing was ragged and short.

Tempest's hands were on Paul's shoulders, pushing him back down onto the couch.

"Come on, come on," he said, clearly worried, "take a breath, Paul. Breathe!"

Paul nodded, and gulped in some air. Slowly, his breathing began to calm down and return to normal. He looked round and saw Tempest, Lauren and Joseph all standing over at him, looking worried. Lauren looked almost sick, and her face was pale; Joseph's face was flushed with concern.

"Paul!" Joseph said in a shaky voice. "We heard you shouting from down the hall."

"Shouting?" Paul replied. "What was I shouting?"

"You were ..." Joseph paused, and cleared his throat. "Well, you were kind of having a conversation with ... uh, I don't know who, but you were speaking in another voice as well as your own."

Paul blanched. "I think I need to see a copy of that DVD," he said firmly.

They watched the film back on the TV in Tempest's office. The session had only lasted for twenty minutes, with a good portion of it being given over to Tempest settling Paul into his hypnotic state and asking him the usual questions. He could remember the comfortable, floating sensation well, with Tempest's voice floating vaguely in the background.

Everyone watched as the Paul on the screen extended his arms in front of himself, reaching out as if to touch someone.

"The shadows," he whispered.

"Shadows?" Joseph asked.

Paul shook his head, unsure how to explain it. "There were ... shadows, things moving. It was stupid, it looked like there were shadows in the darkness, but I couldn't make them out."

Tempest said nothing, but he made a note on his pad and turned back to the screen. Paul then saw his own head snap to the left and begin muttering. After a minute, he began speaking much louder, repeating word for word the conversation he had been having inside his mind with the all-consuming voice that had filled Paul with such a feeling of fear and dread he could immediately feel it returning as he watched.

It had lost none of the immediacy by seeing it on the TV; the shouts his friends had heard from down the corridor had been shocking enough, but to see it actually happening ... it was powerful viewing.

"I'm sorry I let you come here and go through that," Lauren whispered.

Paul shook his head, not taking his eyes off the screen. "No, Lauren, this is fascinating."

"Lauren, Joseph," Tempest said, "can I have some time alone with Paul, please?"

They agreed to go and left Paul alone with Tempest. Paul stood and walked to the window overlooking the Student Union. No-one was sat outside, which was probably to do with the appearance of some dark clouds overhead.

"That didn't go the way I expected," Tempest said casually.

Paul laughed softly. "Yeah," he agreed. "Although I don't know what I was expecting."

Tempur sat down in one of his red leather chairs, but let Paul stay where he was. He wanted the man to feel comfortable.

"And now? How do you feel?"

"Okay"

Paul's tone didn't supporting his words. He caught Tempest's eye, and knew he had been caught out in the lie. He refused to acknowledge it, though - he didn't like talking about his feelings very much, and he hadn't come here to be analysed.

"I ..." he said haltingly. "I don't know how I feel. Not surprised, I know that much."

"How do you mean?"

"I don't know," Paul admitted. "I just know that, now it's happened, it seems ... familiar. Some of the things I saw had ..." he chuckled "... a very familiar ring to them. I just wish I knew why."

Tempest leaned forward - or as much as he could do with his gut being in the way.

"In what way?" he asked. "What did you find familiar?"

Paul opened his mouth to tell him, but his brain suddenly stopped. He suddenly felt very uncomfortable – he wasn't ready to share his feelings with a stranger, he knew that.

"Uh, Doctor," he said awkwardly, "I hope you don't mind, but the session's taken a lot out of me. I think I'm just going to go. I ... well, I really appreciate what you've done for me today, but perhaps we could pick this up later in the week?"

Without properly waiting for a response, Paul gave the doctor a nervous half-smile and a nod, and quickly left the office. Tempest sighed, and leaned back in his chair.

Pushing himself up off the armchair, he walked over to the window.

Droplets of rain had now started to pound the window, as the dark clouds Paul had spotted a few minutes before suddenly began unleashing a heavy downpour. Thankfully, there was no-one outside left for it to soak; except for one.

A blonde-haired, blue-eyed woman was stood outside on the green, by the Union building, strangely unaffected by the rain. Her hair and clothes were untouched by damp, and her vision seemed to be completely unimpaired as she fixed Tempest with a steely glare.

Tempest blinked in shock. "What the hell?" he muttered. "What sort of nutcase goes out in this weather?"

I do, came a voice inside his head

Tempest jumped in shock.

"What's going on?" he demanded. His eyes were still focused on the strange sight outside of his window, but he was having trouble keeping his attention on her; a feeling of panic was rising up suddenly inside his chest.

He suddenly realised that he wasn't experiencing a panic attack; it was far, far more serious than that. He tried to call for help, but the air was abruptly forced from his lungs.

The voice spoke again. *You shouldn't have helped him remember who he was. Now you will pay.*

All the doctor's being was focused on the pain in his chest; his heart felt like it was going to burst through his rib cage. He sunk to his knees.

No, he thought. *Don't let it end like this!*

He didn't even hear the reply in his mind - although he was sure there had been one - as the darkness began to encroach on his vision, and his heavy frame slammed to the floor. The last thing he saw before he lost consciousness was a shining white figure floating towards him, anger in its eyes.

Further down the hall, Paul entered Lauren's office, and smiled as his friends immediately stood, concern in their eyes. Lauren hugged him, and he willingly returned the embrace.

She pulled away from him and gave him a small smile, then went back to her chair. Joseph and Paul looked at each other from across the room, and nodded to each other. They knew each other would always be there for one another without needing to say it - it was just their way. Joseph got up from the visitor's chair and ostentatiously offered it to Paul, making both men and Lauren laugh.

"No, you're alright, I'm happy on the desk. Can anyone explain what just happened?"

"Dunno, mate," said Joseph. "Maybe you're mad."

"Joseph!" Lauren exclaimed.

"What? I was just saying."

"Well, don't," Lauren said sharply, looking scandalised. "You're not mad, Paul."

Paul smiled his thanks; in reality, he was trying not to laugh. Joseph was clearly not taking this very seriously, but Paul wouldn't fall for the bait. Lauren was obviously disturbed by what she had seen - so was he, to be honest, but he was desperate to find the funny side as well.

"Thanks," he said instead, his voice hardly wavering at all.

Joseph picked up on it and shifted in his seat, clearing his throat, but Paul ignored him. Lauren didn't seem to catch the subtlety.

"What happened?" she went on. "What do you remember? What did it feel like?"

Paul drew in a breath, and closed his eyes, thinking back to the session.

"What did you mean about shadows?" Lauren asked, trying to start him off.

"There was ... movement," Paul said slowly, "behind my eyelids. I could ... see movement. I thought it was you two, standing over me - that's why I reached out."

"We didn't come in until later," said Joseph, "after we heard you shouting."

"There was this ... light," he said, feeling stupid as he explained it. "It was a white light, in the periphery of my vision. It became more and more intense, and then this voice appeared in my head."

Lauren leaned forward, which didn't surprise Paul. Any talk about hearing voices would make a psychologist sit up and listen.

"What sort of voice?" she asked.

Paul shrugged. "It was androgynous. When my voice changed, that was the voice speaking to me, in my head. The stuff in my own voice; that was me replying." He shrugged. "I just thought I was talking, you know, in my head - I didn't realise I was talking out loud as well."

"I thought you were messing around," Joseph confessed, "making that voice up, but you weren't, were you?"

"I wish I was, Joseph. Believe me when I say, I wish I was."

"It's a bit ... odd, mate. Hearing voices, no matter what the circumstances."

"Since when did you become a psychologist?" Lauren said to her brother. She then broke into a smile as she turned back to Paul. "What he said."

"It seemed to know me, the voice," Paul said. "I ... I know this sounds weird, but a small part of me felt like I should recognise it as well. I just don't know where from."

"Did it sound like anyone you know?" Joseph asked.

Paul shook his head. "No."

Lauren reclined in her chair.

"Has this ever happened to you before?" she asked.

Paul was surprised by the question. He hesitated, about to deny it, but decided against it.

"Was it when you collapsed at the hospital?"

"Yeah," Paul said. He felt a sudden wave of relief at being able to talk about it without seeming any crazier than he already felt. "How did you know?"

"It was just a guess," she admitted. "I guess we should talk about our dream at some point as well, shouldn't we?"

Paul studied her carefully. This was the woman he remembered as a young girl, always sticking to her older brother for protection - and now, here she was, far more intelligent and mature than Paul had given her credit for. She had had the confidence to talk about the large elephant in the corner of the room, which he had been nervously skirting around the edge of during their entire conversation.

Joseph, however, was eyeing them both as if they were crazy.

"What dream?" he demanded. "Am I suddenly the only sane person in the room? You can't have a shared dream, that's impossible!"

As they spoke, hesitatingly at first, about the dream, their shared experience emboldened them and made them feel suddenly less isolated and definitely less crazy. Joseph listened with a growing sense of unease. The fact that both of them were so clear about the dream, and were able to separately describe the events from when Lauren had been picked up from her own, dreamless sleep in to the world of Paul's nightmare, told him that there was more to this than met the eye. But he also wasn't convinced – his natural scepticism was kicking in, and he told them both as much.

"Same here," Paul confessed. "It's difficult to process. I'm still wondering what the hell this is all about - weird visions, me sharing a dream with your sister. But we can't just ignore it. These things actually *happened*, and we need to find out why."

Whatever Lauren opened her mouth to say was lost in a sudden rush of feet running outside her office. Paul got up and looked out into the corridor; there was a crowd gathered round Dr Tempest's office.

"Everything alright?" he called out.

"Tempest's had a heart attack!" a student shouted back. "Get an ambulance!"

Lauren grabbed a phone as Paul's jaw dropped. Had he been the last one to see Jim alive?

Oh shit, he thought.

QEQM Hospital:
Thursday Evening

Paul, Joseph and Lauren had followed the ambulance in Joseph's car. They ended up going back to QEQM in Margate; Canterbury's hospital had closed its A&E department due to NHS cutbacks. Lauren had wanted to stay and wait for word on Tempest's condition, and Joseph and Paul both agreed to wait with her.

Whilst Joseph and Lauren both seemed able to focus on magazines as they waited, Paul couldn't settle. He had paced for a while then, when that had drawn annoyed glances from other people in the waiting room, stood outside for a while. He relaxed as he felt the gentle breeze against his face. He then guiltily realised that he could be spending this time visiting Adam, who still hadn't woken from his coma. Embarrassed that he hadn't thought of that before, Paul headed over to see him.

As he walked down the corridor of the Viking Bay Wing, Paul hesitated as he saw the door to Adam's private room open. He didn't really want to see Rick so soon after their argument. He turned to go, but stopped when he saw Detective Sergeant Kirby and a nurse step from the room. The nurse walked quickly away towards the nurse's station, where Paul saw her pick up the phone. As Kirby turned to face Paul, the detective did a double-take.

"Mr Finn," he said in surprise. He checked his watch. "What brings you here so late?"

Paul checked his own watch. It was 6.30pm. "It's not that late, Detective."

"I was heading home and thought I'd pop my head in anyway. And then of course ..."

He waved vacantly at the door

Paul frowned. "'Of course' what?"

Paul saw the detective's face go pale as he realised what he had said. "Damn."

"What?" Paul insisted.

He took a step forward and tried to side-step the detective, but Kirby stepped in front of the door, blocking any view Paul might have otherwise had.

"Don't go in there," Kirby said. "Let's go somewhere and talk."

"I'm fine just here," Paul snapped. "Now tell me what the hell is going on, Detective, before I report you."

Kirby took a deep breath. "Adam Wild died two minutes ago, Paul. I'm so sorry."

Paul and Kirby moved to a private room not far from the ward's entrance. There were no windows in the room and Paul was grateful for it. He didn't want anyone to see his red-rimmed eyes or puffy cheeks.

Kirby was used to seeing people cry and it wasn't something he ever grew used to. In a way, he was glad; he always swore the day it became second nature to him was the day he gave up on policing.

"What was it, in the end?" Paul asked.

His voice was croaky, and he took a sip of the water a nurse had brought him. It didn't really make his throat feel any better, but it felt good to have something to do for a moment.

"Hmm?" Kirby replied, who had been lost in a world of his own.

Paul had to disguise a brief moment of irritation at the man which, deep down, he knew was irrational.

"Adam's death. What was it?"

"A heart attack. He -"

Paul's head snapped round and fixed Kirby with a steely stare.

"A heart attack?" he said sharply. "Are you sure about that?"

Kirby nodded. "Due to the circumstances, they're going to perform a post-mortem to confirm it, but, yeah, it's a heart attack." He pushed himself upright in his chair. "Paul, his body underwent a tremendous shock - being stabbed so violently that he had to be forced into a coma to conserve energy. According to the doctors, it's not surprising this happened."

"Doesn't make it right, though, does it?" Paul whispered.

"No," Kirby replied, "it doesn't. And I apologise for the thoughtless way you found out."

Paul waved away the apology. He studied him properly for the first time since they had met. The sergeant wasn't that much older than he was - probably in his early thirties. He also had a relaxed air about him which Paul instinctively liked.

"It's okay," he said with a sigh, leaning back and crossing his legs. "I'd have had to find out somehow, wouldn't I?"

He felt vaguely stupid now for crying in front of a stranger, but there was nothing he could do about it now. They sat in silence for a few moments, Kirby still lost in thought.

"What were you doing here anyway?" the detective asked eventually. "Not that it's any of my business, but it's a coincidence."

Paul nodded his agreement. "My friend's boss had a heart attack. We were there at the time, so we followed to see if there was anything we could do."

"Is that why you gave me a funny look when I mentioned Adam's heart attack?"

"Yeah," Paul replied, and a smile tugged at his mouth. "You're not the only one who thinks about coincidences, you know."

Kirby stood and tried to pace the length of the room, but it was such a confined - and airless - space that he couldn't do it for more than a few steps without needing to turn round, so gave up. Still standing, he spun on his heels and turned back to face Paul.

"Are you still a believer?"

Paul was caught quite off-guard by the question.

"In a god?" he asked. "Yes. Not that I particularly see the reference."

Kirby shrugged. "I'm just curious, that's all. St Mary's is a Catholic church, isn't it?"

Paul nodded. "But I wouldn't call myself Catholic. As my friend Joseph would tell you, I was never a great one for celebrating all the covenants that humans create around a deity."

"I know what you mean," Kirby said.

Sod it, Paul thought. *Why should all the questions be one way?*

"Are *you* a believer, Mr Kirby?"

Kirby was silent for a moment. He sat down and looked at the blank wall opposite him, suddenly deep in thought. Paul wondered if he had overstepped an invisible boundary. He opened his mouth to apologise, but Kirby started speaking before he had the chance.

"My dad was an Anglican," he said, in a thoughtful voice, as if he was thinking about things he hadn't thought about in quite a while. "He kept his faith fairly private - I mean, he never went to church or anything, but he had his faith. My mother ..."

He chuckled, as if slightly embarrassed to admit it.

"She was a die-in-the-wool Spiritualist. She believed in god, as most spiritualists do, but was also a medium. Contacted spirits, spoke to them, believed in spirit guides ... the whole shebang."

Paul watched the detective for a moment, obviously lost in a sudden wave of nostalgia. "You didn't quite answer my question though," he noted. "What do *you* believe?"

Kirby laughed. "I thought you'd missed that one. Well, I've always belonged to the Spiritualist movement. I was a lot more passionate when I was younger, a lot more ... committed, I guess the word is. I even trained to be a medium and ... uh, channelled spirits."

Paul leant forward, suddenly a lot more interested. Before this week, he would have politely smiled and nodded, and then promptly forgot about it. Now, however, things were different; he had experienced things these past few days that he couldn't explain, and Kirby's experiences might be able to help him find some answers. Kirby seemed to mistake Paul's change in posture as a disbelieving one, and quickly shook his head.

"I know, I know," he said with a wry smile, "it sounds completely barmy. Don't think I didn't go through of all that myself when I was growing up. But ..." He shrugged. "I don't know. I've always been able to close my eyes, focus my energy and just ... contact people. Dead people. I've been lapsed for a couple of years ago, what with some personal issues. My faith was shaken, and I ... I don't know, I somehow lost the ability to channel."

"But you still believe?"

"Just about."

Kirby's face was a mask, as if he were remembering things that he had very hard tried to forget. He suddenly shook his head.

"I shouldn't be talking to you about this, you've lost a friend"

Paul felt a sudden stab of guilt; a sob stifled in his throat, and Kirby tactfully looked away.

"I'll be outside if you need me," he said quietly.

He left Paul alone with his grief.

Paul took a few minutes to compose himself - and found that he was thinking about what Kirby had been telling him.

He knew about Spiritualism, of course, from his days in the seminary, but it was more of a general overview. It was while he was trying to remember what he had been taught that the beginnings of a plan started to formulate inside his mind. It wasn't a very complex plan, but might – if Kirby agreed – help him find out if what was happening to him was just a series of dreams or something more real.

Paul found the detective up the corridor at the nurse's station, talking to one of the doctors. Noticing Paul, he smiled his thanks to the doctor and motioned that they should walk a little further down the corridor for some privacy.

"The autopsy will be tomorrow," he said quietly. "They'll leave Adam's body in the morgue until then."

Paul nodded, but said nothing – the thought of his friend being placed in the morgue was an awful one. He tried to put his emotions aside – he could mourn at home but, for now, he needed to focus.

"I ... uh, I wanted to apologise to you," Kirby said abruptly.

Paul blinked in surprise. "Apologise?" he asked. "Apologise for what?"

"For the way I was going on back there," Kirby continued. "Talking about my faith. You're upset about your friend. I shouldn't have dumped on you like that. I'm meant to set a good example as a police officer."

Paul shook his head. "No, I'm actually glad you did," he replied. This drew a quizzical look from Kirby, and Paul explained; "It helped, in a weird sort of way. You really got me thinking."

"What about?"

"Well ..." said Paul, then hesitated. What he was considered was well out of the ordinary.

Kirby leaned against the wall, openly curious. "You've got me interested now," he confessed. "Go on, it can't be any more bizarre than some of the things I've heard in my life. I'm a cop, remember."

Paul laughed. "I'm not so sure about that. Just ... hear me out before you start thinking that I'm a complete madman. "

Ten minutes later, Paul stepped into Adam's room.

Well, he thought, that didn't go as bad as I expected, he thought. *At least he didn't laugh in my face.*

Kirby hadn't immediately dismissed Paul's plan out of hand. It had boiled down to two favours. First, Paul being allowed to have a few minutes to say a proper goodbye to Adam. He knew that it would give Kirby a chance to think more about the second favour, which was, after all, the bigger – and more unusual.

As he had told Joseph earlier, he still had a faith – of sorts. Although he didn't consider himself belonging to any religion, his belief in an afterlife still followed a typically Christian vision – heaven and hell, and being judged on the basis of his life.

I wonder where I'll be going, he thought.

As Catholics, he wondered if Wild would have expected Paul to perform the last rites over his body. Paul suspected that his friend wouldn't put that pressure on him, knowing how Paul felt about the large amount of rituals that had built up around the once-simple belief in god.

He pulled up a chair and sat down next to Wild's body.

"Hey mate," he whispered, and laughed to himself. "Wish I was saying that and getting a response, but hey - can't have everything."

It was ironic, but he didn't feel at all ridiculous talking to Adam now he was dead – as opposed to yesterday, when he had felt embarrassed while Adam had merely been unconscious.

He rationalised that it was down to his former life as Father John's assistant priest. When some believers died, if they had been active members of the church, one of the priests would sit with their bodies after their death for a time. Paul had sat with a woman of 97 and a boy of 12, so he was perfectly comfortable speaking to a spirit through their body. He had never had to do it with a friend before, but Paul knew he wanted to say a proper goodbye.

"I feel so bad, Adam," he went on. "I should have been there more, even after I left the church. You and I were good friends, and I hate myself that I lost contact with you."

He shrugged uselessly. "I don't know. I guess I just needed time away from that ... that place which turned its back on when I was in the middle of a crisis. That stupid bishop, with all his petty rules and regulations ... and Father John and me, with all our stubbornness. I wish I'd overcome that before he died."

"But you," he said with a smile, "you were there for me. Even when Father John and I had that huge row, and you were probably angry with me, you would have still been there for me to lean on. "

He sighed, standing up. He began pacing the room, to try and get his thoughts together. "I'm going to have to tell Rick, I guess. He'll want to know, and I'd rather it come from me than from a stranger. I owe him that much, even though we always bicker like children."

He smiled as he stopped by the room's only window, looking out over the front lawn and entrance to the car park.

"I remember Father John asking me once why we couldn't ever get along with each other like you and I did. I couldn't give him a proper answer except for some glib response about a personality clash. Don't know how true that was, but I don't think Father John believed me. He kept trying to bring us together, but Rick and I just couldn't stop irritating each other."

He stared out the window for a while and watched the world go by. It seemed almost cruel that people's lives were carrying on when his friend was lying here, dead.

He watched a group of nurses walk over to the car park entrance and light up cigarettes. He found it mildly odd that nurses of all people smoked; it seemed slightly ironic somehow.

"Rick and I met for breakfast, you know, after your assault," Paul went on. "It was his idea, actually, and I was really pleased. I thought it might be the start of reconciliation, or at least being able to be in a room together for more than fifteen minutes without one of us starting an argument. I was a bit narked though, when I got there. He'd invited a friend of his along, someone called Lucy Golding. Dunno who she was."

He shrugged. "It just irritated me, like he thought we'd need a chaperone to stop us from arguing. Then she and I got into an argument about something completely stupid, and I ended up storming out."

Paul rolled his eyes at his reflection in the window. "Rick actually ended up trying to be the peacemaker. Ironic, huh?"

A thought suddenly occurred to him. "Hey, did you know that Rick's still in Holy Orders? I was bloody shocked when he -"

He had half-turned before he remembered where he was. His cheeks flushed with raw emotion - he had been chatting away to his friend's body as if nothing had changed, as if they were back in Father Simon's office chatting about the past.

Shock quickly overtook his embarrassment as he realised the chair he had so recently been sitting in was now occupied by –

"Lucy," he whispered. "What -"

Lucy Golding waved aside his question with a flick of her hand. Paul felt a surge of anger, but something told him to bite his tongue, just for a while. Self-preservation was the best way he could describe it.

Watching Golding carefully, he moved away from the window towards the chair. She just smiled, refusing to be intimidated, and rose slowly from the chair - she wasn't much shorter than Paul was, in truth, so his hope at intimidating her was over before it had begun. She was looking at him with a small, amused smile on her face, and her eyebrow quirked as he stopped in front of her.

"I'm sorry we didn't end on a very good note this morning, Paul," she said

"You'll have to forgive me if that's not at the forefront of my mind." He motioned to the bed. "As you can see, I've got other thing to think about right now."

"Of course - your friend Adam." Golding looked over at Adam's body, but didn't look the slightest bit remorseful, and certainly didn't offer any type of sorrow. "How did he die?"

Paul shook his head. He didn't really feel that inclined to discuss it right now, especially with this frustrating woman.

"Perhaps another time," he said with absolutely no sincerity. "You'll understand that I'm not really interested in restarting the argument from this morning, or starting up a new one. I'm just here to say goodbye to my friend."

"Where do you suppose his soul has gone?" Golding asked.

Are you being deliberately obtuse? Paul wondered, *or is there a reason to all this? If there is, I wish you'd just get it over and done with, so I can be with my friend.*

"I don't know," Paul said. "Like I said, another time perhaps."

It was a lie, of course, on both counts; he had his faith, and didn't have much of an interest in having any sort of conversation with her, ever.

Golding's eyes flicked away from Adam to Paul. The smirk had left her face and been replaced with a look of curiosity. Paul had to fight that same feeling he had had earlier - the slight flicker of recognition.

Where do I know you from? he wondered.

"You really don't recognise me, do you?" Golding said, a degree of amazement in her voice. "I thought it would have come back to you, especially after the day you've had today."

Paul frowned. "What do you know about my day?"

"Enough," Golding said with a shrug.

"Care to be a bit more specific?"

"Not really. If you're capable of figuring it out, then you will do. If not ... well, you'll just be the pathetic human being I always suspected you were."

Paul felt a sudden rage building up inside of him, seeing this smug, arrogant woman trying to belittle him in front of his just-dead friend.

"Get out," he said quietly. "Get out of here. *Get out!*"

Paul's voice was getting louder and louder, as all his anger, rage and grief that he had been bottling up over the past few days suddenly erupted from him in a fury, and came out in a focused rage at Golding.

Golding's eyes widened in surprise as Paul's voice continued to rise, and the anger continued to seek release. Paul's yells of "Get out!" became more of a bellow, and Golding actually took a step back out of fear as she saw his hands ball into fists.

Paul took a step toward her, and a small part, deep inside, took pleasure at the sight of this obnoxious woman actually being given a taste of fear, instead of the self-satisfaction she seemed to carry with her everywhere.

As his anger began to truly take over, he was dimly aware of the door being pushed open with a great urgency, and the next thing he knew, Kirby's face was in front of him instead of Golding's as the detective pushed himself between them and placed his hands forcibly on Paul's shoulders, forcing him to stop his forward momentum.

Paul blinked a few times, and suddenly his head began to clear. The anger quickly subsided into a black pit deep inside his stomach: it was still there, bubbling away, but he was now able to control it. He took a step back and drew in a deep, ragged breath to calm down. Fortunately, it seemed to work.

The mist cleared from Paul's eyes. He turned away and ran his fingers through his hair, suddenly feeling very stupid and annoyed with himself for losing control so easily.

Looking round, he opened his mouth to say something to Golding, who had backed up against the wall - but no words would come out. What could he say? He had an intense dislike of the woman, as she seemed to have for him and, while he accepted his abrupt lack of control as his fault, he wouldn't just lie to her by apologising profusely.

I know *you*, he thought with a sudden jolt of realisation. *I know you. You're ... you're ... why can't I remember?*

"Because I don't want you to!" Golding spat back venomously, her eyes suddenly blazing with passion and hatred. "That would destroy everything!"

Paul started – *did I say that out loud?*

Golding stormed towards the now-open door, but was blocked by the sudden appearance of Joseph and Lauren in the doorway.

"Are we interrupting something?" Lauren asked, her eyes flicking between Paul, Kirby and Golding. "We can come back if you want."

Joseph caught the look in Paul's eyes. "No, we can't," he said.

He glared at Golding, who gave a snarl and barged past them into the corridor.

"Looks like we came to find you at the right time," Joseph went on, watching Golding go before stepping into the room behind Lauren. "That her?"

Paul nodded, not trusting himself to speak straight away.

Lauren frowned, and looked back at her brother. She had quickly picked up on the tension in the room, but decided that ignoring it was the best position

Coward, she chided herself.

"Who was that?" she asked.

"Some woman that Paul met this morning over breakfast," Joseph replied without thinking.

Lauren looked scandalised, and glared at Paul.

"It wasn't like that!" Paul quickly protested. He sometimes suspected that Joseph liked winding his friend up just for the sake of it. "I met my old friend Rick for breakfast, and he brought her along. You remember Rick, don't you, from my days in the church?"

Lauren nodded. Paul could see that she suddenly had questions about why he had met up with Rick in the first place, and what Lucy was doing at their reunion breakfast. He just wished he could answer those questions himself - especially the second one.

"You alright?" Kirby asked cautiously.

He was still carefully watching Paul, but cast an uncomfortable look at Adam's body. He clearly didn't want to be in the room for too long.

"Yeah," said Paul quietly.

He felt stupid and ashamed in equal measure. It was if he had been somehow disrespectful to Adam's memory, by losing control in here, and was finding it difficult to meet anyone's eye. He eventually looked up at Kirby.

"It was a stupid thing to do."

Kirby shrugged. "I let her in. I shouldn't have done."

They each accepted the tacit apologies in each other's voices, and Paul went on; "Does this affect -"

"The second favour?" Kirby hesitated, then shook his head. "No. Meet me tomorrow morning ... then we'll see what happens."

"Come on, mate," said Joseph, "let's go."

"What about Dr Tempest?"

Lauren answered in a wavering tone; "He's dead, Paul. There was nothing they could do."

Tears sprung, unbidden, from her eyes, and Joseph drew her into an embrace. Paul swallowed, hard.

Damn, he thought. *Damnit all to hell! Why is everyone dying around me!*

"Would you give me one minute?"

Joseph nodded, distracted by Lauren's tears; Paul didn't blame him, and watched as his friend escorted his sister from the room. Kirby followed their lead, and was alone in the room once again.

He looked back at Adam's body, lost in silent thought. They weren't even thoughts about anything in particular - just snippets of memories that he and Adam had shared together over the years. Laughs down the pub, heated conversations about religion, politics - anything.

A single tear ran down Paul's cheek.

"I'm sorry," he whispered.

None of the three friends had particularly wanted to be alone that evening, so had gone back to Paul's flat together.

Paul sat in his usual recliner chair, overlooking the street and watching the world go by. He didn't much feel like doing anything - it would have felt just wrong somehow. Lauren was spending some time cleaning out the backs of Paul's cupboards - something she had felt needed doing for a long time, and certainly Paul raised no objection today. She recognised it as a displacement therapy, but welcomed the distraction. For Joseph's part, he was determined not to react to Lauren's obvious emotions until she needed him to, and instead read a newspaper.

The evening wore on and Paul's eyes began to droop. After a while, Joseph looked up from his newspaper and saw that his friend was fast asleep. Joseph glanced over at his sister, who nodded. After putting a blanket over Paul, they quietly left the flat - and Paul - to his dreams.

The Celestial Observatory:
Present Day

Michael and Gabriel were sat, side by side, on the stone bench. They hadn't moved for quite some time, lost in their own thoughts and memories of 2,000 years ago. If they had been concentrating, they might have noticed Paul's confrontation with Lucy Golding and seen something ... odd about her. They were too preoccupied to notice.

Gabriel found humans fascinating; they crammed so much into their short lives. They loved, cried and died in the blink of an eye but still found time to build up huge cities, societies and dreams. He sometimes wondered what it would be like to live amongst them.

Michael had been shocked by Paul's visit to the Observatory. There wasn't much that could surprise him these days, given the many thousands of years he'd served at the Almighty's side, and the 2,000 years since the Civil War that he had been the Chief Observer of Them - but Paul's visit had shaken him.

In his darkest moments, he found himself thinking back 2,000 years to when he lost his position as commander of the angelic armies to Metatron. After the Civil War, her position had been strengthened by the

Almighty withdrawing into himself, and she had been able to take his position without any protest. Everyone – including Michael – had been stunned by the quickness and ruthlessness of it all.

But, while he was hurt by the Authority's abandonment, he never argued against his new post; it meant that he was able to keep a check on the Earthly realm, and make sure that Metatron was not interfering.

It's the least I can do, he thought, as the idea was mine. *I wish I knew if I had done the right thing.*

He also wished he'd stepped in and spared Gabriel the pain he had suffered. He carried that guilt around with him even now, after 2,000 years, and had been another reason why he had never challenged Metatron's authority; he couldn't bear seeing anyone else suffering in the way Gabriel had. He suspected that Metatron had allowed Gabriel to remain in Heaven for just that reason – as a reminder to him of what she was capable of.

Gabriel shifted on the bench.

"Is it wrong to wonder what could have been?" he asked. "If only we hadn't sent them away?"

"I think about it every day, my friend," Michael confessed. "Every single day."

After a few minutes, both Michael and Gabriel became aware of another presence in the Observatory, behind them. They looked round and saw a semi-transparent figure floating in the corner.

Michael felt a flash of irritation. He'd managed to keep the Observatory free from all violations for the past 2,000 years; no-one had been able to gain access without his express permission. Now, there had been two intrusions in as many days.

Either my powers are getting weaker, or he is getting stronger, he thought. *Maybe the plan is working after all.*

"Don't send him away," Gabriel said quickly.

Michael caught the look on Gabriel's face; he reluctantly inclined his head.

"Be quick. Metatron must not find out."

Gabriel took a careful step towards Paul. The human was coming more and more into focus; he was looking around him with a mixture of confusion, fear and interest. Gabriel held his hands up and smiled reassuringly.

"Don't be afraid," Gabriel said.

He immediately regretted saying it. Of course Paul would feel afraid - as Gabriel would undoubtedly do if their situations were reversed. He remembered when he had last felt such deep-rooted fear; he had to take a breath to not let a sudden rush of emotion rise up in his throat.

Paul shimmered into full focus. Michael glanced over his shoulder at the image on his screen, and saw that Paul's body was still fast asleep.

"How can he do this?" Gabriel asked rhetorically. "He's meant to be fully human!"

Michael sighed. He knew that Gabriel's questioning wouldn't just stop.

"When Paul's gone," Michael said, "you and I need to have a conversation."

Gabriel nodded, his eyes alight with curiosity; he was distracted as Paul's form solidified.

"Where am I?" he asked.

He looked properly at his two hosts. They were both taller than him (although, given that Paul was five foot five, that wasn't overly difficult) and dressed in ... well, nothing much, to be honest. They had covered the ... important areas, but otherwise were naked.

I suppose too much clothing would play havoc with their wings, he thought.

It took a few moments for Paul to fully register the wings on their backs. They were full and majestic, yes, but still wings. He could think of only one group that possessed wings.

"Angels," he breathed.

Michael's mouth twitched up. "Your powers of observation do you justice, Paul."

"How is this happening?" Paul asked. "I'm asleep. I remember falling asleep, yet I'm here. How does that work? Is this a dream?"

"Have you ever heard of the soul?" Gabriel replied.

"Of course I have," he replied. "I used to be a priest."

"We know. We know a lot about you"

Paul glared at both angels.

"Been watching me, have you?" he snapped.

Michael waved at the vast bank of screens. Paul's square enlarged and he found himself staring at his sleeping form.

"Why are you watching all those people?" he demanded. "Why are you watching me? It's my life - you haven't got the right to watch me like this!"

"We've got more rights than you know, Mr. Finn," Michael replied, folding his arms across his chest. "We watch these people because they're special."

A sudden alarm rang in his head. He looked to the main entrance of the Observatory, knowing instantly who it was.

"What?" Paul asked as he saw their reactions. "What is it?"

"Metatron," Michael whispered.

He squared his shoulders, as if determined not to show any fear towards her.

I think I know you, Paul thought, and then blinked in surprise. *Why are you so familiar?*

He shook his head, dismissing that thought for the moment. While Michael seemed very determined to hide his fear, Paul had no such compunction. After all, what could angels be afraid of?

Gabriel gulped. "What's she doing here?" He turned to Paul. "You need to hide yourself!" he said urgently. "Now!"

Paul looked round the room. Aside from the bench that he had found the angels sitting on, and the large wall of images, there was nothing in the room. The ceiling and floor were transparent, and the blackness of the night's sky could be seen through both, leaving the room bathed in moonlight.

"Where?" he exclaimed. "Under the bench?"

Michael gave him a withering stare, and Gabriel glanced at his fellow angel.

"He makes a fair point."

Michael reluctantly nodded and raised a hand. Paul felt a tingling sensation for a moment. He looked down, but nothing had changed.

"What -"

"Trust him," Gabriel said urgently. "Stay absolutely still and don't say a word."

Paul had no choice but to do as Gabriel said. He had heard Gabriel and Michael talk about Metatron on his previous visit, and their reactions told him she was a powerful angel, more so than either of them, so he was not going to do anything to get noticed by her.

Gabriel quickly composed his face into something more neutral, gave one final glance over his shoulder at Paul, then turned away as a third figure entered the Celestial Observatory.

Paul frowned, as he couldn't quite make the figure out. He blinked, to make sure it wasn't his eyes, but it wasn't – it was definitely the figure itself, blurring against any attempt to allow him to see its true form.

Well, that's one mystery solved, he thought.

He now knew the identity of the angel he had met yesterday, after Michael's failed attempt to send him home.

But why did she think I'd know her?

As Metatron approached, Michael and Gabriel inclined their heads in a respectful nod.

"I thought I'd find you here," she said, her voice distorted and still androgynous.

"I've been Chief Observer since my retirement," he said. "I'm hardly anywhere else."

Metatron looked at Gabriel. "And you?"

"I like to keep Michael company from time to time," the angel replied. "And my curiosity is always piqued by their human lives."

Metatron seemed to nod - at least, the portion of white light surrounding her head bobbed up and down for a moment in the movement of a nod - and she turned to face the constantly-moving images.

"The personalities are still firmly in place, I assume?" she barked. "There are no issues?"

"No," Michael replied. "They are perfect. I personally guarantee them all."

Gabriel glanced at him in warning, but Michael studiously ignored him. Paul's interest was raised; he was one of the people on the display, and was worried about Metatron's mention of personalities being "fixed in place."

What's wrong with my personality? he thought.

"That is good news," said Metatron thoughtfully, as if not entirely convinced.

She watched the images for a few minutes, and this time Michael did acknowledge the look Gabriel was giving him. What was she taking such an interest in? Suddenly, without warning, Metatron called up one of the images to the centre of the screen. Paul's stomach did back flips as he saw his own, sleeping, face projected out at him.

"I recognise this human," Metatron said. "I have seen him here, in my office. Yesterday."

"Paul Finn appeared before you?" Gabriel said with feigned concerned. "How would that be possible?"

"Indeed," she said. "How would it be possible? It would be possible, my dear Gabriel, if the barriers separating our worlds had been breached. Of course, that is meant to be impossible ... isn't it, Michael?"

Michael didn't react. He was stood, almost like a soldier, to attention, and his eyes were focused on the middle distance.

"I would not know," he said. "When I was in charge of security, I could personally guarantee the security of every layer of protection from Earth to here." He fixed his eyes onto Metatron's. "Perhaps you should be telling me about our security."

"I answer to the Almighty, not *you.*"

"Are you *sure* about that? Or do you answer just to yourself? I haven't seen the Almighty in many years. He used to give his orders directly to his angels. Can you guarantee that you are obeying his commands, and not your own?"

Metatron took a step towards Michael, fury showing on her face.

"Be very careful," she growled in a low tone. "Do not forget that you remain in your position at my discretion. If you continue to be so ... disobedient, you may well find yourself at the wrong end of an ... accident."

Metatron took his silence as acquiescence and turned to look at Gabriel, studying him carefully.

"Gabriel," she went on, her voice suddenly becoming dangerously quiet, "I am curious; how do you know Paul Finn? I can accept Michael knowing it – he is, after all, our chief observer. But for what possible reason would you have for knowing it?"

It was only then that Gabriel realised his schoolboy error, and his eyes widened.

"I -" Gabriel struggled for a moment, his ability to form a coherent argument broken in the face of Metatron's cool anger. "I've taken something of an interest in them. I find it curious, that they live out such short, mortal lives, and yet accomplish so much. It ... intrigues me."

Metatron was silent, studying Gabriel closely. Paul felt a shudder of fear and was suddenly glad that whatever Michael had done to hide him had worked.

"I choose to believe you, Gabriel," said Metatron, "because I have no proof to disbelieve you. You always have shown an unnatural fascination in these exiles, for reasons beyond my comprehension. Of course, if that is the only reason you have to know Paul Finn, then you will have no idea why - or how - he was able to bring himself here, to our realm, and turn up in my office on two separate occasions?"

"I ... I do not know," Gabriel stumbled.

Michael quickly stepped in to mask the younger angel's discomfort.

"What did he want?" he asked.

"I do not know," Metatron replied. "He stood there like a typically dumb-struck human, asking stupid questions. He doesn't remember me, though, which lends itself to your story that their personalities are still in place, Michael."

Metatron was clearly fishing for information, but neither Michael nor Gabriel were going to give anything away.

"I would hope that no-one is aiding the exiles in any way," Metatron went on. "We agreed this was the best solution. If it should fail, I would have no compunction in resorting to my plan."

She gave Michael an especially sharp glare as she said this, which he returned, eye to eye.

"Understood, Metatron," he replied coolly.

Gabriel quickly echoed his friend's words, averting his gaze as he said them.

What sort of hold has she got over you? Paul wondered.

"Very well," Metatron said. "Michael, watch Paul Finn and his friend closely. Any one of them could be cause for concern, especially given Paul's predilection to appearing in my office. You know I never really approved of this plan. Mine was simpler ... more effective."

Paul frowned. He didn't know what Metatron's plan was, but it didn't sound at all pleasant.

"I shall check in with you regularly," she went on, "but let me know if they do anything out of character."

"Yes, Metatron," Michael said.

This agreement seemed to pacify the senior angel, at least for the moment; without another word, she turned on her heel and strode out of the Observatory.

Michael and Gabriel didn't move until she was well out of sight, and then both breathed out in unison. They glanced at each other with obvious relief. Michael waved his hand and, although Paul felt no different, he knew he was visible again

Gabriel's wings flexed for a moment as he thought out loud; "What in the name of all that is holy do we do now?"

"It would help," Paul interrupted in a sudden fit of irritation, "if either of you could tell me what the hell's going on. I've understood about one tenth of what you're talking about."

"If I'd sent you back properly the first time," Michael retorted, "we wouldn't even be having this discussion."

"We have to send Paul back," Gabriel regretfully said, "then try and seal the breach he's using to get through."

"You wish to send him back?" Michael said in surprise. "Given who he is, I thought you would have wanted him to stay."

"What do you mean?" Paul asked. "Who am I?"

"You're not ready to know that," Gabriel replied, and before Paul could protest, he turned back to Michael. "I would rather him stay here; after all this time, I want him back, but not if means having Metatron do what she is threatening. We know what she's capable of, Michael. Neither of us wants that. I've ... experienced it once, I don't want to go through that again. I can't be that weak again."

Michael was silent for a moment, not knowing what to say. A moment of understanding seemed to pass between them, and Michael clapped a hand on Gabriel's shoulder.

"You're not weak, Gabriel. You never were. You just couldn't stand up to her. If I were in your situation, I honestly don't know if I could have either. I know why you want Paul here, but ... I agree with you, it's too dangerous. We need to send him back."

"Don't I get a say in this?" Paul asked.

Despite himself, he found his irritation lessening as he listened to the two talking. They seemed concerned for him, as well as the consequences if he stayed here.

Michael looked at him and smiled. "I thought you wanted to go home."

"I do," Paul replied. "But I also want answers. Like why Metatron called me an 'exile'."

"It is in your best interest to remain ignorant. You are not ready to learn the truth. It would do far more damage. Go home ... and sleep."

Paul frowned. "I don't appreciate other people -"

"- making my decisions for me."

It took Paul a few seconds to readjust to his new surroundings. His eyes had begun to get used to the brightness of the Observatory, and the real world seemed dull by comparison.

He stood and stumbled around a bit as his brain regained control of its physical form, almost like a drunk man regaining his sobriety. As he leaned against a wall for a moment, he glanced out the windows - it was still dark, the middle of the night. Hardly any time at all had passed in the real world: in his dreams, it had felt like hours.

He mentally reviewed his memories, and they all seemed to be there - the visits to the other realm, the encounters with Metatron, Gabriel and Michael, everything.

"At least they didn't take them," he muttered to himself.

Mind you, he thought, *I wouldn't remember if there were any gaps, would I?*

In any case, Gabriel and Michael would now be working to repair the breach they had mentioned, thereby stopping Paul getting through again – and needing the memories again.

To hell with that, he thought. *I've got more questions than ever now. I'm going to find out what's going on, whether they want me to or not.*

Back in the Celestial Observatory, Gabriel turned to Michael.

"You had something you wanted to talk to me about?"

I'd hoped you'd forgotten about that, Michael thought.

"Don't think you're getting away with it that easily," Gabriel said with a smile. Michael's emotions were sometimes easier to read than he realised.

Michael motioned to the stone bench, his face turned serious.

"Let's talk," he said.

Paul's Flat:
Friday Morning

P aul slept soundly for the rest of the night and woke at eight o'clock; but he didn't feel rested. His dreams had been full of strange imagery, with wings, stone benches and TV screens full of people's faces.

As he shaved, he thought back on the vivid dreams he'd had throughout his life: of huge halls, the feeling of possibility, of passion ... then of shame and judgement. Throughout his life, he'd dismissed them as just dreams; as his brain chucking up deep, subconscious imagery...but what if it wasn't that? What if it was something *more*?

But how are my friends related to all of this?

Lauren appeared in one of his dreams, remembering it after she had woken up. Joseph, too, was involved, even if he tried to deny it: Paul *felt* it.

As he dressed and made his plans for the day, he knew he needed Detective Kirby, who could contact the dead: or had been up until two years ago.

It can't be a coincidence, Paul thought. *I left the church two years ago. There's got to be something in that. It's fate – Kirby is meant to help me.*

Kirby knew what Paul needed from him; Paul just hoped he wouldn't back out now.

Margate Police Station:
Friday Morning

There was one thing DS Kirby hated above all others.

Paperwork.

If it meant he was fitting into a stereotype, then so be it; to him, paperwork was boring and served no purpose other than take him away from the front-line.

That front-line had become more mundane of late; burglaries, thefts, drugs. He hated that it was all so routine; there were times when a murder would shock a community, or a violent rape would hit the news, and the complexities of the case would make Kirby's days fly by.

I sound like a right freak, he realised.

He would have done a day's worth of paperwork, however, if it meant he gained a lead on Adam Wild's murder.

Father Simon had been stabbed once in the chest; he had died mercifully quickly. As best as Kirby could tell, Adam had then come out from the small kitchen and seen the attacker. Adam must had tried to attack the assailant, because the pathologist had found bruises on his body that fitted with a fight, and one particular bruise on his left temple that looked suspiciously like the imprint of a knife's handle.

Unfortunately, the assailant was good enough at his job to win the fight. He had left no fingerprints, random strands of hair or any other type of DNA that would help narrow down the search. There was one partial shoeprint, but not enough to build up any sort of profile.

The only reason Kirby was even assuming the gunman was male was because of the fight. Adam was five foot nine and solidly built at 13½ stone; a woman would have found it difficult to overpower him.

Kirby sighed in frustration; he was running out of leads. The only person he had left to question was Rick Walton, Wild and Finn's fellow seminary student, and that was more for a background picture than anything else. Finn had promised to ask Rick to call him as soon as he had told his friend the news.

It had just gone 9.30am, and Kirby felt like he had barely accomplished anything in the past two hours. He found himself going through emails, filing his paperwork and flicking through the pages of the local paper, seeing if there were any of his cases mentioned in it. There were two, one theft (defendant found guilty, community service) and one aggravated assault (defendant found guilty, two years imprisonment).

I got one conviction, he conceded, wishing it had been two.

He folded the paper up and chucked it over to a passing constable who had wanted it, then took a walk down to the kitchen for a coffee.

He had barely had a chance to flip the kettle on before the same constable popped his head round the door and told him he had a visitor at the front counter - one Paul Finn.

"Damn," Kirby muttered, then smiled. "Obviously wants to make sure I don't do a runner."

The constable gave him a funny look, and Kirby waved him away.

Kirby was in a different building to the front counter – main reception by any other name - so he began the walk over. He had surprised himself when he had opened up to Paul about his Spiritualist beliefs - he didn't often talk about it to anyone, not so much because he was embarrassed by it, but more because he suspected many people would misunderstand. He knew people often got freaked out by the concept of talking to the dead, so he was usually far more circumspect about who he mentioned it to.

Kirby arrived at reception and entered by the public entrance. Paul was stood by one of the notice boards, reading the rather less-than-cheery notices about how to beat drug and alcohol abuse, not to leave your valuables unattended and the upcoming station open day - which Kirby conveniently had off as annual leave.

"Paul," he said.

As he turned, Kirby was surprised; Paul looked exhausted, as if he hadn't slept in a month. He motioned to the visitors' chairs by the entrance.

"Are you okay?"

"Yeah," Paul replied, stifling a yawn. "Just tired, Detective. I didn't sleep well last night."

Kirby smiled. "Call me Kirby. Everyone does."

Paul struggled to find the words. He'd been rehearsing it in his head, but still didn't know what to say. *I've been visiting angels over the last two days, and I want to see how that fits in to these dreams I've been having since I was a kid about being someone else ... possibly in a higher plane of existence, and I think you can help me.*

"Let's go for a walk," he said instead.

They walked towards Margate beach, the famous sands once beloved by Queen Victoria and now beloved by penny arcades, clubs and pub landlords. The seaweed, a perennial problem to the locals, was high today, and council workers were on the beach cleaning it off. The smell was almost overpowering, but both Paul and Kirby were doing their best to ignore it.

"You're here to talk about the second favour, aren't you?" Kirby guessed.

"Yeah," Paul replied. "Yeah, I have. I need you to contact the dead for me."

Kirby sighed. "There must be hundreds of mediums out there," he said. "I haven't made contact with the other side for two years. Why not one of those?"

"Because I know *you*. I think we were meant to meet, Kirby – I know that sounds weird, but I can't believe it was down to chance. Two years ago, I left the church and something happened that stopped you channelling. I believe you're meant to start again now."

"Don't start about fate with me. My situation was different to you leaving the church."

The detective sighed. He stopped walking and leaned on the railings overlooking the beach. It wasn't one he had ever visited as a child - in fact, he couldn't remember a single occasion, and so he had no real memories associated with the place. It was a hot, sunny day, however, and a lot of people were out enjoying it. He wished he could be one of them, but had found it incredibly hard to just unwind and relax ever since ... *it* had happened.

Paul watched the detective carefully. "I know you still believe," he said. "That's why I need you, because of that belief. And I think I can trust you."

Kirby turned to face him. "I need you to tell me everything before I decide."

Paul started talking, and didn't stop until he had told Kirby everything. Kirby listened closely to it all, and then said the one thing that Paul had hoped he would say.

"I believe you."

Joseph Tempur's Home: Friday Morning

J oseph was usually an early riser; years of getting up early to write before school had drummed it into him. Today, however, it had been nine o'clock when he finally dragged himself out of bed. When he arrived home the previous evening, he'd felt too awake to go to bed, so he wrote a chapter of his latest manuscript before crashing out at four in the morning.

He was disappointed when neither Micky nor Lauren answered their phones; Lauren was at work, but he had hoped his best friend would answer his phone, despite his annoying habit of always leaving it switched off.

He'd called them just to talk; he wanted to go over everything that had happened. He had always been a sceptic, always doubting everything he couldn't physically see or touch with his own senses, and so he found it difficult to accept that two people he trusted beyond measure had both had experiences that fell into that category.

The shared dream that they'd had was an example of that. Joseph had read somewhere of people with tumours being affected by strange dreams and images if they pressed on a certain area of the brain, which made him wonder if Paul had one as well.

That would be an incredible coincidence though, he thought. *Mind you, it would be a rational answer that I could understand.*

His mobile phone rang, and he blinked in surprise when he saw it was Paul's mobile.

"Paul?" he asked. "Are you feeling alright?"

"Of course I am," came Paul's voice. *"Why wouldn't I be alright?"*

"Because you're calling me on your mobile," Joseph replied.

"Well, the battery runs down quickly, and I never get a decent signal. It's a piece of crap."

"Since when did you become Amish?"

"About the same time as you stopped being irritating and asking me stupid questions."

"Alright, alright," Joseph laughed. "I tried calling you at home earlier, but you weren't in."

"Yeah, I'm just over in Margate at the moment," Paul replied. *"Listen, your dining room's still ... well, you know, there, isn't it?"*

Joseph frowned in confusion. "Of course it is," he replied. "Where do you think it's gone, to the great dining room retirement home in the sky?"

"No, look," Paul said with a sigh, *"I'm not explaining myself very well -"*

"You're telling me."

"Do you mind if we use it this morning, mate? For a little experiment?"

Joseph was suddenly alarmed. "Paul, you are not coming round here to try your cooking skills out again. I was in bed for three days last time!"

"No, you stupid arse," Paul interrupted. *"Just get your sister round in about an hour's time. I want to try something."*

"What?" Joseph asked. "This sounds a bit suspect to me. Whatever stupid idea you've -"

"*A séance.*"

"A what?"

"*A séance. You know, where you contact the dead. Cheers, Joseph, see you in an hour.*"

"Paul, I didn't actually say -"

Joseph realised that Paul had already hung up. "Bollocks."

Joseph Tempur's Home: One Hour Later

J oseph didn't bother calling his friend back; he decided to keep an open mind about the séance, so that he could say "I told you so" when nothing happened.

There's no such thing as an afterlife, he thought.

He gave the dining room a vague dusting; he only used it when his parents visited. Joseph then called his sister, fully expecting to get hell for bothering her at work.

Lauren swore at him for a bit, asked why the hell she should leave work for something as stupid as a séance, listened as Joseph had suggested it might be useful in explaining her dream, swore at him a bit more, then promised to come. She had no-one supervising her and, if anyone asked, she planned to play the sympathy card with her tumour. Joseph smiled at her mercenary aptitude.

"Speaking of that, sis," he said, "I think it's time you told Paul."

There was a brief silence on the line, and Joseph braced himself for another round of swearing. Thankfully, it didn't materialise. Instead, she sighed.

"He'll just cluck over me like a mother hen," she said wearily. *"You know what he's like. I know he cares, but he forgets I'm a grown woman sometimes."*

"I forget as well sometimes," Joseph replied, and Lauren laughed.

"You're right," she conceded.

Joseph hesitated; he cleared his throat. There was something else he wanted to talk about.

"What is it, Joseph?"

Lauren could always tell when her brother wanted to say something.

I was thinking ..." he said. "This dream you and Paul think you shared."

"We did *share it, bro."*

"All I'm saying is that you hear about these situations, where people with tumours often experience dreams. What if Paul had a tumour? It would explain the dream."

"You're always trying to be the rational one, aren't you?"

"And you love me for it."

Despite the half-hour journey, his sister was actually the first to arrive. She had a key to Joseph's house, and so let herself in while Joseph was casting a final critical eye over the dining room. He was wondering if he should be doing anything else to it to make it more suitable for a séance. He'd never even been to one, so didn't know what was needed.

"In here!" he called as he heard the front door close.

Lauren followed his voice down the hall, and paused as she entered. She whistled in amazement. "Wow. This is probably the tidiest it's ever been."

Joseph shot her a withering glare. "You're being incredibly sarcastic lately, little sister of mine," he said. "I don't know if I approve."

"You're my brother, not my father," Lauren replied, and kissed him on the cheek. She dumped her bag and coat in the corner of the room and sat with a sigh in one of the chairs. "So what was so urgent about this séance that we had to drop everything and meet at yours?"

Joseph wanted the room to be completely clear of anything non-essential, so moved her belongings into the hall, then sat down next to her – avoiding her glare at the same time.

"I don't know," he admitted. "Paul was just insistent that both of us were here." He smiled. "Do you remember that séance you went to with mum, just after James died?"

Lauren snorted in amusement. "Yeah. The medium thought I was single and gay."

"It wouldn't have been so embarrassing if you hadn't still had your wedding ring on."

Lauren nodded, and looked down at her left hand. "I still do," she said softly.

Joseph took his sister's hand tightly in his own and they sat in companionable silence until the doorbell sounded.

"Hi," Paul said as Joseph opened the door. He waved at Kirby, stood a pace behind him. "I forgot to mention DS Kirby was coming round as well. He's a spiritualist who's leading the séance. I've got him up to speed on everything and ... well, so far, he doesn't think we're mad. A bit troubled, perhaps ... well, mostly me, but he's going to try and help us."

Joseph hesitated – then shrugged. "I'll get the kettle on."

Joseph banged around in the kitchen for a bit, suddenly forgetting where everything was. He hadn't been expecting a detective sergeant to turn up on his doorstep to lead a séance, and it had inexplicably thrown him.

After an embarrassing moment where he forgot the location of his cups, Lauren came out to take charge. With a sigh, and a mutter of "freak", she dismissed him from the kitchen and made the tea without a fuss.

As she brought the tray into the dining room, she was surprised to see that Kirby hadn't moved the furniture around or put candles out. She said as much to the detective, who smiled.

"You're thinking that I can't be much of a medium if I haven't got any dripping candles, incense or a crystal ball, right?"

Lauren shrugged as she handed out the tea, trying not to let him know he had hit the nail pretty much on the head.

"Not really," she lied.

"You'd be surprised. They're used for effect. If the medium's not good, they'll use misdirection to hide the fact that the only voice they can hear in their head is their own."

Lauren admired the detective's honesty, and smiled at him as she took her seat. Joseph cleared his throat, and she looked round at him. He frowned at her, and nodded towards Paul. She picked up on what he was intimating, and sighed.

"Not really the time, bro," she half-whispered.

"What?" Paul asked.

Lauren sighed again, cursing her brother's lack of subtlety. Paul listened as Lauren gave a quick précis of the results of her recent tests, the tumour that had been found in her brain, and the plan to conduct a biopsy on it to see if it was cancerous.

As she had expected, Paul was alarmed by the news; she saw the worry in his eyes. However, she was surprised that Paul didn't overdo the concern, as much as he usually did when something was wrong with his adopted little sister. He'd been a nightmare to live with when her absence seizures had first been diagnosed, even more so than her brother.

Then she saw something else in his eyes; wisdom. She was surprised to see it, but also surprised at herself – she had been so focused on being seen as an adult, not as a little sister anymore, that she forgotten to take into account Paul's feelings.

When Paul and Joseph had learnt about her epilepsy, they were still only teenagers themselves, and didn't have the life experience to know how to deal with the news. Now, however, they were grown men, with wisdom of their own to draw on. Both Joseph's reaction two days ago, and Paul's response now, were those of two people who cared about – no, *loved* her, in a brotherly way, and wanted her to be well and safe. She suddenly felt so stupid, for not seeing how they had both grown, through the experiences in their lives, as she had grown in her life.

Paul reached out and squeezed her hand. "I'll always be there for you," he said. "You just tell me what you need."

She squeezed his hand back. "Thank you."

Paul turned to Kirby; he felt a frisson of excitement.

This is it.

"So how do we start, then?" he asked. "Do we need to chant an invocation or something?"

"If you like," he said, "but it wouldn't do much good. An invocation's pretty much like the stuff Lauren mentioned: nice if you like that sort of thing, but not much use. I'm a bit out of practice with all this. I need a few minutes to meditate then I'll start. I haven't done this in two years, so don't be overly surprised if nothing happens straight away."

Paul watched as Kirby closed his eyes and slowed his breathing down. As the detective prepared himself, Paul quickly cleared the cups away, thinking that it would be slightly odd, attempting to contact the dead whilst surrounded by tea.

It wasn't long before Kirby opened his eyes again. He leaned forward and placed his hands, palms up, on the table. Joseph and Paul took the hint and each gripped one of Kirby's hands, and then took each other's free ones.

Kirby was surprised at how easily he was slipping back into the role. His only concern was whether or not he could still access his abilities after all this time. He hadn't been entirely truthful to Paul the previous day – it wasn't because he *couldn't* access his abilities any more, it was because he was frightened to.

The "personal reasons" he had cited was the murder of his sister. She had been killed in an armed robbery, two years ago, when she had refused to give up her handbag. Kirby had refused to conduct a séance after that day; not because he had been scared of finding Rachel's spirit there, but because he was even more frightened of *not* finding her. So he had placed his ability in a mental box, right at the back of his mind, and let it remain there.

Until now.

When Paul had come along and asked for his help, he had just known somewhere deep inside, that the time was right to open the box up again.

He didn't know how his gift worked, it just did. He wasn't worried that Lauren and Joseph seemed to have their doubts, but he was afraid as to who he would – or wouldn't - meet.

Let me show you the way, said a voice in his head.

Kirby closed his eyes to catch the tears. His sister was there, waiting for him to let her in. He started to wonder how, why - so many questions began running through his mind that he didn't know where to begin.

Rachel, he thought at her. *I'm sorry I doubted I'd ever find you. Oh, god, I wish …*

Later, bro. It's been too long, I know, but we can talk later. I need to talk to you about something more urgent; your friends. You need to warn them that they're in danger.

Kirby frowned, alarm overriding his joy. *What sort of danger? From who?*

From forces far greater than me. I'm just a spirit, a … well, it's hard to explain. The physical manifestation of a soul, I guess, but you won't fully understand that until –

Every cell in his body was screaming at him to forget all this and rejoice at being in touch with his sister; but he couldn't do that. Not when more important things were at stake.

Rachel, what can you tell me? What's this all about?

Well, said the voice inside his head, *Paul has found a way to pierce the veil between your world and the angelic realm - and that's meant to be impossible. The veil's been repaired, but someone very powerful knows about the breach and is gunning for Paul.*

Kirby listened for a few more moments, then opened his eyes and looked at Paul.

"You've been talking to angels."

Twenty minutes later, Paul, Joseph and Lauren were sat in Joseph's back garden.

Through his sister, Kirby had repeated everything she knew, which as far as Paul was concerned, was an accurate reflection of what had actually happened. Paul had filled in the details on his second encounter with Michael and Gabriel, but other than that remained silent.

Rachel believed the three of them were in danger, and Kirby wanted to investigate further. He had asked the three of them to step outside while he delved deeper into the spiritual realm.

"My sister is taking a huge risk in speaking to me," he said. "Just a few moments of privacy, that's all I ask."

Joseph couldn't refuse, and led the other two into his back garden.

They were sat in the midday sun with nothing to do except wait. Lauren laid down on the wood chip (Joseph hated mowing grass, so come up with the solution of replacing it all with wood chip and concrete) and closed her eyes. Joseph paced for a while, but soon got bored; instead, he sat down on the garden swing and stared off into the middle distance. Paul was sat on the path, leaning up against the house.

"This is probably the most bizarre thing you've heard, isn't it?" he said.

Lauren raised her eye, opening one eye in a squint to protect against the sun. She had been dropping off to sleep and only half-heard Paul.

"What?" she asked drowsily.

"I was saying how strange all this seems."

"Is it any stranger than sharing a dream, even if my strange brother doesn't believe us?"

Joseph frowned. "How come I'm strange and Paul's not?"

"Because you're my brother," she said, "and I'm allowed to call you strange. If that's all that's bothering you, don't let it. It may be bizarre, but most of this week has *been* weird and bizarre, so a story about angels just gets added to the list."

Paul glanced over at Joseph, who gave an unconcerned shrug.

"As much as it bothers me to say it," he said with a sigh, "I agree with my sister. Don't worry about it. I don't pretend to understand what all this is actually about - or even if I agree that these angels are anything more than a figment of your overactive imagination - but I'm not worried about your mental state any more than usual, mate."

Paul laughed. "Cheers," he said quietly.

A question suddenly popped into his head.

"Lauren, why have you told me about your tumour *now?*"

By now, Lauren had her eyes closed again. She jabbed a thumb at Joseph.

"Ask him," she said. "It was his idea."

Paul looked over at his friend and raised an eyebrow. Joseph shifted in the swing.

"I was thinking," he said, "that your shared dream could be easily explained if you had a tumour as well, and it was pressing against your brain in a similar way to Lauren's. I've read about cases where it can cause hallucinations."

Paul was surprised. "Mate, Lauren and I *appeared* to each other in the dream. We both remember it. You can't explain that by a tumour."

Joseph held up a hand, almost in defence. "Perhaps," he replied. "Perhaps. But shouldn't you at least consider it? After all, what makes more sense?"

Paul released a breath. He glanced over at Lauren, whose eyes were still shut.

"I can set up a scan for you at Canterbury Hospital if you want," she said. "It's in a training partnership with the university, so won't be too hard to do."

Paul barely hesitated.

"Alright," he said. "What have I got to lose?"

They were interrupted by Kirby; he stepped through the patio doors and into the garden. Paul recognised the redness around Kirby's eyes, but didn't say anything.

It must be odd, he thought, *to know your sister is dead and yet still be able to speak to her.*

Kirby sat down next to Paul and leaned back against the wall with a sigh.

"You'll probably think I'm mad," he said. "Just ... don't shoot the messenger."

Paul rolled his eyes. "We've just established the ground rules on that; there's plenty of madness to go round before insanity is officially declared."

"Speak for yourself," Joseph deadpanned.

Lauren sat up. "What did your sister tell you?"

"Well, like I said," he replied, "it seems that Paul here has been visiting angels. They live in another realm - what we'd call heaven, I guess."

"I've been there as well," Lauren added, "and I saw Paul while I was there. We thought it was a ... shared dream." She looked between Paul and Joseph. "If Kirby's right, then all this talk of tumours is way out, isn't it?"

Paul shrugged. "Maybe," he conceded. "But I'll keep the appointment anyway."

"So what now?" Joseph asked.

Lauren smiled at her brother's eagerness to get answers. That was the atheist in him; while she was more of an agnostic, willing to wait and see how things turned out, he always wanted to know the answers then and there.

"More importantly," Paul said, "why are we in danger? If this breach I used to visit heaven is sealed, then I don't see the problem."

I'm sat here, talking about visiting heaven, he thought. *Talk about insanity.*

"That passageway may be sealed," Kirby explained, "but if it can happen once, it could happen again. She doesn't want that happening. She's incredibly protective of her realm and loathes uninvited guests. Anyone who breaches the barrier is a danger."

"But it's not as if I *wanted* to go there," Paul said, frowning. "I just ... ended up there."

Kirby shrugged. "That's not how they see it. If you can pass from one realm to the other without even realising you're doing it, imagine what you'd be capable of *after* finding out."

"I remember one," he said. "She was a nasty piece of work. Metatron, she was called."

Kirby's head snapped round. "Metatron? Are you sure?"

"Of course I am. Is that important?"

"Oh, yes," Kirby replied, a humourless laugh emerging from his mouth. "In holy texts, Metatron is the senior scribe to God, almost a second-in-command. If Metatron is after you, then this *definitely* isn't the end to it."

"Yes, it is," Lauren replied quickly. "You said so yourself. The passage between our realms had been sealed. We can't pass through again, end of story."

"They can't *guarantee* there won't be another breach. See, there's a hierarchy in the spirit world, with archangels right at the top, right through to spirits like my sister. The archangels don't take much notice of what the spirits are doing, so spirits can occasionally make tiny breaches in the barrier to return to our world and talk to their loved ones. But humans sometimes try to follow the spirits back through that rip.

"If they do, it causes such a rip in the world that the angels can easily detect it. The journey can often drive them mad. Either that, or they can be hurt or injured afterwards by … well, suspicious circumstances. Some might call it Acts of God. Whatever you'd call it, people have always been hunted down and punished for breaking the veil.

"That includes you and Paul. And for Metatron to get involved personally … well, she's got her claws out for you."

"How do you know all this?" Joseph asked, fascinated. His first thought had been to get information about what a great article it could make for a national paper - the Spiritualist belief system and how it linked to mental illness. He was strongly fighting the urge to grab his Dictaphone. Instead, he distracted himself by asking, "Was it something that happened regularly in Spiritualist circles?"

Kirby shook his head. "No, although stories get around. There's a cult that exists, the Seekers of Truth, who do it for a … living. Well, I say living … it's not a career path that offers long-term pension investment."

"You're talking about humans travelling to heaven?" Lauren asked. "How?"

"Intense meditation, prayer, all sorts of ways. A few Seekers of Truth would use hallucinogenic drugs to help them on their journey, although that had its own dangers."

Joseph rose from the swing and walked down the garden towards his friends. He sat down on the edge of the bark and looked squarely at Kirby.

"Why?" he asked.

"What do you mean?"

"Why do these people want to do it?" Joseph clarified. "The way I see it, the spirits come back to Earth to comfort their loved ones. But if that's going to happen, then why does this cult want to go the other way?"

Kirby shrugged. "They want to learn about what *else* is out there," he said. "Like astronauts want to explore the universe, the Seekers of Truth want to explore other parts of the spiritual realms."

Joseph was fascinated; although he was sure the Seekers of Truth were completely barking, he knew he could write an entire *series* of features about this.

"How do you know about all this?" Paul asked the detective. "From what I know of cults, they're very protective about what they do. I can't imagine them willingly telling you everything you wanted to know, especially with being a detective and all."

Kirby shrugged. "Being a detective had nothing to do with it," he replied. "But it had everything to do with being a brother."

He looked around at the three confused faces.

"Rachel was a Seeker of Truth."

QEQM Hospital:
Friday Afternoon

R ick Walton was lost in thought as he walked along the corridor. He was hoping Golding didn't find out he'd come here.

I shouldn't be worrying what she thinks.

Despite that, he couldn't help himself. *She scares me too bloody much. All her mind games are starting to get to me.*

As he approached the main entrance, he felt a huge sense of relief. She wasn't there, waiting for him – and an explanation as to where he'd been. He stepped outside into the sunshine, looked round – and the relief vanished.

Golding was leaning against the wall with her arms crossed and eyes squinting against the sun. She looked patient and relaxed, whereas Walton felt nothing of the sort; he almost *felt* the colour drain out of his cheeks. She turned as the automatic doors quietly shut, and raised a questioning eyebrow.

"I wanted to see Adam one last time," he said.

He knew that it hadn't come out anywhere near as smooth as he would have liked; instead, he'd shot his words out like bullets, immediately showing his discomfort. He lowered his eyes and felt ashamed at himself for being scared of her.

She was charming when we first met. Then she realised who I was, and now she just uses me for what she can get. Oh, Paul, what the hell have I done?

"He is … *was* my friend."

Golding sighed, as if she was disappointed by his answer. She pushed herself away from the wall and walked toward him.

"I'll never understand this need to visit dead bodies," she said, her voice dripping with withering sarcasm. "They're *dead*. Their souls disappeared the minute their weak bodies gave up the fight. All that's left is the shell."

"Don't you care even a *little* bit?" Walton snapped, despite himself.

"That's not just any dead body in there, isn't she?" she asked, her gaze piercing him. "You know what that body represents, don't you? It represents your innocence."

Rick felt a wave of anger, despite the truth of Golding's words, and he couldn't help but retort; "That - that *shell* in there was my friend for ten years! He was loyal and dedicated, and probably one of my few proper friends. His body's the only thing I've got left to remember him by, so don't be so disrespectful!"

Golding held up a hand, stopping Walton in his tracks. She had a vague look of distaste on her face at the priest's outburst of emotion; she frowned at him.

"I very much doubt it was *me* that is being disrespectful to his memory," she said. "I would say that you were far more responsible for doing that. I'm bored now."

Walton blinked, caught off-guard at the sudden change of subject. "W-What?"

"This subject bores me to tears," Golding snapped. Her voice was now like solid ice, and Walton felt a shiver crawl down his spine. "I've accessed Lauren's medical records, and I've got what I need. I want to leave. Now."

Walton swallowed, and nodded. He loathed and feared her in equal measure, but she was in charge, and he couldn't do anything about it. He watched her as she walked towards the car.

You're evil, he thought. *And I've sold my soul to you. I'm damned.*

St Mary's Church:
Friday Afternoon

"Paul, why are we here?"

"Well, Spiritualists believe we're placed here to learn. Scientists argue we're here as the end result of biological evolution. Some people -"

Joseph gave him a withering glare. "I meant the church."

"I know, but I wanted to give you a history lesson at the same time."

Paul caught the flicker of a smile on Joseph's face. The exchange helped diffuse the tension; both were nervous at the thought of what they were planning.

When Paul first suggested the plan, Joseph, Lauren and Kirby had all resisted.

"If they're sealing the breaches," Lauren had argued, "then the last thing we should be doing is trying to get through the barrier again. We're safe now."

"No, we're not," Paul had retorted. "Metatron is sure I'm somehow breaching these barriers deliberately. If Kirby's right, she won't stop until we're no longer a threat. I won't just sit back and accept that. If she's going to keep hunting me, then I need to learn more about where she's from. We need to do that on *their* ground."

Even Joseph had grudgingly agreed after that; his reporter's instinct had won out and they'd gone straight to the church. Despite Kirby's tactful attempt to walk in front of his line of sight Paul's attention was drawn to the altar where he had found Adam and Father Simon, just two short days ago. He gulped, hard, as he remembered the blood; he wasn't sure if he would ever get that terrible sight out of his mind.

"Paul?"

He turned and saw Lauren standing at his side, looking concerned. His smile didn't quite reach his eyes as he said; "Just some bad memories."

Lauren nodded in understanding. She squeezed his hand and they walked up the altar, as if heading towards Father Simon's office, stopping at the "top" of the church. Paul looked up and marvelled at the stained glass window. It was a frieze of the angel Gabriel visiting Mary to tell her that she was pregnant; it was beautifully crafted and had been in place since the church was first built two centuries ago.

Joseph and Kirby joined them; Joseph looked distinctly uncomfortable.

"Why are we doing this in the church?" Joseph asked, with more precision this time. "We could have tried it at home."

"It ... feels right." A sudden smile appeared on Paul's face. "If anything happens, I'd like to think we'd be protected by being in a house of god."

Kirby nodded, his nerves swallowed up by excitement.

It's time, he thought.

He closed his eyes and began to focus his mind. He felt Paul and Lauren take his hands, and assumed that Joseph was completing the circle on the other side. His mind reached out, probing, searching - not directly for

Rachel, this time, but for something higher, more ... divine. After a few minutes, he began to feel a tight knot begin to form in his stomach as he struggled to get a connection. He had never been a Seeker of Truth himself, and was having to do it entirely from what his sister had taught him.

You didn't think I'd let you do this without me, did you?

It was Rachel - his beloved sister. He could feel her presence calming him. The knot in his stomach disappeared almost immediately and he realised he was smiling.

How do I do it? Kirby asked her. *How do I get them beyond the veil?*

Are you sure about this? Rachel asked. *This is a dangerous path. If you're caught, the punishments are severe. Metatron is dangerous!*

Paul wants to try and I don't I blame him. He wants answers. He gave a mental shrug. *You died because you wanted the truth, and I couldn't defend you. Maybe I can do it differently this time. I can actually help these people.*

Rachel was silent; there was nothing she could say. Kirby had always believed that Rachel had been killed because she had belonged to the Seekers of Truth, and who could disprove it? Her killer had never been found and she couldn't remember the events leading up to her death. If her brother could help this group cross the divide – and get them back safely – he might well be able to lay some of his personal demons to rest.

I respect your decision.

Thank you, he thought appreciatively.

But you won't be able to go.

The smile on Kirby's face quickly faded.

Why? he demanded. *If you're just trying to protect me from –*

Don't be an idiot, bro, it's nothing like that. Kirby was suitably chastised by his sister's admonishment, and he shut up. She went on; *I have to move three people from Earth to Heaven without a body, and that takes a huge amount of energy. I need a human body on Earth to anchor me – and give me more energy. You're the only one that can hear me, so you're the obvious choice.*

Kirby sighed and reluctantly acquiesced. *Okay. Let's do it before I change my mind.*

Paul was watching the detective with concern; it had been five minutes and Kirby hadn't moved.

Perhaps I should –

There was a noiseless explosion of brilliant white light around him. Paul pressed his eyes shut, but even that couldn't push back the light's brightness. He gasped in shock at its suddenness, and then gasped again as he felt … different, almost weightless. He heard other gasps as well, and assumed it was his friends experiencing the same thing. The brightness of the white light abruptly faded, leaving odd spots of light behind his eyelids. He opened his eyes to see –

Paul was disappointed. He'd hoped to see the Observatory again, or perhaps even the large, open-spaced Chamber of his frequent dreams, but this was just a corridor.

He quickly checked on his friends. Both Joseph and Lauren were blinking furiously, trying to get rid of the light spots before their eyes. He looked around in confusion.

"Where's Kirby?"

Lauren frowned. "Do you think he accidentally went somewhere else?"

I'm right here.

All three travellers jumped at the disembodied voice.

I'm still on Earth. Rachel needed a conduit - and it was easier to use me. It's almost burnt me out, though. I'm going to need to recharge before I bring you back. Take a look around, keep yourselves out of trouble, and I'll ready to get you back in half an hour or so.

"Half an hour!" Joseph exclaimed.

He quietened down as his friends hushed him. "What are we meant to do for half an hour? We only wanted to take a quick look around!"

There was no reply; Kirby had obviously cut off communication in order to rest properly.

Paul knew they had to accept it; he'd rather get back in half an hour than never; *although this is going to be the longest half an hour of my life*, he thought.

It was disappointing that they had arrived in a fairly plain corridor – Paul had been expecting something more … dramatic, given his previous experiences. The only thing "other-worldly" about it was the dimensions; it was a head taller than a "normal" corridor and could have comfortably fit six people walking side by side. At either end of the corridor were dead ends, with additional corridors leading off left and right. It was also absolutely silent.

"So this is heaven?" Joseph asked. The cynicism in his voice was obvious.

"It's different to what I expected," Lauren conceded.

Paul felt suddenly annoyed. "What *did* you expect? Angels on clouds playing the harp?"

Lauren shrugged defensively.

"I don't know," she conceded. "Were *you* expecting corridors?"

Paul didn't reply; he wasn't going to admit it that he hadn't. He arbitrarily picked left.

"This way."

"Are you insane?" Joseph exclaimed. His voice had started to rise in volume again, and Lauren quickly hushed him. "We can't go wandering around," he went on in a whisper. "What if we get found?"

"What did you think we were going to do when we got here?" Lauren asked incredulously.

"I've got enough issues with *being* here," her brother retorted.

By now, they had reached the end of the corridor. Paul looked left and right again; the corridors were exactly the same as the first. He turned to face his friends.

"Okay," he sighed, "it's somebody else's turn to choose."

Ten minutes later, the trio were standing at the crossroads to yet another set of corridors and feeling thoroughly despondent.

"You'd think there'd be signposts or *something*," Paul grumbled.

"Angels don't need signposts," Joseph retorted. "They just know where they're going. In-built sat nav or something."

"Shh," Paul said suddenly. "Can you hear that?"

Lauren frowned and listened carefully. She saw Joseph do the same then shook his head.

"There's nothing there," she said. "You're just imagining -"

She paused as she finally heard it: voices. They were gradually getting louder, as if walking towards them from a neighbouring corridor.

"What do we do now?" Joseph demanded. "Can you get in touch with Kirby?"

Paul shook his head. His heart was pounding, and he suddenly felt a rush of energy course through his body.

"No," he said, "and he wouldn't be ready to bring us back anyway."

"We need to get out of here," Joseph whispered. "Come on, let's go."

Lauren nodded her agreement and began to follow her brother away from the angels, hoping they could at least keep out of sight. After a few strides, she realised that Paul wasn't with them. - he hadn't moved.

"Paul!" she whispered urgently. "Come on!"

Paul shook his head. "They'll know we've been here," he said. "They'll detect our presence. There's no point running."

"Have you hit your head?" Joseph demanded. "Have you fallen down and hit your head?" He jogged back to his friend and grabbed his arm. "Come on!"

"No. We should stay here. I ... I think I know what to do."

"So do *we*," Lauren said in panic. "We need to move."

The voices had become far more distinctive; their owners were clearly about to turn down the corridor. Paul spun round and abruptly pushed his friends against the wall. He gripped their hands hard and Lauren let out an involuntary gasp - a bolt of energy shot up her arm and into her body.

The energy was coming from Paul; it was coursing through his body. He didn't know where it was coming from, but it felt ... right.

Two figures appeared in the corridor, and he swallowed – *hard*. He instantly recognised both angels. One was Michael, who had a commanding – yet comforting – presence. Walking alongside him, however, was an angel that made Paul go cold; it was the shining figure of Metatron. One thing was different this time: her light had dimmed, so much so Paul could almost make out the outline of a face and a body. It was as if he was learning how to see through the protective barrier she projected. He couldn't get the images in focus, but she looked *familiar.*

Why do you think I know you? Paul wondered again.

Neither angel gave any indication that they had seen the humans as they continued their conversation.

"... and we're sure *all* breaches have been sealed?" Metatron was saying. "There are none left for the human to access?"

"No, Metatron," Michael replied, shaking his head. "The security sweep you requested shows up no further breaches in the realm. We are secure."

Paul felt a bead of sweat trickle down his forehead, but didn't dare move his hand to brush it away. The angels were almost level with them now - and they were talking about *him.*

"Do we know how he was able to get through our defences?" Metatron asked. "We've not had a single breach in 2,000 years, and now two in as many days."

"Not yet. I've taken the liberty of instructing Gabriel to conduct a full enquiry."

Metatron stopped in her tracks.

"Is that wise?" she snapped. "His loyalty is still divided, even after all this time. He believes in Them and I suspect he has sympathetic leanings towards the rebels even now. To put him in charge of an investigation ... it concerns me." She leaned forward, almost whispering into Michael's ear. "It doesn't play well against you either, Michael. To be so ... supportive of him. It could adversely affect your status."

Michael merely stood there, blandly looking at Metatron.

"I am content with my status," he replied. "You stripped me of my rank and took it for yourself, but you could *not* strip away my dignity. I am happy to be an observer, because that way I can guarantee that They are free of any harm you might otherwise cause."

Surprise passed across Metatron's features, as if she was stunned that anyone would dare speak to her so bluntly.

Paul smiled. *I don't know much of the politics up here, but it looks like Michael's not afraid to stand up to her. Good – someone needs to.*

They were just past the human trio – if Paul had had any inclination to, he could have reached out and touched her.

Good job I'm not so inclined.

Metatron's surprise was quickly replaced by anger. Metatron opened her mouth to say something – and Paul's heart skipped a beat as Metatron turned her head and looked at him. Joseph's eyes widened in panic.

Run! he mouthed, but Paul slowly shook his head. He realised that Metatron wasn't looking at *him*, merely the spot where they were stood – and invisible. Michael followed Metatron's gaze.

He was frowning as he tried to understand what Metatron was looking for.

"What -" Michael said, but stopped as Metatron stepped forward, almost brushing against Lauren as she did so.

"There's something there," she said. "I can't quite – wait ..."

Paul closed his eyes and allowed the energy that was still bubbling inside him to run completely free. His back arched as huge amounts of strange, angelic power surged through him; Joseph and Lauren's hands clenched around his as they felt it pass into them.

The world became white for a moment, and Paul felt the same lurch in his stomach as the world around him *shifted*.

Joseph staggered as the light spots disappeared from in front of his eyes. Looking up, he realised he was back in the church, right under the stained glass. Kirby was sat in one of the pews, his head in his hands. He looked up as he heard them reappear.

"What -"

"Joseph!"

Joseph looked round at his sister's shout, and saw Paul slumping to the floor; his face was white. Joseph caught his friend as he fell, his heart skipping a beat as he looked down at the now-unconscious Paul.

"Get an ambulance!" Joseph shouted. "*Now*, Lauren – he's not breathing!"

QEQM Hospital:
Friday Afternoon

"Joe, sit down."

Joseph stopped pacing, but he didn't sit. Instead, he stood and looked out the window.

"Joe ... please? Being angry at the world isn't doing you any good, and it's irritating the hell out of me."

He turned, ready to argue - but he saw the look on his sister's face and realised she was right.

As he sat, Lauren placed a hand on his back, but he shook his head. Paul was Joseph's best friend, and he wouldn't take any comfort until he knew his friend was alright. He ran a hand over his face.

"I'm exhausted," he said quietly. He gave a small chuckle and added, "Three times in my life I've been in A&E. Once when you broke your arm, and then twice in two days."

"Yeah ..." Lauren stared at the far wall, not really taking in the half-empty waiting area. "Never for yourself, eh? You're a real giver, you are."

He scowled at his sister, who stared back at him. After a moment, he cracked a smile and gave Lauren a gentle push in the arm.

"Joseph?"

Both siblings looked round and saw Kirby walking towards them.

"What's going on?" Joseph asked, immediately standing.

Kirby smiled. "Good news. Paul's going to be fine. You can see him in a few minutes."

Joseph released a breath he hadn't realised he had been holding. Lauren closed her eyes and gave a silent prayer.

Looking round to make sure no-one could overhear, Kirby cleared his throat and said quietly to Joseph; "What happened up there? What did you see?"

"Nothing," Joseph dismissively replied. "It was nothing."

"Joseph!" Lauren exclaimed. She stood as well, angry at her brother's dismissal of their experience. "We were in *heaven*!"

Joseph spun on his heels to face his sister.

"'Heaven'?" he snapped. "Lauren, it was just some kind of ... of mass hallucination brought on by stress! Paul reacted badly and had a fit."

Lauren stared at him for a moment, overwhelmingly disappointed in her brother.

"It was real." She stretched out a hand and touched her brother's cheek. "I'll take you back and prove it to you."

Kirby nodded his thanks to a nurse who had come out and nodded to him; Paul was ready for visitors.

"Come on," he said, grateful for the interruption. "Let's go and see him."

Paul smiled as his friends entered the bay that, aside from him, was mercifully empty. He wasn't in the mood for having strangers around him today – but he was glad his friends were there for him.

Lauren hugged him tightly, then pulled back, seemingly worried that she would somehow hurt him. He laughed.

"I won't break, Lauren."

She smiled at him. "You want me to punch you in the arm instead?"

"I think I'll live without that pleasure, thank you."

Kirby looked thoughtful as he folded his arms across his chest.

"Paul," he said, "what happened?"

Joseph shot him an angry look. He had told the detective that Paul needed to rest, but Kirby seemed determined to make him talk about his collapse anyway. Paul caught the exchange and held up a placating hand to Joseph; he *wanted* to talk about it.

"Joseph," he said, "we can't pretend it didn't help. We were all there, and we need to open about it."

"Paul, I ..." Joseph sighed. "I know what my mind is telling me, but then I saw you collapse and ... I don't know what's real any more. How can *energy* make you collapse? It's ... not logical."

Paul respected his friend, and knew it must be difficult to voice dissent in front of people who believed, but was glad that he was able to.

"Joseph thinks we had a collective hallucination," Lauren added, trying – but not entirely succeeding – to keep the cynicism out of her voice. "He thinks the stress of that made you collapse."

Paul turned to Kirby. "What happened after we left?" he asked.

Kirby shrugged. "Nothing. I'd just sat down in the pews. You were gone a minute or two."

"No, that's not possible," Lauren said. "We were there at least fifteen minutes. We were … well, lost."

Paul and Lauren related to Kirby what had happened whilst they were there – and even Joseph commented on a couple of points. The more he listened to his sister and friend, the more it reminded him how *real* it had felt. That feeling scared him, and he bit his bottom lip as he tried to find an answer he could accept.

"Paul?"

Everyone looked round to see Christina, the Kiwi nurse that had looked after Paul during his previous visit, stood at the edge of his bed. She was momentarily caught off-guard by the attention she was received.

"Is this a bad time?"

"No, not at all," Paul replied. He saw the file she was holding. "Is that …" He couldn't finish the sentence; nerves twisted in his stomach.

Christina nodded. She avoided his gaze for a moment, confirming Paul's worst thoughts; *you've found something.*

"Tell me," he whispered.

"What's going on?" Lauren asked.

"Paul requested a CAT scan," Christina replied. "He's been getting headaches recently and wondered if they were related to his collapse."

Paul shifted uncomfortably, knowing it was a lie.

A necessary one, though, he told himself.

A CAT scan could often take weeks to organise, but he'd seen this as a heaven-sent opportunity. He glanced at the others; Lauren primly arched her eyebrow and he knew he'd hear more about it from her. Joseph just shrugged his shoulders and Kirby had been called away by a nurse.

"What have you found?" Paul prompted.

Christina breathed out. "There's a tumour," she said. "It's small and localised, but it's there. I'm going to arrange some more tests for you now."

Paul nodded his thanks; he didn't trust himself to speak. Although he'd been expecting it, a part of him been hoping to be proved wrong and for all this to be some horrible joke.

Lauren took the scan picture from Christina. As she as she saw it, she closed her eyes, unable to fully process what she had seen.

"It's the same as yours, isn't it?" Paul asked – and Lauren nodded.

"You've both tumours in the same place, and you're both getting visions," Joseph said in astonishment. "There's got to be a connection here!"

"They're not just visions, Joseph," Lauren growled. "They're real experiences. You've been there at the same time!"

Joseph's eyes lit up. "What if *I've* got a tumour? It could be the common factor we're looking for! What if a tumour is causing us to think we've seen heaven?"

Paul was torn between his two friends. "It would be an incredible coincidence, Joseph," he said, "but we have to at least consider it."

"You're right on the first point, Paul," Christina pointed out. "To find three people with a tumour in *exactly* the same place..." She shook her head. "It's highly unlikely."

"Then do a scan on me," Joseph challenged.

"I can't do a CAT scan just like that. Paul was an emergency. I can't bump someone else."

Joseph tried not to let his annoyance show. He knew that Christina was right, of course, but had hoped it would be easier than that. *Why isn't life like the films*?

He excused himself and walked over to Kirby, who was stood by the nurse's station.

"Everything alright?" Kirby asked.

Joseph nodded. "They've just done a scan on Paul. He's got a brain tumour."

"Doesn't your sister have a tumour as well?"

"Yes ... in exactly the same spot."

Kirby looked amazed. "Wow, what are the odds of that?"

"Not as much as the odds of me having one as well."

Joseph quickly brought the detective up to speed and then mentioned the CAT scan.

"So ..." Kirby said thoughtfully. "You think it'll show a tumour in your head?"

Joseph nodded. "Yes," he replied. "If it does, then we have to consider what exactly happened to the three of us in that church."

Kirby's police training kicked in; *I need to gather all the evidence before I make a judgement.*

"Come with me," he said.

"Where are we going?" Joseph asked in confusion as Kirby reached for his warrant badge.

"We're getting you your CAT scan."

The Celestial Observatory: Present Day

Michael was alone in the Observatory. He watched Joseph as he prepared for his scan.

He reminds me so much of Satan, *he thought*. Such a logical personality – and he wants to gather all the facts to support his opinions.

He turned his attention to Paul. You believe, don't you? You've managed to access that part of you I kept hidden, all those lifetimes ago, and you believe in what's happening to you.

He sighed. *Did I do the right thing, all those years ago?* he wondered. *Or should I have left well enough alone?*

He remembered how it had begun, all those years ago when he was still in charge of the Almighty's armies and everything had been different.

The Celestial Observatory: 2,000 Years Ago

Michael sat on the stone bench and watched the universe drift slowly by. The vast, arched windows showed a clear view of the inky blackness of space, punctuated by the silvery specks of light travelling across the immense distance of the cosmos.

He always came to this place to think, to meditate when things were worrying him. He knew that Lucifer had come here too, for similar reasons. Michael remembered bringing him here for the first time, when he was just a child, and seeing the awe on the young angel's face – and the sheer, unadulterated joy at seeing the universe spanning out far beyond his eyes, and imagining the sheer number of possibilities that were open to him.

I wonder if he ever imagined this possibility, Michael thought. Because I didn't.

"Michael?"

He turned – and leapt from his seat.

"You shouldn't be here," he said in a hoarse whisper. "Your Father has cast you out, Lucifer. You have to go. Now. *Before they detect you.*"

Lucifer quirked an eyebrow, clearly amused at the suggestion. "When have I ever listened to my Father?" He shrugged. "You know we disagree on practically everything, Michael."

"This isn't a laughing matter! You've been cast out of heaven and the kingdom is now at war! I don't even know how you managed to get in here; Metatron's been running around for the last few hours strengthening our defences."

"Metatron? Since when did she outrank you?" Lucifer asked.

"She doesn't. I'm still your father's senior advisor, but you know how her influence has been growing. On something like this, I'm hard-pushed to say no."

Michael exhaled, calming himself. He knew that he was getting angry, and it wasn't at Lucifer; it was at himself for liking the younger angel, at Metatron for being her usual arrogant self, and at the Almighty for listening to Metatron over him. Lucifer was a frustrated son, trying to do his best to stand up to the system, and Michael didn't blame him. In fact, he respected him for it.

"You're a brave angel, Lucifer," he said. "I admire you for getting through without triggering the alarms."

Lucifer laughed. "I've known you for a long time, Michael, so I know where your blind spot is." He smiled wryly. "You'll find it, but I decided to exploit it while it's still there."

"Oh?" Michael's eyebrows shot up. "Is this the advance guard of an invasion force?"

Lucifer became serious. "If it was, would you stop me?"

Michael shrugged and walked over to one of the large windows looking out into space.

"I don't know," he confessed. "So much has changed, Lucifer. I remember the days when your Father was a dynamic, passionate angel, with the kingdom in its infancy. Then, of course, he met your mother, and you and Gabriel breathed new life into ... well, all of us." He leaned forward, resting his head on the coolness of the glass. "And now look at us. Metatron has become a corrupting influence on your Father, and the kingdom is divided."

"I won't just stand by and let him try to conquer Earth, Michael!" Lucifer said hotly.

Michael just smiled, and continued staring out at the stars. "I agree," he said quietly.

"To take over the mortal realm goes against everything I believe in!" Lucifer went on, oblivious. "Everything you and my Father taught me as I was growing up! As a higher race, we have a responsibility to protect the mortals, but not suffocate ..." His voice trailed off he realised what Michael had said. "You agree?"

Michael finally pushed away from the window and turned back to face this younger angel, whom he had watched grow up with a sense of pride. He knew then that Lucifer's time had come, and wondered what he would do with the destiny in his hands.

"Yes," he said simply.

Lucifer strode forward and gripped Michael fiercely by the shoulders.

"Then join me!" he said. "Join us! I have an army of 144,000 angels, all wanting to make a difference, knowing that we're at a cross-roads in our history. With your expertise, it could make a huge difference!"

Michael studied him closely, and surprised himself by being tempted ... just for a moment. After a moment, he sighed and reluctantly shook his head.

"No," he said. He saw the sadness in Lucifer's face, and clapped a hand on his shoulder. "I won't leave Metatron here unchecked," he said. "Someone needs to rein her in. Without me here, there's no telling how much damage she would do. I won't allow that. I can't allow that. It's the right choice ... and you know it."

Lucifer was still disappointed; it was obvious from his body language, but he reluctantly nodded. Slowly, he began to walk back to the spot where Michael had first seen him appear.

"Lucifer!"

The younger angel paused in his stride.

"A moment ago, I mentioned your power. There's another sort of power, you know, aside from the sort that got you here."

Lucifer looked intrigued. "Oh?"

"You faced your Father on the Ruling Chamber floor. You raised an army by power of persuasion. You've stood up for injustice with words alone."

Lucifer digested what his old mentor said, slowly nodding as he processed the words.

"You're the most honourable angel I know," he said, his voice quiet and thoughtful. "Please watch out for my Father, Michael, and serve him well."

"I'll be fair in my advice – you have my word on it, my friend."

Lucifer inclined his head - and was gone.

Michael didn't move for a good while, sadly watching the spot where Lucifer had vanished. Lucifer was right; Michael would soon find the gap in his security network and have to seal it, although it would give him no pleasure in doing so.

I wonder how this will all end, *he wondered again.* Will I ever see you again?

"Michael?"

He turned; Metatron was standing in the entrance to the Observatory.

"Yes?"

"You spend a considerable amount of time here," she said thoughtfully. "Why?"

Michael shrugged. "It gives me comfort," he replied. "And brings back memories."

"Nostalgia." Metatron couldn't quite hide a sneer. "I've never understood it. You should look forward, not back."

"By looking back, you can understand where you're going ... and not make the same mistakes again."

Metatron gave him a long, hard stare.

"Do you have a point?" she asked coldly.

"Only that times change ... and we must change with them. We must negotiate with Lucifer; we can't just ignore their demands."

Metatron shook her head. "No," she said. "I have already discussed it with the Almighty, and he agrees with me. An all-out assault is the only way."

Michael couldn't hide his shock. "You're talking about all-out Civil War!"

"Yes."

"I'm speaking to the Almighty."

Metatron stepped in front of Michael as he headed for the exit.

"It's decided, Michael," she said. "There's no reversing this decision."

"Lucifer is his son!" Michael exclaimed, anger flushing his cheeks red. "He's also -"

Metatron cut him off sharply. "We are at war, Michael. Ready your armies. Unless ... do I need to replace you? I would be more than happy to take control."

"You would not succeed," Michael icily replied. "The armies will be ready, and they will be under my command!"

Metatron gave a curt nod, and strode confidently out of the Observatory. Michael watched her go; he was furious because he knew she had him tied up in knots. As he had said to Lucifer, if she were to take charge of the angelic *forces, the rebels would be shown no mercy ... and her control over the Almighty would be absolute. He still couldn't see what sort of control she had over him, but Michael would do everything in his power to be a constant thorn in her side - and retain the Almighty's ear.*

"I'll keep doing what's right," he whispered. "I swear to you, Lucifer. Somehow, I'll make all this right."

<u>Heaven:</u>
<u>2,000 Years Ago</u>

T he Civil War raged.
    In human terms, the War had been going on for years – angels, however, weren't linked to something so linear and base as mere time, at least in the way humans understood it. So while, on Earth, they were struggling to come to terms with the son of god, the angels were not tied to that moment, and the Civil War raged on throughout human history – and, on occasion, interacted with *human history, despite the rebels' best attempts to keep the War purely in the angelic dimension.*

Angels had always had a fascination for Earth and its mortal inhabitants due to their firefly-like life spans, and that fascination had encouraged the Almighty's quirky fascination in the minutiae of their lives. Many, however, had been inspired by Lucifer's words and passion, especially when the Almighty had waved his son's arguments aside and mated with the human woman named Mary.

Very quickly, the war of words had degenerated into a Civil War, one side fighting for divine will, and the other fighting for free *will.*

Lucifer blazed across the heavenly plane, his wings beating in time with his pounding heart and the fury burning deep inside him. He had followed Metatron down to Earth, who was to meet with Jesus. He and Metatron had ended up having a devastating fight over one of Earth's townships, causing untold damage; one of Metatron's bolts of energy had even exploded in the sky and caused a human to go blind. Lucifer had been unable to stop it, and *Metatron had been able to get away.*

Satan looked up as Lucifer strode into the war room, hidden away deep inside a little-known dimension of space and time that the Almighty, despite much searching, had been unable to find.

"Did you see?!" Lucifer exclaimed furiously. "Metatron is completely *uninterested about the fate of those humans we met. She even blinded one of them, and then pretended to be my Father so she could claim it was a divine intervention. She is so incredibly arrogant!"*

Satan's mouth twitched up in a smile. "I thank the heavens that is one way in which the two of you differ."

"I'm nothing like her!" he exclaimed, scowling at his friend and lieutenant.

"I would disagree with that, my friend. You are both extremely passionate; deeply believe in what you're fighting for, and will go to any ends to win this war. You've even gone back to the start of time to try and tempt early humans away from following your Father's path."

"Satan," Lucifer said, "I ..."

He didn't know what to say because, the more he thought about it, the more he could see his friend's point. Both he and Metatron were key figures in the War, and he had to admit that he had done things that he regretted. He just wondered if Metatron ever had a moment of doubt over her actions, or did she genuinely believe in everything she had done?

Lucifer rubbed a tired hand over his face and sighed deeply. "We're losing this war," he said quietly. "Metatron has been able to get the humans on her side. They seem to want a union between their world and ours."

"It's propaganda," Satan replied, sitting down and eyeing his friend with concern. "Metatron is winning the propaganda war by a long way. If humans knew what was going on, they wouldn't want to be united; you and I both know that."

Lucifer nodded. He felt a wave of weariness flood over him; he loathed every second of this war. He hated the fighting, the constant feeling of being on edge and having to always hide away, living in fear for their lives. Metatron had instigated a full-scale witch hunt for the rebels, and they were always on their guard; it often felt that it was only by Michael's presence that they were remaining so well hidden.

"Why is my Father obsessed with humanity? Why is he is so fascinated with them?"

"What makes you think it's your Father's doing?"

Lucifer frowned. "Does Metatron really have that much sway over him? And why would she have so much interest in them?"

"I hear rumours ..."

Lucifer's interest perked up. "Go on ..."

"Like I say, it's just a rumour, my friend."

"Just tell me!"

Satan laughed. "Alright!" he exclaimed. "I've heard a rumour that, once upon a time, Metatron was a human."

Lucifer's jaw dropped.

"A human *has* become an angel? Is that even possible?"

"*If you believe the rumours, then yes, it is. I wish I could confirm it, but I can't get any more details without arousing suspicion.*"

Lucifer was silent for a moment, processing what Satan had told him. It had changed his view on Metatron's behaviour, and he realised that the only way round it was to put it aside until he could deal with properly.

"*Metatron has become incredibly powerful over the years,*" *he said,* "*and the Almighty is listening to her more and more. Without Michael, I imagine Earth would be scorched by now, or merged with our realm.*"

Satan nodded in agreement, and they watched as, around them, stars whirled in their never-ending orbits, suns burnt their finite amount of hydrogen ... and rebel angels flew through space, on their own missions, each of them dedicated to Lucifer's principles of free will and self-determination.

You've come a long way, my friend, *Satan thought.* A hell of a long way.

"*This war needs to end,*" *Lucifer whispered.* "*We need to win it. I just wish I knew how.*"

Satan grimaced. "*I may have a solution for you,*" *he replied.* "*I doubt if you will like it though. It is an ... all or nothing solution.*"

Lucifer sat forward, intrigued, and listened. When Satan finished, Lucifer nodded.

"*It has the element of surprise,*" *he commented.*

Satan laughed. "*That it does.*"

Lucifer didn't need to think any more. "*Let's do it.*"

Paul's Flat:
Friday Evening

Christina had been reluctant to let the trio leave the hospital. The discovery of a tumour inside Joseph's brain had caused a flurry of interest in them throughout the hospital, and specialists were apparently queuing up to speak to them. However, none of them had wanted to be treated like lab rats and had made a discreet exit – covered by an understanding Kirby.

Paul handed Lauren a glass of wine before sitting down. They were all silent for a moment, lost in their own thoughts. Joseph shifted awkwardly on his end of the sofa.

"I feel like I'm being given the silent treatment," he said.

Paul shook his head. "No, mate, I'm just ... surprised. You could have got Kirby in a load of trouble if anyone found out he was pushing his badge just to get you a scan."

"It was his idea," Joseph protested, then realised he was sounding like a schoolboy. He shook his head and started again. "I ... It felt like the right thing to do. I thought it would help find some sort of common theme – and it did!"

He leaned forward, his eyes lighting up. "We've all got tumours in our head! You heard Christina – that's *never* been known before, not such precise tumours in the pre-frontal cortex." He looked at his sister. "It's the area of the brain that's said to control our personality. Surely that's something. A ... a link of some kind."

Paul laughed. "So we're ... what, freaks of nature?" he asked.

He stopped laughing quickly; no-one else had joined in. The siblings seemed troubled about what they had found out; although he was too, he had just wanted to lighten the mood.

"I'm not saying that," Joseph said carefully. "But we need to acknowledge we've all got these tumours and they could be behind what we've seen."

Lauren slammed her wine glass down on the table.

"Bloody hell, Joseph, we visited another realm: it was another level of existence! You were stood not two feet from Metatron feeling as scared as I was, because it was *real*. You know it was, bro, and I wish you would just admit it!"

"How the hell do you explain these tumours in our heads then?"

"I *can't* explain them! That doesn't just mean I'm going to accept what you're telling me, when I remember how I *felt* this morning! It was so *real*, Joseph – all of it was so real!"

Joseph was suddenly out of his chair, angry more at himself. He could feel himself getting wound up.

"You're so determined to believe, aren't you?" he demanded.

He was trying to settle his tone, but the anger was obvious behind his words. Lauren nodded. She remained seated; a deep frown creasing her otherwise unlined features.

"Yes!" she exclaimed. "Why are you so eager to *dis*believe?"

"Because ..." Joseph sighed. He shook his head with a sudden tiredness and turned to face his sister. "Because someone's got to. I think about what happened this morning and I wonder how we'd ever prove that we visited heaven. Heaven! Surely it's more possible to believe that these tumours are affecting us than almost being discovered by this Metatron ... person." He couldn't bring himself to say the word 'angel'. "Then Paul develops this power to hide us and bring us back safely to Earth." He chuckled as he looked at his friend. "I hope your sudden skills at hide and seek really were successful. What Kirby was saying earlier about her isn't worth thinking about if she realised it was us."

Joseph took a sharp breath. "Anyway, this is all too weird for words. I think we should ..." He trailed off as he caught his sister's eye.

She smiled. "We need our heads examined. You're as divine as my foot."

Joseph opened his mouth to reply, then suddenly saw the funny side. Paul, too, found it stupidly amusing, and laughed. The lame attempt at humour diffused the tension in the room.

Joseph smiled wryly at his sister. "Sorry," he said. "This is how I am. I like to keep a rational head on me."

Lauren bit back her first response. "I like to believe things when they're staring at me in the face."

Joseph leaned against the window sill for a moment, chewing at his bottom lip, then shook his head. "I'm going home," he said, and grabbed his coat.

"Can you ever accept it, mate, what we've seen?" he asked.

He knew that pushing Joseph wouldn't work – he was a stubborn man, and trying to force him into believing something would only push him further away.

"I don't know," his friend conceded. "I just want the truth. I ... need some time by myself, to think things through."

He leaned and kissed his sister's cheek. "We okay?"

"Course we are, stupid."

As Joseph left, Paul looked over at Lauren, who had remained sat on the sofa.

"Joseph's right about one thing, you know," Paul said.

"What?"

"Metatron must have figured out it was us by now. She knew someone was in that corridor. I'll stake money on her working it out by now."

"Hold on," Lauren said, suddenly very confused, "are you saying you *agree* with me? I thought you'd be on Joseph's side."

"Why can't someone be on *my* side for a change?" Paul snapped, then immediately swallowed and gave a wry smile. "Joseph and I aren't joined at the hip, you know. We *can* have different opinions."

Lauren held both hands up in a mock surrender. "Alright, I give in," she said. "So what – you've seen the light? You're convinced that all of this stuff we're experiencing is real? The dreams, the visions, everything?"

Paul nodded. It was more than just believing it; he *knew* it was true. Something inside him was crying out to be heard, and had been ever since he had returned from the other realm. He wished he could explain it; it was both an overwhelming feeling and a subtle knowledge niggling away at the back of his brain, as if it was starting to become self-aware.

"So what do we do now?" Lauren went on. "If Metatron knows we've returned to heaven ... do you reckon she'll come down and smite us or something?"

But Paul wasn't listening; a thought had suddenly hit him.

"Wait a minute," he said slowly. "Metatron was going to seal up the gap that allowed me to get through to the other side in my dreams."

Lauren shrugged. "So?"

"So who let us through again? Even Kirby's sister admitted she was just a spirit and wasn't as strong as the angels. She couldn't have punched through a seal just like that. It would be like a snail punching through a solid oak door."

"You can't possibly know that," Lauren replied. "How the hell would you know what spirits can and can't do?"

"But I *do*," he insisted, then hesitated; "I just don't know how."

He began biting at a fingernail, trying to force an answer out of his uncooperative brain.

Ten minutes later, Paul and Lauren were walking along Broadstairs seafront. Both of them had needed some air, as if the flat had suddenly become very stuffy with the questions swirling around their heads.

Lauren snapped her mobile phone closed.

"Joseph's turned his phone off," she said. "I've left a message."

She leant on the promenade's railings overlooking the beach; she watched the sunbathers and swimmers relaxing and enjoying herself. Paul leant on the railings next to her.

"You think Joseph should have stayed and argued it out, don't you?"

Lauren didn't reply and avoided his gaze.

"I thought so," he said. He sighed and turned to face her. "Look, he has to make his own choices - we all do. He's been an atheist for as long as I can remember, and you've always been an agnostic. I've got to be honest, I'm surprised you've accepted it as quickly as you have; I thought both of you would take serious amounts of convincing."

Lauren looked round in surprise. "What makes you say that?"

Paul shrugged. "It's ... fantastical, that we had to travel to heaven, and the fact that we've all got tumours in our heads ..." He grinned. "It could lead some to the conclusion that there's a degree of sanity missing from our lives."

Lauren laughed, and Paul was glad. He felt that she was taking Joseph's departure far too seriously, and needed to be brought back to Earth a little.

Brought back to Earth, he realised with an inward groan. *What a pun.*

"You're right," Lauren replied. She raised an eyebrow in curiosity. "Since when did you become so wise?"

Paul scratched his head in thought. "Since I left the church," he said with a laugh – although he wasn't entirely joking. "My eyes were opened a hell of a lot. And your brother was there for me when I needed time to get my head together, so I'm going to be there for him while he needs to do the same."

Lauren squeezed his hand for a moment in understanding ... and then frowned in confusion. There was a sudden absence of background noise, and she panicked for a moment that she had lost her hearing. She looked over the beach ... and was immediately alert.

"Paul!" she exclaimed and pointed to the people on the beach. "*Look!*"

Paul, who had been slower on the uptake, turned as Lauren pointed, and blinked a couple of times. It took him a few seconds to take in what he was seeing.

"What the f -"

His voice petered out as he absorbed what was going on. There was a complete absence of noise coming from ... well, everywhere, not just the beach. People all around him were *frozen* in position; there were some caught mid-dive into the sea from the diving boards, some with their arms outstretched waiting for a Frisbee or ball that would never reach them. In fact, the only people who didn't seem to be out of place were those few people sunbathing in the late-afternoon sun – they, at least, weren't going to be moving much anyway.

Paul took in the rest of the promenade; people with suits on and carrying briefcases were frozen as they walked home; elderly people in groups had frozen, mid-gossip; and schoolboys playing football by the bandstand were frozen as they charged down the make-shift pitch.

"What's going on?" Lauren asked in a whisper.

Paul barely noticed as Lauren slipped a hand into his, almost to reassure herself that he was still there and moving.

"I -"

Both he and Lauren flinched as a dot of pure, white light appeared in mid-air. Neither Paul or Lauren were particularly tall – Paul was the tallest by a hair at five foot six – and the light appeared a foot above him, meaning that he had to crane his neck slightly to see it;

despite its brightness, he wanted to see what would happen, and so squinted his eyes to watch it.

Suddenly, the dot of light stretched down all the way to the ground, making it look as if a gash had appeared in the air. It then widened and opened to make an oval hole, much like an eye, but full of bright white light.

Paul felt a sudden churning in his stomach. *Please no*, he thought. *Metatron's found us. We need to get out of here* now!

A figure appeared in the "eye" of white light and stepped through.

Damn! he cursed. *It's too late. Well, I'm not going down without a fight.*

He took a step forward to stand in front of Lauren...

... and blinked hard as the white light, which his eyes had slowly begun to get accustomed to, suddenly sucked in on itself and vanished; it left nothing in its place except the earthly landscape and an angel, looking out of place.

Paul's eyes didn't clear immediately. Blinking furiously, he tried to peer at the shape. "Whatever you want," he said, "you won't harm my friend. Take me, but leave her alone!"

"Why on earth would I want to harm either of you?"

The light spots finally vanished and his mouth fell open in surprise.

"Gabriel!"

Gabriel, Observer and Angel, gave a wan smile and spoke; "You remember when we met in the Observatory, you asked me what I meant when I said I didn't want you to lose you again?"

Paul nodded silently.

"I remember," he replied. "You ... you said I wasn't ready to hear the rest."

"Well …" Gabriel hesitated for just a moment, then continued. "I think you're as ready as you're going to be. The reason I wanted you to stay is with me is … I didn't want to send my brother away again, not when I'd lost him once already."

Paul didn't understand what Gabriel was getting at.

Gabriel laughed. "I think we've got a lot to talk about, don't you?"

Heaven:
2,000 Years Ago

"*T*his is madness.*"*

Beelzebub glanced round to make sure she hadn't been heard. She hadn't meant to speak; it had just slipped out.

Be careful, Beelzebub, *she told herself.* Focus.

She continued moving along the corridor, listening out for anything that would alert her to potential threats.

I can't believe I've actually got this far, *she thought.* Either we have been able to confuse Metatron's security as much as we had hoped ... or I am as good as Lucifer and Satan keep telling me I am.

She was only a matter of minutes from the Ruling Chamber, at the heart of the Almighty's kingdom. Even under normal circumstances, to approach the Chamber with no invitation was considered the height of rudeness, but now, in the midst of the Civil War and for a rebel angel to be approaching, it was treasonous and punishable by death.

Before she knew it, Beelzebub was facing the vast doors to the Chamber. They were fourteen foot high and etched with the Word of God, his judgements passed down through the Ages. Beelzebub noticed that two new judgements had been added to the bottom of the doors;

Thou Shalt Follow Your God Unto Death and The Word of God Is Law – To All.

Beelzebub rolled her eyes.

"How very subtle, Metatron," she muttered. "I can't imagine anyone has missed their meaning."

She hesitated, realising the importance of this moment. This will either be my salvation or my death.

Knowing that it was now or never, she raised her hands and the doors slowly parted.

I am *good, she thought with a smile.*

She walked into the Chamber with a confidence she didn't entirely feel; looking round, she absorbed the sight before her. It was almost empty; the Almighty was sat on his throne and looking down towards the Debating Floor. Michael was nowhere to be seen, which – on a normal day – would be unusual, but today he would undoubtedly be in the vastness of space, leading the forces of God against the rebels.

Beelzebub found herself missing his reassuring presence but, before she could feel any nostalgia, she realised why the Almighty's attention was on the Debating Floor. There, looking back up at him, stood Metatron and –

"No!" she whispered urgently.

Gabriel was knelt on the floor next to Metatron; his face was bloodied and bruised, his left wing was missing feathers and his right arm looking damaged, perhaps broken.

The Almighty looked up, a tired and sad expression on his face; at his reaction, Metatron's head snapped round and saw Beelzebub, her shoulders sagging in shock.

"Welcome, Beelzebub," she snarled, a snake-like smile flashing across her face. "Please do come in. We've been expecting you."

A sudden rage filled Beelzebub up from deep inside her as she saw Gabriel's damaged body. He had been their advance guard, sent to scout the kingdom for any improvements to their defences before Beelzebub came in. They hadn't heard from him within the agreed three days, but the rebels had decided to risk going ahead with the mission anyway.

Part one of the mission was going on outside these walls, with the rebels launching an all-out assault against the Almighty's forces. They knew that Michael would be leading the attack, and that his unwillingness to see fellow angels being harmed would stop his soldiers from doing any harm, merely push them back. This would give Lucifer, Satan and Beelzebub the chance to try different routes into the Chamber and force the Almighty to stand down.

But the Almighty and Metatron were expecting them; they had caught poor Gabriel and tortured him.

They've been waiting for me, Beelzebub realised with a swooping feeling of horror.

Gabriel couldn't raise his eyes to meet hers, and she understood.

I forgive you, Gabriel, she thought at him – although she wasn't sure whether or not he heard her thoughts or not since there wasn't even a flicker of acknowledgement. She tried to mentally raise the alarm to her friends, but the Chamber was well-shielded.

"You tortured him," she said in disgust. She looked at the Almighty. "You allowed this to happen? Against your own son?"

She walked down the steps, determined to go to Gabriel and check on him. She glanced up at the Almighty, but he wouldn't meet Beelzebub's eyes.

Good, *she thought.* I hope you feel ashamed of yourself for letting this happen.

She looked round as Metatron laughed, a harsh sound against the emptiness of the Chamber, and gestured with a hand. Beelzebub felt a sudden lurch, and went crashing to the ground. No matter how much she tried to fight against it, she couldn't get up. She was, however, able to move her head, and looked up to see Gabriel now facing her, a tear falling from his left eye.

I'm sorry, *he mouthed, and she nodded as much as the pressure would allow.*

"Did you really think your plan would work?" Metatron asked, disdain dripping from every word. "I've been expecting like this for some time; an all-out attack on our territory. Even without Gabriel's ... fascinating testimony, I would have suspected something was wrong from the moment your rebels began their raid. But then Gabriel told us everything ... and I began to prepare for your arrival."

Beelzebub noticed Metatron's use of the word "I"; she moved her eyes to the Almighty, who had sat back in his throne and was strangely silent.

Why aren't you stopping Metatron? *she wondered.* You're the Almighty! *You* should be commanding this room, not *her! She froze as realisation flooded over her.* She's got a mental hold over you, she thought. She is controlling you – but how?

Metatron caught the look of desperation Beelzebub was giving the Almighty; she gestured with her hand again, dragging Beelzebub to her feet and bringing her, unceremoniously, closer to Metatron and Gabriel. Beelzebub was now floating off the ground and, no matter how she tried, she just couldn't move.

"You look at me when I speak," Metatron growled "Is that understood?"

Beelzebub growled, the deep, low rage still bubbling away inside her. "I do not answer to you," she furiously replied. "I answer to Lucifer and, through him, the Almighty."

Metatron laughed loudly. "You answer to the Almighty?!" she exclaimed. "You have fought against him for two decades, and now you claim to answer to him? If you answered to him, you would have never rebelled!"

Beelzebub could not – would not – remain silent at such an accusation. Despite being in Metatron's power, she wouldn't just stand by and let that insult go unanswered.

"You are wrong!" she retorted. "You are wrong. *I have never stopped believing in the Almighty. I believe he's capable of making mistakes, like any angel, and he should never have tried to unite Earth with our realm. I took a stand against that, because it was the right thing to do … but that doesn't stop me respecting my leader. This realm needs to change, Metatron, and I know the Almighty will accept that change if it means our factions are reunited."*

The anger in Metatron's eyes coalesced to hate, and she moved forward as if to strike Beelzebub. Before she could, she was halted by a resounding "Stop."

The Almighty stood from his throne and began to walk down the steps to the Floor. Beelzebub's eyes widened; she had never known the Almighty to step down onto the same level as "normal" angels. Only Metatron and Michael had ever been allowed to stand on the same, or similar, levels at him. If she had full control of her body, she knew that she would be kneeling by now, almost without thinking. As it was, Metatron, although her surprised attention was on her leader, was still keeping her stock still.

"*You Speak Of Change,*" the Almighty said in his deep baritone. "*Do You Know What Effect Your Changes Would Have On This Realm ⋯ And The Entire Cosmos? A Democratic Heaven With No Unifying Figure ⋯*" He shook his head. "*It Would Cause Chaos.*"

Beelzebub shook her head; she couldn't believe that she disagreed with him, the Almighty. She respected him unswervingly, and had unquestioningly followed his leadership for so many centuries. It was difficult to understand that she now opposed him. She had stood on this floor before, debated and discussed options, but never openly disagreed with him.

"Almighty ..." she whispered, "... all this war, all this devastation we've brought on ourselves and the people of Earth ... for what? For your desire to unite the heavenly and physical realms into one? Could you not at least accept the possibility that we have caused more damage to Earth by trying to influence them than if we had left them alone? In answer to your question – yes, we have considered the effects that our changes would have. A democratic heaven, where we can all have a voice ... that would be a heaven worth fighting for, rather than against. If you were to stand aside now in favour of us, and make humans truly responsible for their own actions ... that would send such a powerful signal."

"A signal?" Metatron scowled. "The only signal that would send is that we are weak. We need to be strong and united, Beelzebub, and you fail to see that. You and your rebels are the cause of everything that is wrong in this realm."

"No," Beelzebub replied, "you're wrong. You *are* the cause."

"*Why?*" the Almighty asked thoughtfully. He either did not see – or care – the astonished look that Metatron gave him.

Beelzebub's eyes were still fixed on the Almighty's deep, soulful eyes. She would not do him the dishonour of looking away.

"If we stand aside now, and allow humans the free will to live their own lives, we are showing our true, divine selves. A race of beings above such things as war, hatred and jealously -" She glanced at Metatron, then turned back to the Almighty, "- are a race of beings that humanity can aspire to. You, Metatron, typify everything that is wrong in heaven, and you have been influencing the Almighty to follow your path."

She began choking as Metatron took control of her throat.

"Enough!" Metatron angrily exclaimed. "You know nothing *of my life!* Nothing*!*"

"Let her go, Metatron!"

Beelzebub couldn't help but smile as she recognised the voice behind her; it was Michael. Metatron sneered at him.

"What will you do if I don't?"

Michael's eyes blazed with fire. "I've stood aside for far too long as you've corrupted the Almighty's mind. I won't let you do any more harm."

Metatron laughed. Beelzebub's throat was suddenly loose, and she fell to her knees, exhausted by the effort of trying to breathe. She glanced up as Michael stepped onto the floor; he was wearing his angelic armour, and his sword was sheathed, but his opposite hand was wrapped tightly around the hilt.

"You're responsible for the angelic armies," Metatron said to him, "not interrogation. This is my purview, and you have no right to interfere."

"Maybe not," Michael replied, "but the Almighty does."

He turned to the Almighty, and bowed his head in the proper gesture of respect.

"Almighty," he said. "You have led this kingdom now for untold aeons, and I have been honoured to stand by your side. However, since Metatron's arrival, she has served to corrupt your rule with violence and hatred. My counsel is no longer welcome, and Metatron seems determined to undermine all the good this kingdom can achieve. I suspect that, in reality, even this plan to merge the two realms is her idea, and not yours, isn't it?"

"How dare you!" Metatron exclaimed. "I loathe humanity! They are weak and insignificant. Why would I seek a union between the two realms?"

Beelzebub pushed herself to her feet. "Stand aside, Metatron," she said. "It's over."

"It's not over until I say it is."

Her hand was raised before any of the other angels could react, and Michael, caught off-guard, went flying across the Chamber. Beelzebub raised her hands to fight back, but Metatron moved quickly and snaked an arm round Gabriel's throat. Despite his injured state, he valiantly tried to prise her off with his good arm.

"Metatron, stop this," Beelzebub said. She glanced to her right and saw the Almighty watching the fight. An odd expression of confusion was on his face, as if he couldn't quite focus on what was happening.

What's happened to you? she wondered.

She realised that she was alone again. Michael was hurt; his wings had been badly hurt by the collision with the wall. Gabriel's injuries from his torture, as well as the *hand around his throat, were obviously painful, and Lucifer and Satan hadn't arrived yet.*

If they're even coming. Have they been attacked somewhere else?

She saw Metatron look at the Almighty in alarm. He was blinking, almost as if he was coming around from a sleep. Metatron nodded at him, and Beelzebub felt rather than saw the energy transfer between Metatron and the Almighty.

Has Metatron been controlling his mind? *she wondered.* That's meant to be impossible. But Metatron's one of the most powerful angels I've ever *known, even more so than Lucifer. That explains everything!*

"Almighty," she said urgently, "listen to me. It's not too late; I can help you. Metatron is controlling you. These thoughts are not your own!"

"*What Good Would Come From Me Standing Aside?*" the Almighty asked. He seemed unaware of Metatron's actions, and deaf to what Beelzebub had just said. "*What Will That Accomplish? Speak To Me, My Angel, And Give Me Your Thoughts.*"

Beelzebub looked at him in astonishment. He genuinely wanted to know her thoughts, and it caught her off guard. Even after all this time, he still didn't hate her; despite the rebellion and everything that had happened as a result of it, he still considered her one of his own.

She recovered herself when she realised that his love of all *his angels made his complicity with Metatron and her torture of Gabriel even worse – whether he was under Metatron's control or not, some part of him had to still be* him.

"You standing aside could mark a new age for our realm," she replied. *"To wash away the mistakes of the past, allow Earth to chart its own course, and –"*

"Stop - now," Metatron said, her voice dangerously quiet.

She pushed Gabriel to the floor; he fell on his bad arm, causing him to cry out in pain. Beelzebub reached out to help him without thinking. His body was clearly at the very edge of its ability to heal itself.

In the name of all that is holy, *Beelzebub thought,* you were tortured by Metatron of all people. How the hell could you do that to him, you evil, evil bitch?

She realised, in that moment, that she had failed – she had looked away at the critical moment, out of compassion for Gabriel, and Metatron taken the initiative. She darted towards the Almighty and placed a hand on his chest. Her hand glowed with energy and the glazed eyes and confused look returned to the Almighty's face.

"Leave him alone!" Michael bellowed.

He tried to struggle to his feet, but his legs buckled from under him and he collapsed back to the floor. He cried out in frustration; Beelzebub could understand that feeling, because her body had been frozen again as soon as she had moved towards the Almighty and Metatron.

After a moment, Metatron removed her hand ... and staggered backwards, apparently drained by whatever she had done to the Almighty. She quickly recovered, blinked, and fixed her eyes onto Beelzebub.

"I cannot allow you to live after what you have seen."

Her voice wasn't its normal pitch; the power she had transferred to the Almighty, plus the effort it was taking to control Beelzebub, was clearly taking its toll on her.

"Almighty ..." Beelzebub said desperately, but she could see in his face that it was too late.

The Almighty inclined his head, turned and began ascending to his throne. He paused on a step for a moment, turned his head to look behind him, and then continued walking.

"*My Son Has Arrived.*"

The double doors to the Chamber burst open again and Lucifer and Satan ran in, their wings ruffled and chests heaving, as if they had just flown at full speed to get here – They probably have, *Beelzebub thought.*

"Beelzebub!" *Lucifer called out. His knees buckled at the sight of Gabriel, bloodied and battered, on the floor of the Chamber. Seeing Michael slumped against the far wall, he took a step towards him, but stopped; he seemed to recognise that they'd lost.*

"No," *he whispered.*

"It's too late," *Beelzebub whispered, a tear falling down her cheek.* "She's betrayed us."

Metatron seemed to have regained her energy. She flicked her hand again and both Lucifer and Satan were thrown violently off their feet; landing hard on the ground, they were trapped inside individual columns of light.

"What a happy occurrence," *she said with a wicked grin.* "The ringleaders are all here."

"You evil* bitch!" *Satan bellowed.* "How could you torture Gabriel? How? He's your -*"

"He's a* traitor!" *Metatron exclaimed.* "You're all traitors!"

She drew a breath, as if she hadn't expected to give quite such an impassioned outburst. She looked down at Gabriel, as if truly seeing him for the first time in his current state. She didn't flinch once, even when Gabriel looked up at her, his pain obvious in his eyes.

"I did what I had to do," Metatron said coldly, and turned away.

"It's you that's the fallen angel, not any of us," Michael growled from across the Chamber.

Metatron glanced at him, but her angry expression didn't change. "I'm doing what I have to do for the kingdom," she said. "You've been feeding secrets to the rebels, haven't you?"

Michael gently nodded his head. "I remained here, at the Almighty's side, to try and shield him from the likes of you."

A smile appeared on Metatron's face; it didn't quite reach her eyes.

"You failed."

She looked up at the Almighty, now sat on his throne with his vacant expression intact.

"Almighty," she said. "We must kill these traitors now, all four of them. And then we should parade their lifeless bodies throughout the realm, for everyone to see. I suspect that will bring about an end to the fighting extremely quickly."

The Almighty's eyebrows knitted together as he thought about that statement.

"*No*," he said slowly. "*They Should Not Die*."

Metatron was rendered speechless as she registered what he had said.

"What?" she demanded.

"*My Sons Shall Not Die. I Do Not Wish It. There Has Been Enough Death. You Must Find Another Way, Metatron. I Am Tired of Death*" The Almighty paused, then added; "*I Am Tired.*"

Joseph's House:
Friday Evening

Joseph threw his keys down on the sideboard.

Thank god I'm home, he thought with relief.

He closed the front door and started towards the kitchen, but something made him stop. A noise from the lounge made his ears prick up and the hair stood up on the back of his head.

There's someone in there, he realised.

His first instinct was to call the police, but he knew that the intruder would have already heard him close the front door.

Looks like it's down to me, he thought, adrenaline suddenly surging through him. *You're in my bloody house, pal, and I've got the right to defend it.*

He looked round the hall for something to use as a weapon, but there was nothing within reach that was heavy enough. His mind went blank; he didn't know what to do next.

The decision was taken out of his hands when the living room door was yanked open. Joseph jumped, and swore to himself for being so skittish.

"Joseph!"

He blinked. "Rick? What the hell are *you* doing here?"

"I ... err ..."

Joseph was shocked at how much Walton had changed in the past two days. He was no long the self-assured, confident man Joseph remembered; he was pale and sweaty, with dark bags under his eyes – and seemed terrified of something.

Or someone.

"I came here to hide," Rick stuttered.

His eyes darted up and down the hall, as if to reassure himself that no-one was there. "I'm sorry, Joseph, I know what this looks like, I ... oh, hell, I don't know. I needed to get away from her, and she won't think to look here. Can you ... can you forgive me for just breaking in like this?"

Joseph studied him for a moment. *What are you so frightened of?*

As the adrenaline wore off, he realised that there was no point getting angry; with Walton so shaky and paranoid, anger wouldn't solve anything right now. Joseph indicated towards the living room.

"Let's go and talk."

Once they sat down, Joseph fixed Walton with a steely gaze and said, "Why don't you start from the beginning?"

Walton nodded and swallowed. "I ..." He hesitated, struggling to find the words, and ran a shaking hand through his hair.

"Rick?" Joseph prompted.

Walton closed his eyes and breathed out, obviously trying some sort of calming exercise. It didn't seem to do the trick but, after a minute or so, his breathing had at least become more regular and he seemed, at least temporarily, more focussed.

"You remember Lucy Golding?" he asked.

Joseph nodded. He couldn't *not* remember her, given Paul's reaction to her arrogant attitude over Adam Wild's death, and her performance during their breakfast.

"Our relationship is slightly more ... complicated than I first admitted to Paul."

"I guessed," Joseph deadpanned. "You said you two knew each other from school?"

Walton shook his head. "I don't even know where she went to school," he confessed.

"So where *did* you meet?"

"I was in Africa, working on a Christian training project for kids. I'd been travelling for a little while before that, and ended up there more by chance than anything else."

He paused, as if realising he had raced ahead. "I left the church not long after Paul did," he explained. "I wanted some new experiences, away from this place. The youth camp was a good place; I just don't think it deserved the angry man I was then."

He seemed to find his confidence the more he talked, so Joseph decided not to interrupt. It seemed to be leading somewhere, and he wanted to know where.

"Back then, before I left, I was angry with being passed over for promotion ... again," Walton went on. "Father John was so convinced Paul would come back, he couldn't see that Adam and I were still there, and I was extremely ambitious."

He smiled. "Times change. Anyway ... I went travelling instead, to see if I fitted in somewhere else. I was drifting, not really sure where I was going, until I settled in Africa ... must have been about six months ago. After a couple of weeks, Golding turned up and we begin talking. She ... had a plan, and it fed right into my own insecurities." He leaned back on the sofa, suddenly unable to meet Joseph's eyes. "And jealousies."

"Paul," Joseph realised.

Walton nodded, his eyes still down-turned.

"What happened then?" Joseph prompted.

When the priest didn't reply, a look of shame still ingrained in his face, Joseph snapped.

"Rick!" he growled. "You've come into my house to hide: I think I've got the right to know what from! Now tell me what happened, or I'm calling the police, right now."

Walton seemed to realise he was skating on thin ice, so continued his story.

"Golding knew about my history with Paul; I never asked how, or why, because she seemed angry at him as well, and I liked that. I was angry with him because he seemed to cast a shadow over my life, even when he wasn't around. I'd had to escape half way round the world to try and get away from that. She never told me why she was angry with him, but she wanted to seek him out for some reason ... and that was good enough for me. I felt Paul ... needed to be knocked down a peg or two, for always succeeding over me."

Joseph frowned. "I can't imagine thoughts of revenge would go down very well with your superiors in Africa ... if they knew, which I assume they didn't."

Walton shook his head. "No, they didn't," he replied. "I kept that quiet."

Joseph didn't push that any further – he was more interested in the events following their fateful meeting.

"She convinced me we should travel back to the UK and look for Paul," Walton went on. "I took a job working at the seminary where Paul, Adam and I did our training."

"What did Golding do when you got back?"

"She was looking for Paul," Rick replied. "She was struggling to find him."

Joseph quickly did the sums in his head. "He would have still been travelling then."

He tried to keep the sadness out of his voice, although he doubted Walton would have noticed in any case. Paul's 18-month absence had been tough on Joseph, although he would never admit it. The two of them had been best friends for more than fifteen years; when Paul left the country, and then come back after a year and a half with a girlfriend in tow, Joseph had wondered if he would still have a place in his friend's life.

Joseph was surprised to realise that Walton was more like Paul than he had realised. Both had gone travelling to try and sort out their demons but, while Paul had started to resolve his, Walton had gone down the opposite path and surrendered to his.

"Why was Lucy looking for Paul?" Joseph asked. "What reason could she have for disliking him? I've known him for half my life – I'd *know* if he had ever come across anyone called Lucy Golding. The only women who probably have any right to be angry with him are Kerry and Marie."

Walton shrugged, rubbing away at his tired eyes with the balls of his hands.

"She wouldn't ever tell me," he said. "I tried asking her, but she refused to even discuss it. She hasn't been with me constantly over the last six months; she'd often go away for days at a time."

Joseph sighed. "If you don't mind me saying so," he said, "you don't exactly seem to be carrying the same hatred of Paul that you had in Africa."

"Yeah. Since I've been working at the seminary again, I've been remembering all the good times I used to have." He suddenly smiled, briefly lost in nostalgic reminiscence. "The more I remembered the good times I had with my friends, the more I began to lose a lot of my anger. Within a few weeks, I ... well," he said with a shrug, "I started to remember the reasons why I liked Paul."

"I'm glad you just came to your senses," Joseph said. "How did you break it to Golding that revenge had fallen a long way down your list?"

Walton swallowed and looked down. "I didn't," he said in shame. "I never could. By that point, she ... I ..."

He stumbled for a moment as he tried to find the words.

"I never found the nerve," he finally admitted. "She was never around for more than a couple of days, but she'd always come back, like she was watching me. I think she suspected, because she was always pushing me to look for him ... and getting more frustrated every time I came up blank. She'd be furious if she didn't think I'd done enough." He glanced at Joseph. "I've become very good at lying, in the last few months. Her patience was beginning to wear thin until this week."

Joseph looked at Walton in a new light – this man, who had always projected such an air of confidence, was just as scared as they all were, with his own failings, fears ... and weaknesses.

I'm glad I'm not the only one, Joseph though. *I'm terrified at the thought of Lauren and Paul being right. What would I do then? I've defined my life as an atheist ... how could I continue to define myself when that's taken away from me?*

He shook his head to shake those thoughts away. "What changed this week?" he asked. He answered his own question. "You found Paul."

"When ..." Rick cleared his throat and shifted on the sofa. "When Adam was attacked," he went on in a hoarse whisper. "I heard about it... on the news. I went straight to the hospital. Paul and I met there. Golding ..." He shrugged, avoiding Joseph's gaze. "She never said, but I assume she found out about it the same way I did, and invited herself along to breakfast when I told her about it."

Joseph frowned in confusion. "If Lucy's got this hatred for Paul, why would she want to meet him for breakfast?"

Rick shrugged. "I wish I could tell you," he replied. "She never confided in me that much."

Joseph was silent for a moment, then, sighing, he pulled his phone out of his pocket and typed out a brief text about Walton to his sister; he didn't bother sending it to Paul, as it was doubtful he'd receive it before Christmas.

He chewed on his bottom lip for a moment as he watched the text send, then looked up and was about to ask Rick another question when -

"I should have thought to come here first."

Joseph's head snapped round.

"Golding!" Rick exclaimed. Fear quickly etched itself into his face. He jumped to his feet, and the small amount of colour in his cheeks vanished. Joseph jumped to his feet as well, anger, rather than fear, pushing him up.

"How the hell do you get in here?" he demanded.

Golding was stood by the lounge door and giving him an appraising look; Joseph felt like a pig being sized up for its bacon. His hackles, already on edge, rose even more. When it was clear Golding wasn't going to give an answer to his question, Joseph squared his shoulders and took a step forward.

"Get out of my house, right *now*," he said angrily.

His hands were curled tightly into balls and his anger rising with every second he watched the smug, arrogant woman in front of him look round his front room as if it was nothing more than a hovel. Her eyes eventually settled on Joseph.

"What if I don't?" she said. "Will you hurt me? I'd forgotten what a violent species humanity was, you know."

Joseph refrained from saying the first thing that came into his head, as that would only make her comment true. It seemed oddly worded, though; *She* looks *human enough*, he thought. *And how did she get in here in the first place? I* know *I locked the front door.*

Through gritted teeth, he asked in a controlled tone; "Are you going to leave?"

Golding rolled her eyes; despite having broken into Joseph's property, she obviously couldn't see any problem with what she'd done.

Paul managed to bring her down a peg or two at the hospital, Joseph remembered. *If I have to do it as well, then so be it.*

Joseph reached out for the phone next to the sofa, but was stopped by Golding's hand snaking out and grabbing his arm.

"I wouldn't, if I were you," she whispered. There was a menacing undertone to her voice that hadn't been there a minute ago.

Walton was still pale and shaking, clearly terrified at being found. "Golding, I -"

Golding's eyes narrowed as her head turned to face him, and he stammered to an awkward stop under her intense gaze.

"You have nothing to say that interests me," she said in that same undertone. "Traitor."

Joseph tried to wrench his arm away from Golding, but his eyes widened in surprise as he began to pull. Golding had a vice-like grip on his arm, and he couldn't get out of it; she didn't even look as if she was making any effort in maintaining the grip.

"What the -" he began.

Golding smiled; it was a mirthless smile, though, that went nowhere near her eyes. Turning back to Walton, she raised her eyebrows; "My poor little Rick. Why don't you tell Joseph the *real* reason that Adam ended up dead?"

"You said ... you said no-one would ever need to know."

"I lied," she replied. "I thought you humans knew all about that."

"That's the second time you've said that," Joseph said, curious despite himself. "'You humans.' What does that make you?"

Golding rolled her eyes. However, she seemed to be considering what he said.

"Perhaps now is the time," she muttered, half to herself. "Now that I'm so close ..."

She glanced at the cowering Walton, who fell to his knees. Joseph watched him carefully – there was more than just terror in his eyes, although that was there in abundance.

If I believed in such a place, Joseph thought, stilled into silence by the man before him, *I'd say he's seen seven types of hell.*

"Please," Walton whispered, looking at Golding. "I'll pay for what I've done. I swear."

"It's too late for that, don't you think?" Golding turned back to Joseph. "Rick didn't exactly tell you the whole truth a moment ago. The reason he knew about Adam being attacked ... was because Rick was the one who attacked him."

It took a moment for Joseph to understand. He looked down at Rick, who sagged back against the sofa; he seemed almost defeated, now that the truth was out.

"I won't believe that," Joseph said softly. "Rick, tell me she's lying."

Walton looked back at Joseph; the terror in his eyes slowly fading, to be replaced with a blank, resigned look. That alone told Joseph everything he needed to know, but he still wanted the priest to say it.

"Rick," Joseph said. "Tell me. Tell me what happened."

He felt Golding's grip loosen from his arm, but he had no immediate urge to pick up the handset. Instead, he remained focused on Rick; the blank look still stared back at him.

"I ...." Walton swallowed. "I ... killed Adam and Father Simon."

Joseph was stunned. He suddenly felt used; during their conversation, he had come very close to actually feeling sorry for Rick. Despite everything, he had been able to overcome his anger and hatred - and actually rediscover the friendship he and Paul once had.

If only any of that was actually true, Joseph thought in sudden disgust. *You're a murderer.*

Walton must have seen the disgust in Joseph's eyes, because tears began welling up in his eyes.

"Everything else I said was true!" he protested. "I swear to you! I've learnt from my mistakes. I was just too afraid to stand up to *her*." He nodded at Golding. "She wanted to find Paul, but wasn't having any luck. One day, she came and told me that if I were to injure Adam and the new priest, Paul would want to visit him -"

"*Injure* him," Joseph replied "How did it get from that to *killing* him?"

Walton stared, open-mouthed for a moment, as if his brain had slowed down. "They fought back," he whispered. "I ... I didn't know what I was doing. I panicked and ..."

He trailed off, realising the weakness of his argument. Joseph still couldn't hide the disgust from his face as he realised the depths this pair would go to just to get to Paul.

"They fought back so you *killed* them?" he said. "You murdered them!"

Walton didn't say anything; instead, he lowered his eyes and allowed the tears to stream freely down his face. Joseph turned back to Golding and saw that the arrogant sneer was still on her face; he had to fight the urge to wipe it off.

"Why was it so urgent to find him that you had to kill two people to do it?" he demanded.

"Because drastic times call for drastic measures."

Joseph reached out again for the phone, and Golding held up her hand to stop him. Surprised that she didn't grab him with her vice-like grip again, he paused.

"You're an accomplice," he spat, "and Rick has killed two people! I'm reporting this."

"I don't think so," she replied coolly.

Joseph laughed at her audacity. "You're in *my* home and you're telling *me* what to do?"

Golding looked at Walton. "You've done your duty," she said. "I can have my revenge on all of them now that you've led me to Paul and his friends. You're no longer necessary."

Without warning, Walton flew through the air and smashed into the wall, his head colliding with a sharp *crack* against the mirror. He hung there for a moment, eyes widened in shock, then his body slid down to the floor – leaving a streak of blood behind him.

"No!"

Joseph checked for a pulse. He needn't have bothered – the vacant, staring eyes alone could have told him that Walton was dead.

How did she do that? he asked himself. *She didn't even touch him.*

He was too much in shock to feel any anger; he knew he would do, when his brain caught up, but for that moment, he felt numb. She was far stronger than him, having killed a man with a flick of her wrist - and didn't seem to even be the slightest bit concerned about it.

How can I fight someone like that? he thought with a surge of despair.

Standing up, he shook his head. "I don't understand," he said. "I don't understand any of this. You want revenge against Paul – and now me. Why? I don't even *know* you!"

"Yes," Golding replied quietly, "you do. You just don't remember."

Joseph frowned. "What are you talking about?"

Golding smiled, and stepped briskly forward to again take Joseph firmly by the arm. This time, he didn't object – a quick glance down at Rick reminded him of Golding's power.

"Look at me," she ordered

Joseph looked up automatically. He stared into her eyes – and felt his stomach lurch as a sudden, inexplicable flash of recognition washed over him.

"No ..." he whispered. "It's not possible."

Golding regarded him, her eyes taking in his face. "So," she went on, "a part of you can remember me. How is that possible? I thought I wiped every trace of me from your brain."

I don't know, Joseph thought, *but I wish with all my heart I* didn't *remember you.*

With a sudden, frustrated sigh, Golding tightened her grip on Joseph's arm, making him cry out in pain.

"You're coming with me, so I can find out exactly how you've kept a part of your memory alive after so many years."

Joseph's head began to spin as he watched Golding start to *change*, her features physically altering to turn her into the person he now remembered -

- and, in a burst of blinding white light, they were both gone.

Heaven:
2,000 Years Ago

Michael barely noticed his journey through the corridors of Heaven; he was too focused on – and worried about – the task in front of him.

His physical injuries had almost completely healed in the intervening weeks; he could walk for the most part without any pain. His right wing still hurt when he flew, but he had been assured that would disappear with exercise.

His worries stemmed from the plan that they were currently putting into action – his plan. Soon, he would be separated from his friends, the so-called rebels; he had spent a decade apart from them and now, despite having them back, he knew they would be gone again in a matter of hours. All 144,000 rebels had been rounded up by the armies he commanded – or, rather, had commanded.

The Almighty's surprising intervention had staved off the execution of the leading rebels – although Michael knew that Metatron's command to "kill everyone" had more than likely included him, so he was grateful for that small mercy. However, given what the punishment for rebellion actually was, he wondered if death wouldn't be the kinder mercy.

And it was he who had devised it.

If I hadn't done something and taken it straight to the Authority, *Michael thought, and not for the first time,* Metatron would have done her utmost to find a way round the ruling and killed all the rebels, regardless of what the Almighty said. At least, this way, I've given them a fighting chance of survival.

He entered the Celestial Observatory; it was mercifully empty – most people were out on the upper extremities of the kingdom, watching the rebels being transported down to Earth.

The punishment for the rebels was unconventional, yet amazingly simple; to live out the remainder of their immortal days on Earth, in human form. Metatron had strenuously argued against this, as she pointed out that humans weren't immortal, and natural-born humans would be likely to start questioning where they had come from. Michael had been forced to accede to the logic of this, and decided to instead reincarnate the angelic spirits into different, normal-length human bodies, each of whom would die off after a purely-mortal life span.

He sighed as he sat down on the stone bench, savouring the view of space; he savoured it even more than usual today, knowing that he would never be able to look on it from here in the same way again.

Metatron had also insisted that they remember nothing of their angelic lives, and so their fate had been sealed; they're as good as dead now, *Michael thought. He had hoped to spare them the worst of her excesses by giving them a safe haven on Earth, but now that was stripped away from them; their memories and everything that made them ... them were being taken away. His plan, which was the best of a worst bunch, had suddenly become a death sentence by proxy ... unless he took action.*

So he had come up with a last-ditch attempt to help save them.

"I wondered how long it would take you to get here."

Michael span round to see Metatron stood in the far corner of the room, resting against the wall. She pushed off the pure white surface and walked casually towards Michael. For his part, Michael refused to allow himself to be intimidated by her.

You may have won this time, Metatron, *he thought,* but I won't bow down to you. I've let you get away with more than enough, over the years. Not any more.

"I'm here now," he replied bluntly. "Ready to take on my new role."

He obviously hadn't been completely able to keep the frustration out of his voice, because Metatron gave him a faint smirk.

"You are fortunate to have *a job," she said. "If it was up to me, you'd be joining the rest of those ingrates down on Earth."*

Michael felt a wave of uselessness flood over him – because she was right. The Almighty had intervened, despite being in some sort of thrall to Metatron, and insisted that Michael were to stay. Metatron had countered by demanding that, if he were to stay, he had to be demoted, due to his overt support to the rebels in the Ruling Chamber.

"How are you doing it?" he asked. "Keeping control of the Almighty? He's always been the most powerful out of all of us. How long have you been controlling his thoughts for? Was it before you gave him his children, or after?"

Metatron shrugged. "What does it matter?" she said. "I'm commander of the angelic armies, and you're ..." She laughed. "You're nothing, so your opinion doesn't really matter."

Michael took a step forward, eyes burning with a sudden hatred ... then stopped. What else could he do? He knew she had control over the Almighty, but how could he now prove it? All the rebels were now imprisoned, he no longer had any direct access to the Almighty, and he knew that Metatron would be watching his every move. He knew he was now as much of a prisoner as Lucifer, Satan and Beelzebub.

Metatron saw the look of realisation on his face and nodded approvingly.

"I suspect I may enjoy this punishment more than your death," she said. "This way, I can see your pain day after day ... after century."

She waved a hand, and the windows polarised. Individual images came up on the screens, showing each of the rebel angels being forced into their new forms, the first of many human bodies they would experience throughout their lives. Michael saw the devastation in their eyes – some fought it, some had given into it completely. But all were now facing a fate worth than death.

And so am I, *Michael thought as he watched Metatron stride confidently out of the Observatory – and his new working space.* I can only hope that my plan works out. If it doesn't ... then we might as well all be dead.

Broadstairs Sea Front: Friday Evening

Paul's was struggling to process everything Gabriel had told him. He and Lauren were still on the promenade, along with the angel, who was patiently watching their faces run through a range of emotions, from surprise to shock to disbelief.

"Okay ..." Paul said. He realised he didn't know what he was going to say after that. What *could* he say, after everything Gabriel had just told them? The story of the events leading up to the Civil War, the Civil War itself, and the imprisonment of the rebels seemed fantastical.

"Sounds unbelievable, I should imagine," Gabriel said with a degree of understatement.

Paul was silent for a moment, struggling to decide which of the many questions running through his head to ask first.

While he thought, Lauren interjected. "Are you actually telling us that there are 144,000 human beings on this Earth that are actually angels hidden away inside human bodies?"

"Yes."

Lauren laughed quietly to herself. She turned to look out over the frozen landscape, with the swimmers and sunbathers locked in position as though they were in some sort of photo.

Paul glanced at her for a moment, then looked back at the angel in front of him.

"So what are you saying?" he asked. "That Lauren and I are two of these rebels?"

It was Gabriel's turn to laugh. "What I'm *saying* is that you're more than just ordinary rebels." He pointed at Paul and Lauren in order. "Lucifer and Beelzebub. My brother and one of my best friends."

Celestial Observatory:
1,000 Years Ago

M ichael had been Chief Observer for a millennia, and he was losing hope.

A thousand years to the human race was a long time; the 144,000 had lived so many lives and accumulated so many experiences and memories; if only they were allowed to remember them, from one lifetime to the next. Michael had noticed some of them could occasionally remember a brief snippet of a previous life, but they were always dismissed as merely dreams or the work of the Devil.

The Devil, *Michael thought with a laugh.* How ironic.

For an angel, however, a millennia was different – Michael had lived many times that, so a mere thousand years was the blink of an eye.

Michael sighed; he had hoped that his plan to ensure the human-angels remember their angelic lives would have worked by now, but it seemed that he'd done his job better than he expected ... and that he had failed.

Have I condemned them to a fate worse than death? he wondered for the hundredth time that day.

He buried his head in his hands and drew in a breath. He tried to focus his mind through meditative techniques he had learnt, but none of them seemed to work. His mind was unfocused and ragged. Guilt surged through him as he felt the enormity of what he had done – come up with the plan that had condemned his friends to this fate.

Should I have allowed Metatron to kill them? Would that have been the kinder option?

"Michael?"

Michael looked up in surprise; no-one ever troubled him when he was on duty here in the Observatory. He was a social pariah – Metatron had made sure of that, with veiled threats as to what she would do to anyone who seemed too friendly towards him. Michael didn't care what people of him anymore, and was actually quite glad of the privacy.

So it was with intense shock that he saw Gabriel walking towards him.

"What are you doing here?" he asked. "Metatron won't be pleased if she finds out."

Gabriel sat down on the stone bench beside Michael and cast a quick glance over the wall of screens, before turning back to the observer.

"My mother can think what she wants."

Michael's eyebrows raised in surprise. "I haven't heard you call her that in ... I can't actually remember the last time." He made a face. "I'm sure I would have heard if your relationship had improved to that extent."

Gabriel shrugged, his now-immaculate wings following the line of his shoulders. He looked back to the screens and leaned forward, as if trying to find someone amongst the constantly-moving images.

"She never was much of a mother to me," he said. "Any vestiges of a filial bond that barely existed in the first place were destroyed during the Civil War."

They sat in silence for a few minutes until Gabriel expelled a deep breath.

"You tried to defend me, when I was ... tortured."

"I didn't do a very good job."

"You tried," Gabriel retorted. "That was enough. I'll never forget that."

Whenever Michael had seen him over the past millennia, there had been a haunted look in his eyes, a definite slump to his shoulders, and a weariness that Michael could definitely sympathise with. They were both survivors of the War and both felt that the wrong side had won. Now, however, he saw a different side to Gabriel; he had a glint of something else in his eyes, and Michael was intrigued by it.

"How are you?" he asked, emphasising the words so that Gabriel knew he wasn't just asking to be polite.

Gabriel smiled. "I'm better than I have been in a long time," he replied. "I had an ... epiphany last night."

"Oh?"

"You have a plan that you've kept from Metatron."

Michael hadn't confided in anyone about his plan; he felt there was no-one he could trust.

"Why do you think that?" he asked.

Gabriel looked at him carefully. "My mother is a clever angel, but she is also an arrogant one. She is convinced that no-one is more clever than her, and now she has won, no-one will rise up against her."

A fraction of a smile touched his lips. "But she forgets about you, Michael. You are defeated, but that does not mean she has won. You care about your fellow angels, and you would have not suggested your plan without a second, private part. Metatron has no empathy, so she cannot consider how someone who is defeated would have the cunning to put a plan into action. You used her arrogance to create a plan right in front of her that is so simple she would not consider."

Michael opened his mouth to deny it, but closed it again. He had no desire to lie to Gabriel's face, but was not ready to reveal his secret yet.

"It's okay, Michael," Gabriel went on, seemingly to pick up on Michael's hesitation. "You don't have to go into details, but I just wanted you know that I am here if you need me."

"Why are you coming to me now?"

Gabriel shrugged. He stood up and walked a few paces to stretch his legs.

"I don't know," he admitted as he turned back to the older angel. "It's taken me a long time to get over what Metatron ... my mother ... did to me to end the War, and how I've been treated since they won. I've spent the past thousand years being shunned by people I once called friends, ignored by my mother and have a Father who I haven't seen since the Civil War. I need a friend right now."

Michael understood what Gabriel was saying – he, too, felt alone. He could sympathise with what Gabriel had said, even regarding the Almighty. His beloved leader, whom he had served faithfully for so long, had shut himself off from the entire realm; only Metatron now had access to him. Michael and Gabriel knew that keeping him isolated meant that Metatron could maintain her control over – and she had threatened to kill the 144,000 if either of them revealed the truth.

He stood and smiled at Gabriel. "I could do with a friend as well."

Broadstairs Sea Front:
Friday Evening

Fascinated, Gabriel watched Paul stride along the promenade, carefully avoiding the people-statues. Lauren was following two steps behind; she wasn't as used to walking, or at least used to walking at Paul's speed. Gabriel was on the *other* side of the promenade barrier, where there was nothing but a sheer drop down to the beach, about twenty feet below; he was using his wings to gracefully fly alongside them.

"This is interesting," Gabriel was saying. "When Lucifer needed to think, he used to fly. It's interesting that you need to move fast to think too."

Paul paused and looked at Gabriel, trying to work out whether or not the angel was winding him up.

Probably not, he decided on reflection.

He could hear Lauren gratefully drawing in breaths as she leaned against the railings.

"Sorry," he said. "I forget how fast I'm walking. It helps blow away the cobwebs though."

Lauren smiled. "So does flying, apparently."

They both looked at Gabriel. He had soared away, enjoying the sensations of the wind against his angelic skin and the sun's rays hitting him through a filtered ozone layer – feelings that he rarely experienced. He hadn't yet revealed everything to the two angel-humans below him and knew he was prevaricating.

Let them have another few minutes of innocence, he thought.

Far below, on the promenade, Paul released a breath. "So what do you think?" he asked Lauren in a tone that was intended to be casual, but was actually loaded with meaning.

Lauren glanced at him, then went back to watching the awe-inspiring sight of seeing an angel flying far above her head. "I think we got what we wanted," she said. "We *did* ask."

"Yeah ..." he replied. "Yeah, we did."

Gabriel flew back down to join them, his massive wings landing him gently on the ground.

"You have many questions."

It wasn't a question so much as a statement. Paul nodded.

"Not so long ago, Michael said that I was nowhere near ready for all this knowledge," he said. "How can I be ready now? What's changed?"

Gabriel just stood there, maddeningly calm – but it was Lauren who answered his question.

"Yes it has, Paul," she said. "Something *has* changed."

He frowned, still not understanding. "What?"

"You managed to transport us back from heaven under your own power."

"Yes, but ... I ... Well ..." He stumbled to a halt, and glared at Gabriel. "You know about that, don't you?"

Gabriel nodded, trying – and failing – to hide the smile from his face.

"How?"

"Metatron and Michael were walking down a corridor when Metatron felt a presence," Gabriel replied. "She couldn't pinpoint it, and it disappeared after a moment. Michael went straight back to the Observatory and saw you on the monitors discussing it at the hospital."

Lauren was instantly alarmed. "But won't that mean Metatron will know about it as well?"

"Metatron shouldn't be a problem," Gabriel replied. "Michael altered the records – your conversation has been deleted from the archives. She has suspicions, of course, but nothing concrete."

Paul nodded his thanks. "Gabriel, you need to come with us and talk to Joseph. He's struggling to believe all this, so it would really help it coming from you." He hesitated. "Actually, I think *I'll* really benefit from hearing it again. It's all a bit ... mind-blowing."

"I understand," Gabriel said with a laugh. "Being told you are the leader of a group of rebels that was imprisoned for his beliefs ... well, it'll take some time to understand."

"Wait," Lauren interrupted, a thought suddenly occurring to her. "You're telling us all this, but none of it's ringing any bells with me. I've seen this sort of thing happen in films; when a person tells them the true story of their lives; all their memories come flooding back. Well, I've got to be honest ... I don't remember anything."

Paul looked at her and raised an eyebrow.

"Well," she conceded, "actually, I can remember all this past life stuff." She frowned and looked intensely thoughtful. "Wow, that suddenly makes sense. I've *lived* all those lives, haven't I? I've *been* all those people?"

Gabriel laughed. "Not quite," he said. "*Beelzebub* has been all those people. You're just the latest in a line of humans to host her."

Seeing Lauren's sudden disappointment over her face, Gabriel realised that he could have phrased that far better. He quickly changed the subject.

"Your angelic memories can be restored, but I would rather Michael discuss that with you."

"Okay," said Paul, "we go and get Joseph, you tell him what you've just told us, then we ..." He slowed to a halt and frowned. "What then?"

Gabriel hesitated. He looked at the pair of them, and wondered for a moment about Michael's plan. *They've been human for so long ... what will happen when we try to dig down and find Lucifer and Beelzebub? My brother and my friend ... are you still in there?*

"I ... think I'd rather talk about it when we're with Michael," he replied.

He was aware that he wasn't making a very convincing argument, but didn't want to have to tread those muddy waters without Michael by his side. In truth, he didn't know if Paul and Lauren would survive the process, and he felt extremely uneasy about that.

"Alright," Paul replied, seeming not to pick up on the apparent problem. "Let's go and get Joseph."

He grabbed his mobile phone out of his pocket, ignoring Lauren as she scoffed at it. The phone was at least five years old, brick-like, and needed charging every few hours to keep it going. Paul kept it out of nostalgic value more than anything else; in reality, he was ambivalent towards mobiles – he hated the thought of constantly being contactable, which was why he so often left it off, and would have got rid of it were it not for the fact that it irritated his friends more by keeping it.

Lauren got her own mobile phone out and waved it in front of his face. "Now *this* is a mobile phone, Paul. Touch screen, 8 meg camera -"

"Wow … I don't care," Paul replied, smiling at his friend. "A phone's a phone to me. And you've got a text."

Surprised that Paul could even tell what a text symbol looked like, Lauren opened the message; it was from Paul. She read it out to Paul and Gabriel.

Paul frowned. "Why has Golding been searching for me?"

"Let's go and get him," Gabriel said. "Put away your phones – there are quicker ways of contacting your friend."

Paul's eyebrows arched. "Well, forgive me if I've forgotten how to do it," he retorted. "It *has* been over two thousand years since I've last used my powers, so I'm a bit rusty."

Gabriel ignored the sarcasm, and turned his head slightly to the side. After a moment, he frowned, and pressed his fingers against his temples as he focussed his energies. Lauren was the first one to notice his sudden depth of concentration.

"What's wrong?" she asked.

"Nothing," Gabriel replied automatically.

The frown, however, didn't go away. Paul stepped forward and grabbed Gabriel's arm.

"Tell me what's wrong," he demanded.

Gabriel was caught off-guard for a moment; he heard his brother's voice in Paul's.

"Lucifer?" he whispered.

Paul blinked. "I'm still Paul. What's happened to my friend?"

"He's … he's gone."

Lauren and Paul exchanged a frightened look.

"What do you mean?" Lauren asked. "This is my brother! Gabriel, you need to find him!"

The angel held his hands up to forestall any more protests, and his eyes went unfocused for a moment. Paul was about to ask a further question, but was interrupted by a muted cry of alarm from Gabriel.

Lauren jumped. "What?"

Whatever she had been expecting, however, was nothing compared to what Gabriel said next. Her blood ran cold.

"Metatron has him."

Heaven:
Present Day

J oseph's staggered back in shock as the white light disappeared; it was so quick that it left him breathless. He was stood in a large auditorium, with rows of tiered seats arranged in a semi-circle around the room. Looking up, he squinted to try to see the top row – and failed.

How big is *this place?*

On his right were some more steps – not as many this time, perhaps two dozen or so – which led to an ornately-decorated luminescent throne. It wasn't made of any precious metal that Joseph recognised; instead, it seemed to shine from within itself. It was empty; he was intrigued as to who sat there.

Golding was in front of him, the smug smile on her face as irritating as ever. However, there was something more this time, something deeper. Joseph looked at her closely, and saw something else in her eyes. It was a pool of loathing and malice that seemed, at this precise moment, to be directed entirely at *him*. He had already come to realise that there was a lot more to Lucy Golding than met the eye, but he wondered what there was about her that he couldn't see. She had shown him her true self for a moment, back in his house, but he couldn't quite see it here, or remember what it was – except that it hurt and was *horrible*.

"Who are you really?" he asked. "You're not plain and simple Lucy Golding, I know that."

He strained to remember what Golding had shown him, but it was as if she had taken away the knowledge almost as quickly as she had given it to him.

Golding laughed. "That's true," she said. "Perhaps it's time to show my real identity. I'm eager to get out of this skin anyway; it's always made me uncomfortable, being this ... weak."

Joseph winced as a sudden bright light surrounded Golding; there was no warning, it was just there. A sense of foreboding surged through Joseph as he witnessed Golding's figure start to morph; there was only one person he knew that had ever projected such a light round themselves, and he didn't even believe that she existed.

Metatron.

The light quickly faded, and Joseph was almost disappointed to see that there wasn't much of a change to her – she was a few inches taller now, but other than that, she could have still been mistaken for human.

Then Joseph saw her wings.

His eyes almost bulged out of his head as he realised what they were, and that they were real; he had spent much of the afternoon denying precisely what he was now looking squarely at. He also realised that this was the first time he had seen Metatron without the white light surrounding her.

"You were right about one thing," Metatron said. "I'm so much more than plain and simple Lucy Golding. Tell me, Satan – how do you cope with being limited to purely human? I've felt so constrained in a flesh-and-blood body."

Joseph blinked, his mind spinning in confusion.

"'Satan'?" he repeated. "What are you talking about? My name's Joseph Tempur! What the hell is this all about? Don't think I'm going to take any crap from you just because you're real! This ... this is all making absolutely *no* sense whatsoever!"

Joseph realised that he was becoming hysterical, but didn't care. He felt he was casting about without a safety net, and needed something to anchor himself to – like an answer to any of his questions.

Metatron looked at him curiously, seemingly lost in thought for a moment.

"What's that I detect in your head?" she asked. "Is that -?"

She barked another, harsher laugh.

"I see what Michael's done, right there inside you!" she exclaimed in understanding. "Oh my word, how simple; how could I miss it?!"

"In my head?" Joseph repeated. "There's nothing in my head ... well, except my -" He stopped as he realised what Metatron was talking about. "The tumour."

Metatron nodded her head, her eyes alight with fascination. "I wonder how it works," she muttered, half to herself. "Are your memories inside it, Satan?"

"Stop calling me that! My name is Joseph and I -"

Metatron held up her hand, and Joseph stopped talking, surprised by her eyes dragging themselves up and down his body.

"So human," she said. "I wonder if anything would happen to you if I did ... *this.*"

She waved her hand in a languid motion – and Joseph's head exploded with agony. Memories, thoughts and voices flooded through his head, and he felt lost in a world that he suddenly didn't recognise.

A Different Realm:
Present Day

P aul couldn't see anything. He blinked a few times, but there was nothing for his eyes to focus on. There was *nothingness* all around him, as far as he could see. He couldn't even be sure how far that was, given that there was nothing to judge distances by.

"Where are we?" he asked. "Heaven?"

"Not quite," came the reply.

Paul was confused. Gabriel, who was stood in front of him, hadn't moved his mouth; it was only when he saw Lauren turn her head did he look over his shoulder to see Michael.

He gave them both a weary smile, and Paul was instantly reassured; he couldn't quite put his finger on why, but just knowing Michael was involved was comforting.

"Hello, Lucifer," Michael went on. "How are you?"

Paul held up his hands. "Please don't call me that," he pleaded. "I'm just plain old Paul Finn. I don't have any of Lucifer's memories. I'm just ... me."

"You're so much more than that," Gabriel said from behind them. "Both of you are."

"And you *do* have Lucifer's memories," Michael said softly. "You just don't know it yet."

Lauren had a more pressing issue on her mind. "Where's Joseph? Gabriel said that Metatron's got her?"

Michael nodded. "Yes," he replied. "We're meeting in a side dimension, away from prying ears. This is where the rebels executed and planned the Civil War. The Almighty and Metatron were never able to find it, even after they tortured Gabriel. He never gave up that secret, and I'm glad of it. It means this remains our most valuable secret."

"You haven't answered the question," Paul noted. "If Metatron's got Joseph, then he's not safe. Where is he, and how do we get him back?"

Lauren nodded. "He's my brother," she added. "I'll do anything I have to go to rescue back. Tell me what we can do."

Michael studied her carefully for a moment, and Lauren flushed. She felt as she was under a microscope, and suddenly felt very small. Flushing with an unexpected anger, she snapped.

"I'm not some study!" she said sharply. "Stop looking at me as if I'm an insect!"

"Apologies," Michael replied, abashed at her retort. "It's just that you remind me so much of Beelzebub, it's … frightening."

"Part of her personality was bound to leak through," Gabriel added.

Lauren's anger didn't subside. "Stop saying that! I'm Lauren Tempur, not Beelzebub, and if she's in my head, then she can just get the hell out!"

"It's not as easy as that," Michael replied. "She's inexorably linked with you – if anything, you're a part of her, not the other way round."

Lauren didn't know what to say to that, so decided to just ignore it. "And my brother?"

Michael sighed. "If Metatron has him anywhere, I imagine it will be in the Ruling Chamber. She likes to intimidate people, and the Chamber certainly has that effect."

"Why has she got him?"

"Metatron has been obsessed with the rebels ever since their defeat," Michael explained. "If she could have, she would have them slaughtered, removing the problem. The Almighty wanted them alive, and I've been making sure she keeps to that order. He doesn't show himself to us anymore, but I remind Metatron of his authority over our realm at every opportunity. However, something's changed; she's taken one of the lead rebels captive. I imagine she'll kill him after she's satiated her own curiosity - and then move on to the remaining rebels."

"Michael, do *you* know why Metatron was looking for me for so long?" Paul asked.

"Because of what you mean to her, above all other angels," Michael said quietly. "We can consider that later. Metatron will undoubtedly kill Joseph when she is finished with him, and so *he* is now our priority."

"So let's go," Paul said firmly. "We need to get him."

"It's not as simple as that ..." Michael replied. "They will be in the Chamber, with the surrounding area secured. She has been blatant about taking him from Earth, so doesn't care who knows. That means she's prepared for anyone who'll try and rescue him."

Lauren was visibly agitated as she turned to Paul. "There's got to be something we can do. I'm not going to just leave him there with *her*."

Paul knew there was nothing he could do, at least without access to Lucifer's memories, and he wasn't sure that he *wanted* access to them. The whole idea blew his mind, the fact that another entity was living within him ... or was a part of him; he couldn't work out the logistics of it.

He blinked, and realised that Lauren was looking to him for an answer. *I don't know what I can do*, he thought guiltily. *I want Joseph back as much as Lauren does, but how the hell are we going to do that? We're just human, not –*

His eyes widened as a thought occurred to him. As his mind began to whir, he caught the look in Lauren's eyes, and realised that she was thinking the same thing.

"It would be incredibly risky," he said quietly to her. "Gabriel and Michael *want* their friends back. What if they just ... override our personalities? What if we didn't exist anymore?"

Lauren swallowed. "I'd risk it, to save Joseph." She glanced over her shoulder at Gabriel. "I don't think they *would* do that to us. But that doesn't mean we should both do this."

Paul opened his mouth to protest, but Lauren stopped him with a glare.

"You know it's the right thing to do," she said. "One of us needs to stay as we are, to anchor the other one. I'm going to need someone to remind me of Lauren Tempur."

"What makes you think I'll let you go?" Paul retorted. "You stay here with Michael and Gabriel, and I'll bring Joseph back."

"Like hell you will!" Lauren exclaimed, her voice carrying across the empty white void. "He's my brother, Paul! I'm going to get him, and that's all there is to it!"

"I'll go with you, Lauren," Gabriel said. "I'll help you with what you want to do."

She gave the angel a level gaze. "How do you know what I want to do?"

"Because I hope that, if our circumstances were reversed, I'd be willing to call on *my* hidden angel to help my recover *my* brother, no matter what the cost."

He glanced at Paul, who felt another pang of guilt. *This is as close as he's got to his brother for over 2,000 years ... and now I'm staying as I am and not bringing Lucifer back. Am I doing the right thing?*

"Paul, we need you for something else."

Paul looked at Michael and raised a quizzical eyebrow. He had been chastised by Lauren's forceful words, and knew better than to argue with her. *I have to remember that she's not a little girl anymore,* he thought. *I have to let her go, if she's that passionate about it. I hope whatever Michael wants me to do can distract me while she's gone, because otherwise I'm going to be terrified for her.*

"What?" he asked.

"Help me get to your Father and make him see sense. I think I know where he is. Metatron's controlling him and we need to stop her. Now that Metatron is distracted by the rebels, I wonder if a human might succeed where I've failed."

Paul nodded, thoughtfully – Michael was talking a lot of sense. "I can't promise anything," he said. "But I'll do my best."

Lauren turned to Gabriel again. "I need you to help me, but ... I don't understand. Where is Beelzebub? Is she just stuffed away inside my head?"

It was Michael who replied. "Yes ... and no," he said. "When the rebels were given their first human forms, they were cut off from all outside contact, in an unconscious state. The only way humans would know that the angels were sharing their souls was by the occasional dream, and that's only if they were particularly susceptible."

"'Occasional dream'?" Paul repeated. "I've had the same recurring dream at least once a week since I can remember. I'm in this huge Chamber, waiting for my Father to appear and pass judgement on me and my friends."

Michael and Gabriel exchanged a significant glance, which wasn't lost on either human.

"What does that mean?" Paul asked.

"I don't know if it means *anything*," Michael said. "Except that Lucifer was an extremely strong personality. Even though he's unconscious, some of his memories are still leaking out. What you're remembering is the day when the Almighty and Metatron disagreed on your punishment, and you ... well, Lucifer ... and the other rebels were banished to Earth."

"Gabriel," Lauren asked, "how did you manage to escape banishment?"

Gabriel, quietly and with shame hanging on every word, told her how Metatron tortured him for information, forcing him to betray his fellow rebels in exchange for his life.

"What's worse," Michael added, "is that Metatron is Gabriel's mother."

Paul was appalled. *What sort of sick individual does that?* he thought. *Tortures her own son?*

He realised that Lauren was giving him an odd look.

"What?" he asked.

"Paul ..." she said quietly, as if unsure whether or not she should continue. "*That's* why Metatron was looking for you. She's your -"

But it wasn't necessary; Paul's brain had caught up with Lauren. If Metatron was Gabriel's mother, and Gabriel and Lucifer were brothers, then...

"No ..." he whispered, half to himself. "*No*! That ... that woman is not my mother! I remember my mother – she died when I was fifteen years old and she was nothing like that evil ... creature that masquerades as an angel!"

His voice was cracking, full of emotion, but he didn't care. He was Paul Finn, not Lucifer, and he wouldn't have his own mother's memory defiled by some vapid creature here in heaven, of all places.

"Paul," Michael said, holding his hands up placating, "Lucifer *is* you, and *you* are Lucifer. You're part of each other."

Paul shook his head. "No," he replied, "I won't accept that. I'm *not* Lucifer. I'm Paul Finn, and she -" he pointed at Lauren, "is Lauren Tempur, nothing more. We're not some angelic beings who just can't remember their angelic lives, we're *human*! And Metatron is *not* my mother!"

"The rebels, when they were imprisoned on Earth, were merged with their human hosts, so that the two sides became totally united," Michael explained. "This meant that one could not be extracted without killing the other. Metatron forced us to do this, because she knew any rebel sympathisers -"

"That's Michael and I," Gabriel noted with a half-grimace, half-smile.

Michael nodded, then continued; "She knew that we wouldn't, in all good conscience, be able to separate them, given that we'd be killing the human hosts and quite possibly the angels as well."

Lauren took a step back, away from the group. She suddenly looked very frightened. "I take it back," she said. "I don't want Beelzebub's memories returned, especially if it means killing me. I'll be no good to Joseph dead, and I doubt Beelzebub would that that interested in rescuing my brother."

"Lauren," said Michael with infinite patience, "let me finish. I was able to intervene, secretly, and stop that from happening. I developed a method of keeping the two personalities separate throughout each human incarnation. This would mean we could one day recall Lucifer or Beelzebub's personality without killing either angel or human."

"The tumours," said Paul in realisation. "You used the tumours."

"Yes. With each succeeding generation, the tumours I implanted grew bigger." Michael smiled. "You wouldn't recognise them if you saw how small they were in Lucifer's first host. When they reached a certain size, they were designed to automatically trigger certain processes in the human brain and reactivate Lucifer."

Paul knew that every second they were talking was a moment wasted, but one question in his brain demanded asking.

"Is that why you said I wasn't ready?" he said. "Because my tumour wasn't the right size?"

Michael nodded. "I'm glad you understand," he said "Somehow, though, you were able to access Lucifer's memories through the tumour – and use it to transport yourself here that first time completely by yourself. I still don't understand how you were able to do that."

"I don't care about tumours," Lauren said bluntly. "I just want to get Joseph back." She hesitated, as if caught in the midst of an internal debate. "If that means I have to access Beelzebub's memories to do it, then so be it. Do whatever you have to do."

"Let's go speak to the Almighty," Paul said to Michael. He looked at Lauren. "Be careful."

She rolled her eyes at him, but a small smile touched her lips.

"I could say the same to you … Lucifer."

The Almighty's Private Chambers: Present Day

Paul and Michael left straight away, leaving Lauren and Gabriel behind in the white void. To avoid detection by Metatron or any of her agents by transporting straight to the Almighty's suspected realm, Michael grabbed Paul firmly by the wrist, beat his wings, and began the long flight there.

He watched in fascination as the pure white background abruptly changed to interstellar space, the stars like dots against the pure black background.

How am I not suffocating? he thought.

That thought was quickly pushed aside as a wave of dizziness flooded over him as the background began to push past him at incredible speeds.

He looked ahead at Michael, who still had a firm hold of his wrist. He was looking intently ahead, focused on the journey. His face was set in concentration, as if trying to remember the way.

Paul realised that he was far too quickly adjusting to the sensations of flying, and his eyes began able to focus on the speeding swirls of light that were flying past him at the speed of light. He swallowed hard, and closed his eyes.

I don't want to get used to this, he thought. *I need to stay* me, *for Lauren's sake if not for mine.*

In what felt like both a moment and an eternity later, the sensations in his stomach stopped, and he felt his feet touch something solid. He opened his eyes again, and he and Michael were now outside a solitary, one-story farm cottage building. Whatever Paul had been expecting, this certainly wasn't it.

The Almighty lives here? he thought. *That can't be right* - god *doesn't live in a farmhouse.*

He looked around; the house itself was in the middle of an endless row of green fields, with a blue sky overhead. Horses were galloping in the distance across a paddock, and there was a general feeling of peace and calm over the whole scene that gave Paul a settled feeling for a moment. He breathed out, and the knot in his stomach returned. Looking at Michael, he blinked in surprise as he saw confusion on the angel's face.

"What is it?" he demanded. "What's wrong?"

Michael opened his mouth to speak, but no words came out. He looked confused and upset by what he saw.

"I didn't expect it to be like this," he whispered. "I didn't ... I don't understand."

Paul couldn't help but feel a surge of fear run through him. *If* you *don't understand,* he thought, *then we might as well give up now. I sure as hell don't know what to do.*

He took another look out at the meadow. "Well, if it's any comfort, I didn't exactly expect to find the Almighty living in a cottage."

"Neither did I," Michael muttered. "We've known for a long time that this was where the Almighty lived, but I didn't know it looked like ... *this.*"

A mixture of surprise and horror was mingled into his voice, and Paul turned to face him. "Like what, exactly?"

"So *human.*" Michael returned Paul's gaze, and the look of confusion was still there. "Metatron restricted access to this location after the Almighty moved here, on the grounds of security. She's too obsessed with Joseph to realise we've broken through her seals, but she'll discover it eventually." He blinked. "We should begin."

Paul wasn't entirely convinced, but he nodded anyway. *What am I going to say to him?* he wondered. *He thinks I'm his eldest son, and I don't remember. I don't even think I want to remember any of that. The Almighty's meant to be the divine ruler here, but this house doesn't look very divine. How am I meant to get him to make Metatron to step aside, when Michael and Gabriel haven't even been able to get this close in 2,000 years?*

Paul stood at the front door.

"I don't know what to say," he confessed. "To the Almighty. How am I going to convince him that Metatron is evil if he's under her power?"

Michael studied him for a moment, and a small smile touched his lips. "You'll think of something," he replied. "Lucifer would have done. And yes," he added at the look of annoyance on Paul's face, "I know you're not Lucifer. You're Paul Finn. Although you sometimes remind me so much of him, it's hard to see the difference."

Paul scowled at him, and made to open the door. He glanced round as Michael took a step backwards.

"You're not coming in with me?"

Michael shook his head. "No," he said. "I think my presence would only … complicate things. It's better if I stay out here. Don't worry – I have faith in you."

Paul mentally shrugged, opened the strangely-normal front door, and entered the Almighty's strangely-human home.

A Different Realm:
Present Day

"Are you sure about this?"

Lauren nodded. "As sure as I'll ever be. I'm just concerned about Beelzebub's personality overriding my own."

"She was always a very forceful personality," Gabriel replied. "But she was also very moral – she'll do everything she can not to hurt you, I'm sure of it."

Lauren didn't reply, and Gabriel seemed to understand. There was nothing he could say to quell her nerves; she was determined to rescue her brother from Metatron's clutches, and if it meant calling on Beelzebub to help her, then so be it.

"Is there a ceremony you need to perform or something?" she asked.

Gabriel raised an amused eyebrow. "What is it with you and ceremonies?"

"What do you -" Lauren paused, and laughed. "Those screens. You saw us doing the séance."

"The human fascination for ceremonies and rituals never ceases to amuse me."

"I wouldn't say that to Paul if I were you. He used to be a member of the Catholic church."

Gabriel's face quickly became a mask of concentration, and Lauren swallowed.

This is it, she thought. *What will happen to me after this? I hope I remember who I am.*

She watched Gabriel closely as he touched her forehead.

"Don't worry," he said, "Michael has taught me what to do. It sounds very easy."

Lauren's eyes widened in shock. "You mean you've never actually done this -"

A flash of energy stopped her question in its tracks. Lauren could hear a strange double echo inside her mind; it was almost as if she *felt* Beelzebub emerged.

Lauren saw random memories flying past her eyes: Beelzebub and her friends standing in front of the Almighty; fighting in battle during the Civil War; seeing Gabriel, his body damaged almost beyond recognition on the floor of the Ruling Chamber ... feeling the pain of imprisonment as her form was crushed into pure memory and inserted within a human host, then subsumed by the human.

She swallowed, feeling a sudden sadness threatening to overwhelm her. It was a strange sensation, having the entire weight of someone's memories released into her mind, and she felt her knees buckle as she struggled under the weight of them all.

What – What's happening?

Lauren almost jumped out of her skin at the voice inside her head – it was at once incredibly familiar and totally alien.

Beelzebub? she asked.

Who are you?

My name's Lauren. I'm ... well, it's complicated.

I'm inside you, aren't I? You're one of my human incarnations.

... Alright, maybe not entirely complicated, then.

I've ... not been conscious over the years, but I remember being imprisoned. Where's Lucifer? Satan?

Lauren hadn't expected to get around to the subject quite so directly, but she swallowed and decided to go for it.

I'm glad you asked. Satan's ... consciousness, I'd guess you'd call it, is currently held in the mind of my brother, who's being held captive by Metatron. I want to get him back – and I was hoping you would help me.

Metatron? If she's got your brother, then I have to tell you but he's dead already.

He's not dead! Lauren took a breath, knowing that she had been overly vehement with her denial, but she couldn't – *wouldn't* – believe that her brother was dead. Not yet. She had to try and save him, no matter what. *He needs my help to get out of there ... and I need yours.*

Why do you need my help? Beelzebub sounded suspicious, and Lauren understood that – if their situations were reversed, she would probably feel the same.

Because Metatron is so incredibly powerful, and I'm just human. Gabriel's here with me, and I won't ask him to stand against her alone, not after what he went through the last time. I need your power, your ... strength against her if I've got any chance.

Beelzebub was silent for a moment, and Lauren wondered if she had gone. She realised, however, that she hadn't – Lauren could still *feel* her consciousness hovering there in the back of her brain, just out of reach.

You must love your brother a lot if you're willing to stand up to Metatron. The last time we tried that, I ended up here.

I'm willing to take that chance.

Beelzebub was silent again, then said; *what about Lucifer? Where is he?*

Paul – Lucifer – has gone with Michael to visit the Almighty. They thought they might be able to make him see sense, or at least find out what this hold is that Metatron has over him.

He's gone to the Almighty? Beelzebub sounded appalled. *We need to go after him – there's so many traps surrounding his apartments, they could be killed as soon as they set foot inside his quarters!*

Lauren wasn't surprised by her reaction; she knew now that Beelzebub's relationship with Lucifer was at least as close as hers was to Paul, and knew she would want to do the same thing if it wasn't for Joseph.

Michael's with him, Beelzebub! It's not as if he's gone by himself. Come and help me get Joseph back, then we'll give those two back-up. But I'm not going anywhere without my brother.

A warning tone entered Beelzebub's thoughts. *Even after all this time, I think I could still overpower you without a second thought if I had to. I could just take over your body and go after Lucifer and Michael.*

Yes, you could do that. But I know you won't.

How?

Because I've seen your memories – I know what you're like. You're compassionate and kind ... you were horrified by what Metatron did to Gabriel. How can you stand by and let that happen again, to Satan this time?

Lauren hated herself for using the guilt card, but knew she needed to do it; Beelzebub was very much like her, in that she *felt* very deeply, and hated seeing people in pain.

Alright, Beelzebub said. There was a tinge of reluctance in her voice, but also a tinge of respect, that Lauren had stood up to her. *Let's go rescue Satan before it's too late.*

It's Joseph, actually.

Excuse me?

Lauren was startled – Gabriel had been so silent in the conversation, she had almost forgotten he was there.

Yes?

Satan and Joseph are actually the same person ... in a way. As, indeed, are you both.

Shut up, Gabriel.

Gabriel smiled; Beelzebub and Lauren had spoken in unison, and it was impossible to tell them apart. They were both stubborn, strong-willed and incredibly compassionate about those they loved, and he was filled with a new-found confidence about facing up to his mother.

Let's go.

The Ruling Chamber:
Present Day

Joseph pushed himself off the ground, groaning in pain as he did so. He had a horrendous headache. Rubbing his hand over his face, he tried to mentally push it away, but without much success. The headache was pounding away in the centre of his forehead and threatening to spread itself even wider.

He looked out through half-closed eyes and struggled to focus on his surroundings. Nothing seemed to have changed since he had abruptly lost consciousness – *I haven't been moved. Is that a good or bad thing?* – and Metatron wasn't visible, so he spent a moment quickly going through a mental checklist, checking that nothing was broken.

He had a strange double-take moment as he touched on memories that weren't his and yet were right there in his head. Memory after memory lined up for his attention, and he almost passed out again as they jumbled and overlapped together, each demanding attention.

These are Satan's memories, he realised, without quite understanding *who* Satan was.

Taking a deep breath, he began processing the memories, and very quickly understood who the angel inside him was, and why he was there. He felt a sudden wave of guilt for his hard-line denials towards Paul and Lauren.

Where are you, Satan? If you're there, shouldn't I be able to hear your voice?

"What's wrong, Satan? You look like an angel who has lost something."

Joseph's head snapped round. Metatron was at the very top of the throne podium, and she was sat – no, *draped* – over the throne. Her legs were resting over one ornate arm, and the hand that she was using to rest her head on was positioned on the other.

Joseph stood before her with a confidence he didn't entirely feel. His legs almost gave way under him, but a conscious effort made him stand upright. He knew running would be pointless – Metatron would be able to stop him before he was even half-ways towards either set of doors. So, instead, he looked upwards and gave her a steely glare; he refused to allow himself to be intimidated by her, even sat in that chair.

"That's the Almighty's throne," he said angrily, the memory immediately there. "You have no claim to it."

Metatron laughed, a cold, hard sound that had no mirth behind it at all. "I have *every* claim to it," she replied. "The Almighty is under my control now. He spends all his time at his ... country retreat, I think you would call it. In his absence, I rule this kingdom, and have become very efficient at it."

Joseph was inwardly appalled – this horrible, cruel angel had become dictator in all but name, and no-one had been able to stop her.

"He was always so fascinated by humanity," Metatron went on. "I've given him everything he wants; a human body, human experiences ... a human house."

Joseph blinked in shock. He didn't know why, but he felt a deep gut-wrenching pain, almost grief-like, as he realised how the Almighty had been imprisoned.

"You've made him human," he whispered. "You've reduced the Almighty to human."

Abruptly, Metatron pushed her legs off the side of the throne and leaned forward, her face contorted in anger.

"If he could remember even a small amount of who he really is, I'm sure he would appreciate the irony," she said. She was spitting the words out, each one condensed to pure fury. "He wanted to be united with humanity and I have *given* him that wish, in the same way that the 144,000 were. I have imprisoned him in a body of flesh, and been able to rule heaven in his place."

She cocked her head to one side, and the anger in her face turned into fascination.

"Who *are* you?" she asked with interest. "I've opened up the tumour inside your mind, which should have brought out Satan's personality. I'm curious to know whether or not he's taken over ... or if he's too weak to, and I'm still talking to poor, human Joseph."

Joseph opened his mouth, but couldn't answer. He hadn't realised that Metatron had *intended* to release Satan, presumably to drown out Joseph's personality.

So why am I still here? he wondered.

Something began to dawn on him as his brain continued to process memories. He *was* feeling different in some way – more knowledgeable, and... different. It took him a minute to understand, then he turned his head slightly, mentally caught sight of something – and didn't immediately understand.

How would I have known that that used to be the Almighty's *throne? I mean, I know I've got Satan's memories, but it's a hell of a lot to process. I don't know if I could have pulled up that information right away – my memories are still...*

His peripheral vision had caught sight of something over his right shoulder, and his stomach lurched. He looked again to confirm that he hadn't been hallucinating.

"Oh, damn," he whispered.

Right there, on his back, were a full set of wings. He looked back up at Metatron, who had risen from the throne. Her face was full of shock as she, too, saw his wings.

"How have you done that?" she asked. "I meant to trap Satan in a human body. How have you got his wings?"

Joseph smiled, suddenly understanding. "We've merged," he replied. "You've merged us into one being – we've got the memories of both. Satan is back ... and I am *angry*."

Inside The Almighty's Private Chambers: Present Day

Paul closed the door behind him. He was half-tempted to turn around and flee - but he resisted.

This needs to be done, he thought, *and perhaps I'm the one to do it.*

He looked around; if he'd been surprised at the exterior, then the interior was ... shocking. The cottage effect was continued; he had walked straight into the front room, with a comfortable three-piece suite, a grandfather clock in one corner, and a large, open fire was burning away along one of the long walls. Cooking smells were coming from a kitchen down a corridor at the back of the room. Paul assumed that there was a bedroom down there as well.

Do any angels need to sleep? he wondered.

He realised he was just putting off the inevitable. *Should I just introduce myself? What am I going to say to him anyway? Regardless of whether or not he's under Metatron's power, he's still a deity.*

Taking the bull by the horns, he called out a "Hello?" and took a tentative step towards the kitchen.

"Hello!" came the cheery reply.

That hadn't been the response Paul had expected; a challenge, perhaps, or at least some kind of curiosity, would have been more normal than the happy shout. He hesitated, wondering what to do next; his mind had gone blank. The question was answered for him when the voice called out again; "Come into the kitchen! I'm just doing some baking – I don't like to leave the oven!"

The Almighty's baking? Paul thought. *Have I gone insane?*

It was then that Paul realised what was going on: *This isn't his home, this is his* prison. *Metatron's imprisoned him here, so she can do what she likes to him.*

He had to work hard to contain the anger that was threatening to bubble over inside him. *And she's not just imprisoning him,* he thought. *She's humiliating him as well – because she can. You evil bitch – you're the one who deserves to go to hell.*

Paul was at the entrance to the hallway before he realised that he had obeyed the voice without question. He frowned, unable to say *why.* The voice reminded him of a kindly grandfather or uncle, and yet it had also brooked no argument – which was why his legs had automatically taken over.

The normality of the house continued into the kitchen. An island hub housed the oven and work surfaces, with cupboards around the outside of the room for storage. A back door led out to the fields and a small vegetable patch.

He realised he was gawping, so he stepped over the threshold for something to do. He looked around in confusion – the source of the voice was nowhere to be seen.

Then, all of a sudden, he was.

It wasn't due to magic or any angelic power; instead, the person behind the voice stood up from the other side of the island, clutching a spatula. He had short, white hair, a beard, and was wearing a cardigan. It almost made Paul's heart ache at the sight of this man – no, this angel – reduced to this.

Paul automatically took a step backwards at the speed that the Almighty stood up. The Almighty jumped in surprise, then laughed. Putting the spatula down on the side, he said; "Sorry about that. I dropped one of the biscuits down the back of the oven."

"No problem," Paul replied. "My name's Paul. I hope you don't mind me popping in?"

The Almighty shook his head. "No, no, not at all," he replied. He looked around, evidently searching for something. "It's actually nice to have some company. Not many people visit these days."

"What are you looking for? Maybe I can help."

The Almighty shook his head. "Don't worry – I'm looking for my oven gloves. I know I left them here somewhere; I'll find them."

As he continued to search over the kitchen, Paul took a seat at one of the island's seats, in an area that obviously doubled as a breakfast bar.

"I'm sorry, what was your name?" he asked. "I didn't quite catch it."

"My name?" The Almighty was at the far end of the kitchen now, looking in the cupboards for the missing oven gloves. His face was obscured by the cupboard door. "I thought I told you?"

"No, you must have forgotten to mention it."

"Oh, well, my name's … It's, er … Oh."

Paul watched the Almighty carefully. He paused in his search, his face still hidden.

Metatron's made you forget everything about yourself, Paul thought in horror. *What sort of hold has she got over you?*

The Almighty stepped away from the cupboard and looked at Paul, concern in his eye.

"Why can't I remember my name?" he asked, his voice suddenly small and frightened. "No-one's ever asked me that before; I've never had to … think about it. I've never worried about it."

Paul looked down, feeling vaguely ashamed. Who was he to say that this wasn't what the Almighty wanted, that he hadn't been a complicit part in all of this, and actually *chose* this life. He looked again at the confused man and a single word emerged in his brain; *Father!*

The nagging feeling at the back of his head, the one that he had been conscious of for the past week, suddenly *pushed* itself forward, awakened by the sight of the weakened Almighty. Paul flinched in shock as a wave of understanding coursed through his body; the nagging sensation was Lucifer, trapped inside Paul's own mind. He was such a powerful personality that he could never fully be suppressed. However, what Paul hadn't considered was that *he* was a forceful personality too - his life had made him that way. The death of his parents, his excommunication from the church ... the events of the past five days, had all made him who he was, and he *wasn't* just going to give it up without a fight.

Your *Father, not mine!* he shouted at Lucifer. *I'm trying to help him and my friends. This is* my *life, not yours! Your turn will come, just not yet! Now back* off!

Paul blinked, and he was back in control. He was surprised that Lucifer had acceded, but then felt his consciousness still there, at the back of his mind. It was that same nagging feeling as before, but now Paul could tap into it on a more conscious level. He did so now, tentatively, and realised the depth of love Lucifer had for his Father – and realised that the Almighty would *never* had agreed to this level of submission to Metatron. Despite his love of humanity, he was still proud to be of angelic stock, and chief of all the angels – whatever Metatron had done to him, it had been done against his will.

The Almighty was watching Paul.

"Are you alright?" he asked. "You look a bit peaky."

Paul nodded. "Yes, I'm fine, thank you." He smiled broadly. "Actually, I've never felt better. It's starting to all make sense now."

The Almighty continued to look at Paul, now looking more concerned for Paul's state of mind than about his own. He walked forward and leaned on the central island.

"Do I know you?" he asked. "You look awfully familiar to me."

"We've never met," Paul replied with. "But there's someone in here -" he tapped his head "- who knows you."

"I think you should leave now," the Almighty said. "You're frightening me. Please leave."

Paul set his jaw. "No," he said. "If you want me to leave, then you're going to have to make me. I know you have the ability to – can you remember how to use it?"

The Ruling Chamber:
Present Day

Metatron's eyes blazed with shock – and anger.

"No," she spat, "that's impossible. Human and angel *cannot* merge!"

Joseph-Satan smiled. "You are wrong," he said. "You succeeded in doing it without even realising it. I have all of Joseph's memories *and* all of Satan's ... as well as my wings."

Metatron strode down the steps from the Almighty's throne. "You're lying," she said. "It's a trick!"

Joseph-Satan's eyebrows quirked up in amusement. "You should know all about tricks, Metatron. It seems that your time as a human has dulled your senses... use your power, you'll see that what I'm telling you is the truth."

Joseph-Satan's comment about being human clearly angered Metatron; as she reached the bottom of the stairs, she raised a hand as if to slap him across the face. He didn't flinch, merely smiled as shock registered on her face. She *felt* the human and angelic sides within him, and saw that they were fused together.

"No ..." she whispered.

"Yes."

Joseph-Satan beamed – his mind had expanded beyond his comprehension. Suddenly, everything made dizzying sense; it was incredible, as if he had been asleep all his life.

Whenever I saw shadows behind my eyelids ... they were just shadows of Satan, moving around in his sleep. I could see him, and I still didn't understand! I'm so glad my eyes are open now – it's incredible. Terrifying, but incredible. I have ... power!

Out of the corner of his eye, he saw Metatron move angrily forward; before she could do anything, a bolt of energy emerged from Joseph-Satan's left hand and hit her in the stomach; it made her fall backwards and skid along the floor.

It was at that moment that Gabriel and Lauren (and, technically, Beelzebub, albeit in disembodied form inside Lauren's head) appeared outside the doors to the Ruling Chamber.

Gabriel frowned. "Strange," he said.

Lauren glanced away from the massive doors towards the angel.

"What?" she asked.

"I didn't expect to be able to get so close to the Chamber," he admitted. "I thought Metatron would block close-range transport."

A thought from Beelzebub appeared inside Lauren's mind. "Unless she's injured ... or dead."

"It would take more than one angel to kill her," Gabriel replied. "If Joseph is alone with her, I doubt get close enough to injure her."

"Well, we're here now. Let's get in there."

Gabriel nodded, swallowing nervously. He hadn't been looking forward to this moment; he'd only had sporadic contact with his mother since the Civil War and he was content with that. She had deliberately tortured him, forced him to betray his friends, and then tossed him aside. He had wished on several occasions that he could have been banished with the other rebels – by remaining here, he had to endure the knowledge that his mother didn't care enough to get rid of him.

Pushing his fear aside, he raised his arms and reached out with his mind. He felt the doors open. He was confused - no traps had presented themselves.

Odd, he thought. *Perhaps Metatron* has *been injured.*

He wasn't surprised to discover that he didn't care.

Joseph-Satan looked round as the massive entrance doors, above the level of the debating floor, opened. He beamed as he saw Gabriel and –

"Lauren!"

His sister smiled back, and took a step towards him. Joseph-Satan frowned as she stopped at the top of the steps leading down to the debating floor, a look of fear and confusion suddenly crossing her face.

"What?" he asked.

"Joseph ..." she whispered. "You've got wings."

"Don't worry, sis. It's fine. Really, it's okay."

"'It's okay'?" Lauren repeated, still in shock. "*You've got wings!*"

"Look, I'll explain, alright? Just ... Lauren, I need your help. Please?"

Joseph-Satan held out a hand, and both Lauren and Beelzebub saw their own loved ones in his eyes. Still not fully understanding, but accepting, Lauren nodded.

"How sweet; the family is reunited."

Joseph-Satan's head snapped round, to see Metatron walking towards them from the far side of the Chamber – unharmed.

"But -" Joseph-Satan began. He knew that Satan had always been a thinker, a debater, but he had the strength and power of any angel, even after all this time.

Metatron laughed. "You can't have believed that a single blast would stop me," she mocked. "You merely surprised me. I assure you, that won't happen again."

"Mother ..." Gabriel said.

He and Lauren stepped down onto the debating floor. There was no warmth in his voice, and Metatron's face reflected his feelings.

"My son," she replied, "I suspected you were involved. Michael is too, I assume? I should have killed you when I had the chance, but the Almighty wanted to show you compassion."

Lauren was appalled. "This is your *son*, Metatron," she said angrily. "How can you want to kill him?"

"My relationship with my children is *none* of your concern."

Joseph-Satan was surprised at the venom in her voice.

"For someone who wanted to see humanity and Heaven merged into one realm," he said, "you don't appear to have much liking for them ... us ..."

He took a step back in surprise as Metatron laughed. It wasn't just a polite laugh either, but a true, deep laugh, as if he had genuinely amused her.

"You think I'm in favour of uniting the two realms?" Metatron asked, her laughter now under control. "I *loathe* humanity. Their lives are so small and petty ... and worthless. They're so concerned with their own frailties and problems that they never allow their painfully limited little minds to be opened up to the wonders of the universe, like mine was. They have all these puny little religions that profess to be the one true faith ... and yet they fail to see that the Almighty could just be worshipped in the privacy of their own heads if they wished, without all their materialistic ... trappings. The only reason I let them live is because the only thing I hate more than humans are angels who rebel against the natural order, and I wanted to see them *suffer*. You, Satan, and Beelzebub here – and Lucifer, and all the others – were fighting my cause for me, far better than I ever could, and I can now watch them suffer for their crimes against Heaven, by living out small, insignificant little lives ... and I can *enjoy* watching them suffer."

Gabriel's mind was reeling. All this time, he had thought it was Metatron forcing the Almighty to merge the physical and spiritual realms together – instead, it had been down to the Almighty, and the rebels had played right into her hands, making it easier for her to divide and conquer.

"No, I won't accept that," Joseph-Satan said slowly, his voice thick with shock. "You've even got a human alter-ego. You've been visiting Earth in human form."

Metatron looked at him, and Joseph-Satan had a flash of how Gabriel must have felt over all those years. It was as if she was searching his very soul for deceit, lies and wrong-doing – both angel and human had to summon up every inch of courage not to buckle under the gaze.

"I used that human shell for a purpose," Metatron said. "I was searching for Lucifer ... my *other* son .... as he was the only angel I could not sense whenever I wished it."

Lauren frowned. "Why would you need to know where they all were?"

A smile snaked across Metatron's face. "Because I was humanity's Jailer."

Inside The Almighty's Private Chambers: Present Day

"What the devil are you talking about?"

The Almighty and Paul faced each other across the kitchen island; Paul was struggling to hold his nerve, worrying that the Almighty would remember his identity any minute and banish him to kingdom come.

"Don't you remember *anything?*" Paul demanded. "About who you really are? You've lived here, imprisoned inside this ... this fake farmhouse for such a long time, you've forgotten everything that used to be important to you!"

"But I like it here," the Almighty protested. "I'm safe here, from ... from ..."

Paul shook his head sadly. "It's her, isn't it? You're afraid of her. Metatron."

"Who?"

"Metatron. One of your senior angels?"

"Angels!" The Almighty laughed, his fear suddenly distracted by his amusement. "I don't know where you're from, lad, but round here, I promise that there's no such thing as angels!"

Paul didn't know what to say; he had been sure that Metatron would have checked up on him. She wouldn't have left it to chance that -

"You'd know her by a different name," he realised. "Lucy Golding."

The Almighty winced. "Don't say that name! She knows when I'm talking about her! Please, just leave!"

Paul shook his head. "I'm staying right here."

He began walking down the side of the island towards the Almighty, who was watching Paul closely.

"You're so ... human," Paul whispered. "You're the *Almighty*, not some ... some biscuit-baking old man!"

"You're talking rubbish," the Almighty replied. "I don't understand what you're talking about. I'm ordinary."

"Ordinary? How can you be ordinary! You can't remember your name because *she* never had one! How do you know Lucy Golding?"

"She ... visits me from time to time," the Almighty replied. "I don't know why – I can't remember. She ... she always ..."

He had been walking backwards, to maintain the distance between him and Paul, and stopped talking as his back hit the wall. Paul stopped too, leaving a gap between them. He glanced out the window, and saw the idyllic scene outside – four horses were galloping round a paddock, the sun was shining and there wasn't a cloud in the sky.

Too perfect, he thought. *Too false.*

"What does she do to you?" Paul asked.

The Almighty swallowed. "There's ... pain, and darkness ... I can't always remember ..."

Paul released a slow, quiet breath. *She's suppressing his memories*, he thought, and knew that it was Lucifer telling him that. *We need to find a new tack. This isn't getting me anywhere.*

"Please ..." the Almighty begged. "I don't know who you are, but please, just leave me alone now. Let me live my life in peace."

Paul shook his head. "This isn't life. This is imprisonment."

It started to become clear. Metatron's ambition and desire for power would never have allowed her to remain second fiddle to the Almighty and Michael forever. Metatron had overcome that by dividing and conquering;

once the war was won, she had demoted Michael to observer and blocked his access to the Almighty. She alone controlled access to him; with no-one else allowed to see him, she had sent him off to this prison, with only the occasional visit from her needed to ensure he wasn't beginning to remember his old life.

"Perfect," he muttered, half to himself. "She's thought of everything. Except for us." He swallowed and addressed the Almighty again. "Metatron didn't consider the possibility that we would find you. She built up the defences around this place so that angels would never be able to get here by themselves ... but she didn't even *consider* the possibility that humans would ever be able to travel here. And that's all I am ..." He smiled. "I'm just human."

The Almighty looked at him as if he were mad. He was clearly frightened, and nothing seemed to be sinking in. Paul gave a start as the Almighty suddenly turned and grabbed the door handle. As he opened the door, Paul raised his hand – and the door slammed shut.

There was a moment's stunned silence, then the Almighty turned back to face Paul. "Who *are* you?" he asked.

"Just plain old Paul Finn," he replied. "And ... yet, I'm more than that. I ... wish I could explain it to you."

He knew what he needed to do; although he was frightened of trying it, he knew that it was time to try. Before the Almighty could react, Paul grabbed his shoulders. He ignored the imprisoned angel's protests; mentally, he looked inside himself and said, *Lucifer, I know you're there. Help me get your Father back. Get me into his mind, and let's find the part of him that's still* him.

What if there isn't any part of him left? Lucifer demanded with a mix of anger and fear. *What if* this *is all that's left?*

Then I don't honestly know if we can defeat Metatron.

The Ruling Chamber:
Present Day

Gabriel stepped angrily in front of his mother, absorbing the full sharpness of her glare without flinching; after her torture, there wasn't anything worse she could do to him.

"*You* were the Jailer?" he said.

There was a fury in his voice that surprised Lauren. He had always been so softly-spoken and calm: to see Gabriel angry was a strange sight.

He went on; "All this time, you spread the word that *Michael* was the Jailer. For a long time, I actually believed you as well. Even when I saw through your lies, I wasn't able to discover who you had chosen to fill the role ... and I couldn't have considered you, not with your eldest son down there."

Metatron looked back dispassionately, and didn't reply; if she had been affected by his words, she didn't show it.

"I don't understand," Lauren said. "Gabriel, why are you so angry? If the rebels were imprisoned, surely they would need a jailer?"

Joseph-Satan was the one who answered. "This isn't a jailer in the normal sense of the word," he said. "As Jailer, Metatron was responsible for keeping the rebel population suppressed by any means necessary, and if that meant torturing or killing someone to do it, then so be it. The Jailer was given special dispensation by the

Almighty to use any means necessary to keep the rebels under control. If one of them showed even the slightest sign of remembering their angelic origins, she could do anything she wanted to get them under control – including kill them. As Jailer, she had instant access in her mind to all the 144,000 at any one time."

"An angel does not kill angels" Gabriel snarled. He was practically shaking with fury. "Even in the Civil War, we were so careful *never* to kill."

Lauren was surprised at how much her brother knew.

"So, Metatron was the Jailer ..." A light dawned. "... and one of the rebels was her son. When she could no longer sense him, she travelled to Earth herself and decided to search for him herself."

"Exactly," Gabriel replied, then spoke again to Metatron; "I always thought that torturing one son would be enough for you. But it wasn't, was it? You'd have been willing to kill Lucifer if you had to, like you would have killed me if I hadn't broken."

Lauren's heart felt like it was going to break as she listened to Gabriel; she couldn't imagine what he must have had to endure, knowing that his mother was causing him such agony while his Father watched, unwilling or unable to help.

Gabriel took a step closer to his mother, so that he was practically breathing in her face.

"I don't understand why you had to stand against us," he said, "if you were against the alliance too. The whole reason for the Civil War was because we believed the Almighty was *wrong* ... that humanity deserved a chance to stand by itself, rather than with us. If you'd stood with us, we could have won!"

Metatron shook her head wearily, as if she was talking to a simpleton who hadn't understood a word she had said. Lauren felt a sudden surge of anger well up inside her at the sheer arrogance of the woman.

"You just don't get it, do you?" Metatron said. "I would never side with *you*, a pathetic bunch of rebels. My two sons ... beloved leaders of the rebellion!" The sarcasm in her voice was obvious. "You wanted independence for Earth. I wanted Earth *crushed* ... as well as those who threatened my power. Earth is a weak, mortal place, its inhabitants full of lust and desire. It has always been such a wicked place. I would never side with a rebellion that wanted to *save* them."

Gabriel was taken aback by the sheer venom in his mother's voice, and Lauren couldn't blame him. *Why does she have such a deep-rooted loathing of Earth?* she wondered. *What have we ever done to her?*

"It must have hurt when the Almighty didn't listen to you," Joseph-Satan said. "You won the War and had the opportunity to obliterate all of the rebels ... and Earth. But the Almighty said no, didn't he? So in response, you took control ... you banished the Almighty."

Metatron stared at him, but didn't say anything - Joseph-Satan took this as tacit agreement. He was aware that everyone was watching him, and he wanted to capitalise on the moment. It felt good, to be here again on the floor of the Ruling Chamber, having a chance to argue his case.

Despite the fact it feels like the first time, the human part of him thought.

"But then," he went on, beginning to pace the length of the floor, "after you banished the Almighty, you could have found a destroyed us all anyway." He spun on his heel, turning back to face Metatron. "So why didn't you?"

Gabriel let out a sudden gasp, and Lauren, who was stood next to him, looked round in surprise. His eyes had widened, and he was looking at Metatron in shock.

"It's because of who you are," he whispered. "You hate humanity, but you couldn't quite bring yourself to destroy them ... not when your own descendents might still be down there, living amongst them. Your arrogance ... you didn't want to see your own bloodline die."

Lauren was confused. "You mean Lucifer?" she asked. "Couldn't she have just saved -?"

"No," Gabriel said, cutting her off, "not just her *angelic* bloodline. Back in the mists of time, Metatron was once human. What was your name again? Enoch?"

A low, warning growl rumbled from Metatron's throat. Joseph-Satan watched her carefully as she squared up to her son - he was reeling from the shock of Gabriel's revelation.

"Is that true?" Lauren asked. "Metatron, were you human?"

Metatron ignored her, her eyes focused entirely on her son.

"You're a disgrace," she spat at him. "You were always weak. Your problem has always been that you *cared* too much ... cared for other people. You could have been so much more."

"More like you, you mean?" Gabriel retorted, his voice now raised in anger. "I was proud to follow my brother; I did it before, and I'd do it again in a heartbeat! And this time, I'd hunt you down and kill you, *Enoch!*"

Lauren saw Gabriel's hand move a fraction of a second before Metatron did, but it was still too slow. The faintest glow covered his hand, but Metatron was faster; her right hand, glowing and crackling with energy, came out and struck Gabriel square in the throat.

His body jerked and shook for a moment, as the energy bolt circled his throat and neck.

"No!" Lauren screamed.

Joseph-Satan darted forward, but he was too late. Gabriel's body crumpled to the floor and Metatron watched him fall without emotion.

"*This* is worse than torture," she whispered.

There was silence in the vast Chamber. Lauren and Joseph-Satan looked in despair down at Gabriel's body. Lauren didn't even know if angels had a pulse – if they did, she knew that Gabriel would not have one.

He was dead.

A tear fell, unbidden, down her cheek.

"That was your son," she whispered. "Your *child.*"

"He was nothing but a disappointment to me," Metatron replied, her voice as cold as ice.

"He was my friend," Joseph-Satan replied. Tears had formed in his eyes, too, but he refused to shed them, not when he was so angry. "You heartless *bitch*."

Metatron laughed. "Is that meant to wound me, Satan?" she asked. "Mere words."

In that moment, something snapped inside Joseph; he knew that Metatron had to die – and he would do anything in his power to do it and avenge Gabriel.

Metatron saw the look of pure hatred in his eyes, because the laughter quickly stopped, and she looked thoughtfully at him for a moment.

"You really think that you could beat me?" she asked. "In a fair fight, you think *you* would win, when my own son was powerless to stop me? You really are hopelessly naive."

Lauren saw the energy crackle round Metatron's hand. She saw the hand being raised, she saw it aimed at Joseph, she saw the energy discharge, she *felt* –

Inside The Almighty's Private Chambers: Present Day

Paul and Lucifer were working together, pushing through the defences Metatron had created around the Almighty's mind. It was agony, and every ounce of concentration they had was focused on their task, but soon they cried out in victory as they ripped away the last layer – and found the Almighty's soul.

Images, sounds and feelings all coursed through Paul's mind at such a speed it was almost painful. He was coping with the pressure far better than Lucifer had expected; he was still alive, for a start.

Lucifer felt a singular joy at being awake, even trapped away inside a human form; to him, the memory of first being compressed and imprisoned felt as if it was only yesterday. That joy was only dampened by having to witness the Almighty – his Father - reduced to living like a hermit. His instinct had been to take over the body he was in and drag his Father out of his stupor. However, Paul's strong words had convinced him that killing an innocent was cruel – and he would never do that, because that would make him no better than Metatron.

Paul buckled for a moment, drowning under the weight of an eon of memories.

Help me, he begged, and Lucifer responded with all his might ... and the efforts of a human and an angel together made more of an effect than either would have been able to do individually.

The sheer *volume* of memories washing over Paul was awe-inspiring – the Almighty truly had the weight and history of the entire cosmos on his shoulders. He was surprised to learn that the Almighty had come into being *after* the cosmos, but Lucifer was completely blasé about it; to the angelic realm, it was common knowledge.

Imagine the rewrites all the holy texts would have to go through if they ever found out, Paul thought ... and then wondered if he would ever be able to return home and talk about it.

He felt a sudden wave of fear shudder through him, and realised it was coming from the Almighty.

What is it? he thought. *What's wrong?*

"I Remember," the Almighty replied, his booming, all-encompassing voice once again at full strength. *"I Remember Everything. I Remember What I Lost."*

What did you lose? Paul asked him.

"Everything. How Can I Reclaim My Position When I Have Allowed Such Wanton Hatred In My Name? All I Sought Was For Unity Between Our Realms. Instead, One Of My Sons Is Banished To Earth For All Eternity And The Other Is Tortured By The Angel I Allowed To Rule In My Name. How Can I Live With The Shame Of That?"

Because you can't let Metatron win, Paul replied. *She's corrupted your peace, and tried to reduce you to a forgetful old man. It's time to fight back.*

"I Do Not Deserve To Win. I Was Weak Enough To Give That Angel Power Over Me, When My Wisdom should Have Seen Through Her Plans. I Am Ashamed – I Do Not Deserve To Be The Almighty."

I know about shame, Paul thought. *I have felt shame and run from it. It gives me comfort to know that the Almighty, the god I've always believed in, can be as fallible as me. If you, of all the hosts of angels, can be brought down by a woman, and be captivated by her beauty ... if you are as fallible as anyone of us, then I don't feel bad about my past, about what I've done.*

But, he added, *if you are refusing to come back to take your rightful place on your throne because of your shame and embarrassment, then you are an incredible disappointment to me ... and your sons.*

This time, it was Lucifer who spoke. *Father, I'm here, inside Paul's mind. I agree with him – you need to take heaven back from Metatron.*

"Lucifer ···?" The Almighty sounded shocked to hear his son's voice. *"You Are Here?"*

Yes, Father, I am here with you. I urge you to consider Paul's words – he is right. We need *you ... we need you to lead ... and help us stop Metatron.*

"You Need Me?" The Almighty's sudden, sad laugh boomed throughout Paul's head, and he flinched. *"You Need Me? I Recall It Differently, An Eternity Ago In The Ruling Chamber· You Wished Me To Step Down· You Have Your wish, My Son·"*

Not like this, Father! This *is not what I wanted! Metatron has turned everything into a nightmare, and I won't stand by and watch her destroy everything you've built.*

The Almighty was silent for a moment, obviously considering his son's words. Paul felt, at an instinctive level, that he was touched by what Lucifer had said.

Paul remembered the story Gabriel had told him, how the two brothers, plus Satan and Beelzebub, had stood before him, and demanded that he step down in favour of a heavenly republic. Well, he *had* stepped down – albeit forcibly – and Paul had seen the consequences. He understood Lucifer's desire to reinstall his Father on the throne, to unite the angelic realms against the tyrannical Metatron.

It's a shame Lucifer's dream of a republic never saw fruition, he thought. *I wonder if human history would have been any different as a result.*

He felt a stirring deep within himself, and was momentarily confused; he then realised that he, Lucifer and the Almighty had become so intertwined that it was difficult to see where one
ended and another began. Paul felt a surge of panic well up inside him as -

"Do Not Worry. You Are Yourself Again; You Have Not Lost Who You Are."

Paul blinked, adjusting to his new surroundings. He looked round; the farmhouse and surrounding land had vanished into nothingness and had been replaced by the blackness of space. There was a brief moment of terror deep in the pit of his stomach as he realised he was in outer space and still breathing, then closed his eyes again and focused.

You're alright, Paul, you're alright, the Almighty is keeping you alive.

Paul opened his eyes again, and found himself looking deep into the oldest, wisest eyes he had ever seen. They were eyes that were both sad and happy at the same time, old and young, angry and peaceful.

"Almighty," he whispered. "Is it really you?"

He then realised that he was still tightly gripping onto the Almighty's shoulders, and quickly released them.

"Sorry."

The Almighty laughed; a deep, rich sound that made Paul smile at the sheer joyousness of it.

"Do Not Apologise. You And My Son Have Brought Me Back From The Abyss. For That, You Will Always Have My Gratitude."

Paul took another look around him – there was *nothing* of the Almighty's prison in sight.

"What happened?" he asked. "Where -"

The Almighty raised a hand. *"It Is ··· Complicated· Suffice To Say ··· I Willed Myself Away From That Horrendous Place, And It Became So·"*

"Almighty!"

Paul and the Almighty both looked round, and saw Michael barrelling towards them at full flight. It was a disorientating sight for Paul, to see an angel flying through the depths of interstellar space, his wings at full width.

"Michael" The Almighty replied, spreading his arms expansively wide to mirror the wide smile on his face. *"My Friend·"*

Michael pulled himself upright just as he reached the group, and paused in mid-air, smiling and breathing heavily. He laughed, then leapt forward and hugged the Almighty.

Paul jumped in surprise at this. *Is that allowed?* he asked Lucifer, still buried deep inside his head. *Won't Michael be ... well, in trouble for touching the Almighty?*

You're not far wrong, Lucifer replied, a hint of amusement in his voice. *Michael's different, though. He served my Father faithfully for eternity; if anyone's earned the right, it's him.*

The affection between the two angels was obvious, and genuine, much as Paul's friendships with Joseph and Lauren were. A lurch of guilt sudden stabbed at him; he hadn't thought about either of his friends since entering the Almighty's cottage / prison.

The Almighty seemed to pick up on this, as he gently released himself from his friend's happy embrace, and looked carefully at Paul.

"You Have Come Here With Others," he said, and Paul nodded.

"Yes," he said. "You would know them as Satan and Beelzebub ... they are my friends Joseph and Lauren. I promised that I would go to them when I had ... helped you."

The Almighty glanced at Michael, who nodded. There seemed to be an unspoken communion between them for a moment, then Michael turned to Paul.

"They are in danger," he said bluntly. "They are with Metatron. I can't see inside the Chamber, but I know something is wrong. You need to go to them, now."

Paul frowned. "We should all go!" he protested. "Now that the Almighty's back, all this will be sorted out! I don't think I can do this alone – I need you!"

"*And I Will Be There,*" the Almighty replied reassuringly. "*You Must Understand ··· I Am Going To Help You, But I Have Been Imprisoned For Two Millennia· I Need To Fully ··· Recover· I Will Need Michael's Help To Transport Me To Our Kingdom·*"

Paul had to swallow his first reaction, one of frustration.

He will *join us*, Lucifer said from inside Paul's mind. *Let's go ahead.*

Paul couldn't be sure, but he thought he heard a hint of humour in the angel's tone. *After all, we've just broken the Almighty out of prison ... if we can do that, then what else can we do?*

Paul smiled, and focused his eyes again on Michael and the Almighty.

"Don't be long," he cautioned them.

The Almighty inclined his head. "*You Have My Word·*"

Paul turned to Michael. "I need you to get me there. I wouldn't know how to do it."

"I think you can," Michael said with a smile. "You were able to transport yourself from *Earth* to the kingdom ... this is just a small jump by comparison."

Paul was thrown; he genuinely *didn't* know what to do. His transport to Heaven the last time had been accidental, as had the trip back. He thought of Lauren and Joseph, caught in the Ruling Chamber with Metatron, and a surge of panic leapt up from his stomach.

I need to get to my friends! he thought urgently. *I need to be with them now!*

An odd, yet now-familiar, feeling took hold in his stomach – as if he was being pulled *sideways* through space.

"What the -" he exclaimed - and disappeared.

The Ruling Chamber:
Present Day

In that moment, something snapped inside Joseph; he knew that Metatron had to die – and he would do anything in his power to do it and avenge Gabriel.

Metatron saw the look of pure hatred in his eyes, because the laughter quickly stopped, and she looked thoughtfully at him for a moment.

"You really think that you could beat me?" she asked. "In a fair fight, you think *you* would win, when my own son was powerless to stop me? You really are hopelessly naive."

Lauren saw the energy crackle round Metatron's hand. She saw the hand being raised, she saw it aimed at Joseph, she saw the energy discharge, she *felt* the energy slam into her.

There hadn't been time for a conscious decision – it had been pure instinct, driven by her desire to protect her brother, to jump in front of Metatron's energy blast.

The beam ploughed into her midriff; she felt as if it had driven all the air out of her body. She collided with Joseph, and the siblings fell to the floor, Lauren landing on top of him. She cried out in pain, immediately pressing her hands to the wound. Metatron seemed genuinely surprised by Lauren's actions, but quickly recovered.

"As you wish," she said. "If both of you choose to die, then so be it. It won't be the first time I have killed a human; Dr Tempest ... Rick ... you humans are just so fallible and weak."

She raised both hands, still glowing with the same energy. Joseph tried to shift Lauren's weight without hurting her too much, but knew that it was too late.

"You're a coward, Metatron!" he bellowed. "Trying to kill us when we can't fight back! Is this how you killed Tempest? When he was defenceless?"

"Yes," Metatron casually replied, "he died because he was weak – as you are. You're still thinking like a human, Joseph. Your sister is dying. If you didn't allow your emotions to get the better of you, you could have just burnt through her to get to me, and done her a kindness as well. Instead ... I win."

She threw her arms forward, and Joseph instinctively closed his eyes against the impending blasts – and blinked when they didn't materialise. Metatron's hands were still glowing with energy, but it was frozen in place.

Joseph looked round in confusion.

"Paul!"

Despite himself, Joseph couldn't help but smile broadly as he saw his friend stood at the double doors of the Chamber. Metatron, on the other hand, seemed ready to explode.

"I should have killed you when I had the chance!" Metatron growled. She still had her hands up in front of her, as if by that posture alone she could regain her powers.

As he walked quickly down the steps, Paul looked closely at Metatron. It was the first time he had seen her without the white light surrounding her, and she was remarkably familiar. Suddenly, a smile lit up his face.

"Lucy Golding," he said. "What a good disguise – I never guessed."

"How are you doing this?" Metatron snarled. "You are human!"

Paul shrugged. He stepped down onto the Debating Floor and came face-to-face with the tyrannical angel.

"You'd be amazed," he replied. He tapped his head. "I've made a new friend up here. Mind you, you'd know all about that, wouldn't you ... Golding?"

Metatron was seething with anger, and again tried to throw her energy bolts, but this time at Paul. He just stared at her, a glimmer of humour in his eyes.

"Paul! Help me!"

His head snapped round. Joseph had managed to extricate himself from underneath his sister. She was sliding in and out of consciousness; Joseph had found her pulse, which was weak and thready. He glanced in concern at her face, and his heart skipped a beat as he saw how pale and clammy she was. His eyes moved to her midriff, where her hands were still clutching her wound, and he didn't dare prise them away. He glanced at Paul.

"She's dying," he croaked with emotion. "We need to do something."

Paul was gripped with panic as he saw Lauren's wound. He turned to look at Metatron, who smiled a feral grin; she had lowered her arms and was watching the scene with intent pleasure.

"I can't help you like this." She nodded towards her hands, which were still covered in the swirling mists of energy that couldn't go anywhere.

"And if I released you?" Paul asked, willing to consider any possibility to help his friend.

"Do you honestly believe I would even consider it?"

Paul's face curled up in anger for a moment, and his fists bunched up into fists. "You could help," he said. "Prove to me that your soul isn't entirely lost."

Metatron continued smiling and turned her back on Paul. She began tracing a slow, languid circle around the natural bend in the floor.

With a wave of Paul's hand, the Chamber doors slammed shut. Metatron paused in her walk, glanced over her shoulder, and raised an eyebrow. A moment later, apparently unconcerned, she went back to her pacing.

At least I'm keeping you where I can see you, Paul thought. He knew she wouldn't be any trouble all the while Lucifer had control over her powers, so he could concentrate on Lauren.

He did a brief double-take as the wings on Joseph's back finally registered in his brain.

"What the -"

Joseph scowled at his friend. "Is this really the time?"

Paul dumbly shook his head. After a moment, he realised that he was still staring, absorbed, as he realised that they were real *wings* on Joseph's back. He shook his head again, and looked down at Lauren.

"Hey beautiful," he whispered. "You're going to be okay, you know that?"

Lauren looked up at him through glassy eyes, and a faint smile emerged on her lips. Paul felt her brow, and inwardly winced; she was freezing cold, yet had a thin layer of sweat forming on her face. He glanced at Joseph, who returned his gaze – each man saw the truth.

"You never ... were ... very good at lying, Paul," Lauren gasped.

Paul gave her a wan smile. "Maybe not," he said. "But I'm going to do everything I can to save you. I'll get Lucifer to -"

"No ..."

Lauren shook her head, and Paul stopped talking. He wanted to argue with her, tell her she was wrong, but he couldn't – because he knew Lucifer wouldn't be *able* to help, and Lauren knew that too, because Beelzebub was whispering it to her in *her* ear.

If I were in my own body, Lucifer was saying at the back of Paul's mind, *then I might be able to do sometime. We can heal by touch ... Lauren's wound is bad, but I could have done something.*

"Then take over my body," Paul protested, a tear dropping from his eye. He placed a hand over Lauren's, positioned over the deep, nasty wound in her stomach. "Use my body to heal her. Do whatever you have to, *please!*"

I can't, Paul, please ... I can't. *Your body is human, not angelic – it would take days for a new angelic body to form, and Lauren hasn't got that kind of time.*

"There's got to be *something* you can do!" Paul demanded through his tears. "*Lucifer!*"

But Lucifer was silent, lost in his own grief for his dying friend.

Lauren gently touched Paul's cheek. "Stop ... crying," she said slowly through ragged breaths. "You shouldn't ... cry over ...what might have been."

Paul nodded, and gripped her hand tightly. "I'll try," he said. "No promises, though." He attempted a smile. "Just hang on, Lauren. Michael will be here soon, and he can help you."

Lauren just smiled at him. "Where's my ... brother?"

"Right here, sis ... right here."

Joseph moved so she could easily see him. She smiled as her eyes focused; her face briefly contorted as a spasm of pain coursed through her. Joseph swallowed a desire to cry out in sympathy, and scrubbed the back of his hand across his face to brush away the tears. His other hand took hold of her free one, and he squeezed it tight.

"I came to ... get you, Joe," she said as the pain subsided from her face. "I knew you'd be here ... I wouldn't leave you ... along with ... *her.*"

Joseph nodded, unable to speak. He glanced up at Metatron, who was still strolling around the perimeter of the Debating Floor, seemingly without a care in the world. Unable to look at her any more, he turned back to his sister.

"I would have done the same for you," he said. "You're my sister ... no matter what anyone says about these angels in our heads, you're my sister."

Lauren gave him a small smile, which made his heart leap in grief. "And I'm ... proud to have you as my ... brother. Even if ... you're completely ... stubborn and pig-headed sometimes."

Joseph laughed, and Paul and Lauren joined in. Lauren's laugh quickly turned into a cough through, and Paul leaned forward. He raised her head slightly and rested it on his legs.

"Try to sit up a bit more," he said quietly. "It'll help."

Lauren waved his urging away with her eyes. Another spasm of pain passed through her, and it was obvious this one had been worse than the last.

"Who made you ... a doctor? It doesn't ... matter, anyway."

Joseph bit his lip, hard, but couldn't keep the tears away any more. He took her hand again, and folded it in his own hands. A single tear formed at the edge of Lauren's right eye.

"You're so much more than just human now, Joe," she said quietly, finding a brief second wind. "You can choose whichever destiny you want."

Joseph shook his head. "I'd give it all up in an instant if it meant I could keep you here with me."

Lauren smiled at him. "Just think of it as ... my next ... adventure."

Her eyes began to glaze over; her head turned away.

"Lauren ..." Joseph began, but lost his words.

Lauren's eyes were glazed over and unfocused – but, just for a moment, Joseph swore a frown of concentration formed on her brow as she focused on something in the middle distance.

"Oh, my ..." she whispered.

Joseph looked round at where she was looking, but there was nothing there, except for pews upon pews of seating.

When he looked back, she was gone.

"No -" he moaned. Grief stabbed through him like a knife, and he doubled over as it wracked him like a physical pain.

Paul had seen Lauren's eyes close and the last breath expel from her body; he was sobbing quietly, his own eyes squeezed shut as if he could block out the pain of what just happened.

Tears ran freely down Joseph's face, and it felt as if the grief was strong enough to kill him. He couldn't only feel his grief for his sister, but Satan's grief as well, for his beloved friend Beelzebub, who had died with Lauren.

The grief threatened to overwhelm him as he kissed his sister's fingers and laid them gently on top of her other hand, taking care not to disturb it; he had no desire to see the corrosive wound that had killed her, although Satan's memories certainly provided his imagination with plenty to think about.

As his tears continued to fall, he felt a different emotion begin to coalesce, deep inside him. At first, he struggled to identify it, buried deep as it was amongst the painful waves of grief. Then, suddenly, he knew what it was.

Paul opened his eyes as he saw a movement next to him; Joseph was standing up, a strange look on his face. His wings seemed to almost *flex* behind him as he stood, as if they were providing a natural counterbalance to his motion, and Paul found himself again transfixed by them. He didn't pretend to understand what had been going on; his momentary joy at being reunited with his best friends had changed to crushing grief at Lauren's abrupt and devastating death. For the first time, he saw Gabriel's body lying across the floor, and he realised how much pointless death had been caused by all the fighting.

He realised that Joseph was staring at Metatron, hatred and anger burning out of his eyes.

"Joseph ..." he said slowly. "What are you doing?"

"What I should have done two thousand years ago," he replied.

Metatron was sat on one of the pews, leaning casually back against the back rest with her legs crossed. She was looking with complete disinterest at the scene, and didn't react to Joseph's anger. The golden energy around her hands looked out of place, and there was an air of arrogance exuding from her, as if she owned the room; which, in her eyes, she did.

"Paul," Joseph said, loudly enough for Metatron to hear, "give Metatron her powers back."

Paul blinked in shock, the surprise pushing his grief into second place for a brief moment.

"Are you kidding?" he replied. "Metatron's powers are the cause of all this in the first place. Lucifer's hold over her is the only thing stopping her from killing *us* as well." He lowered his voice. "At least wait until Michael and the Almighty get here – when the numbers are four to one, I'll be a lot more comfortable."

Joseph looked down at his friend. "She just killed my sister. I am going to make her *pay* for what she's done, but only with her hands free. She deserves the chance to defend herself."

"She just killed your sister in cold blood, and you're offering her a fighting chance?"

Paul was amazed that Joseph was even considering it. He walked over to his friend and, doing his very best to ignore the wings, placed a hand on his shoulder. "She's a murderer. You've seen what she can do ... and if you've somehow merged with Satan, then his memories will tell you how powerful she is. If Lucifer lets her go ..."

Joseph nodded. "Then I'll be giving her a chance to defend herself, which is far more than she gave Lauren ... or Gabriel ... or Rick."

"Rick?" Paul blinked. "She killed Rick too?"

"He was no longer needed," Metatron said from across the room. "He was a waste of space. I thought you'd be pleased, Paul ... after all, you and he never did get along, did you?"

Metatron's voice was back to its cold, haughty tone. He turned to face her, and she stood from her seat to face him.

"There's one thing I want you to explain to me," Paul said.

He was trying to keep his voice as neutral as possible, whilst fighting every urge to join with Joseph and attack her where she stood.

Metatron shrugged, obviously disinterested. "What is it?"

"Why am I so important?"

Metatron looked briefly confused. "What do you mean?"

"You weren't able to find me when I left the church. Why was I so important to you that you *had* to find me?"

Metatron gave a harsh-sounding laugh, and began walking down the stairwell to the Debating Floor once again.

"Because my son was ... *is* locked away deep inside you, Paul. Well," she added, "perhaps not so deeply any more. After all, he's managing quite well with *this*."

She waved her hands briefly in the air, and both Paul and Joseph tensed for a moment, then relaxed as nothing happened; Lucifer's shield seemed to be holding. Metatron stepped back onto the central floor and stopped, staring at Paul.

"I wanted to see what you were like," she confessed. "I was ... curious; you had somehow managed to hide yourself from me. I wanted to see if you had changed, become something ... *more* than my son had ever been, maybe even someone I could have been proud of." She smiled. "I found out you were excommunicated from the church for an affair. You were quite ... repressed before that, I understand."

Paul flushed, despite himself.

"I was Jailer to the 144,000," Metatron went on, "but I couldn't find *you*. I wanted to know if you somehow become more than the sum of your parts. I even recruited a human – the seemingly-useless Rick to help me – but then I failed."

Joseph stepped forward, standing side-by-side with Paul. It also meant that Lauren's body was totally shielded from Metatron; it was a small gesture, but a defiant one.

"Why couldn't you find me?" Paul asked, then staggered back in surprise as a sudden overwhelming knowledge suddenly flooded into his brain.

I began to wake up, Paul, Lucifer said from his hiding place. *I wasn't conscious for very long, and I couldn't do anything ... except, at some level, know that if I was awake, Metatron would soon realise. So I was able to hide you from her and keep you safe.*

Metatron's snake-like smile slithered its way across her face. "I see you understand," she said. "The more I couldn't find you, the angrier I became. I eventually forced Rick to come back to your home town, and I discovered how loyal you were to your friends from the church, even after everything that had happened. So, I gave Rick his orders."

"Kill Adam Wild."

Metatron gave another diffident shrug. "Kill, injure, whichever was easier," she replied. "It brought you to me, didn't it?"

Paul was no longer surprised by Metatron's casual approach to life; she had made it quite clear what she thought of humanity. He was struggling to feel *anything* aside from the grief that kept threatening to overwhelm him at any moment.

"So now you've found me," he said with a sudden weariness. "What are you going to do with me, now that you've seen what I've become?"

Metatron shrugged, a second of uncertainty showing in her face before it was washed away by the hard stare that she could have patented. In that second, Paul was curious to know about her background – how had she got to this point, where she was so filled of hate and bile that she just couldn't see the good in anything?

"A part of me just wanted to see you," she admitted. "To see if you were any less of a failure than your brother."

Paul and Joseph both glanced down at Gabriel's crumpled body, and a shiver ran up Paul's spine.

"And?" he asked.

Metatron pursed her lips. "You're worse. You can't even hold my energy in place without detecting a trap."

Everything seemed to happen in slow motion; Metatron's hands rose up and the energy circling her hands *pulsed*, then shot forward. Paul's eyes widened in panic and he reacted with a purely human response, pushing his hands up in front of his face. Lucifer, buried deep inside his brain, couldn't react in time; he saw the energy coming towards him, but knew that anything he could do would just burn up his human host ... and kill *him* as well.

After what felt like an eternity, but was – in reality - only a couple of seconds, Paul staggered back under an onslaught of heat crackling by his cheek. Confused, he opened his tightly-clenched eyes and peered through his fingers.

Metatron's golden energy was half-way across the space between her and Paul; it was being stopped however, by a stream of blue light – blasting out from *Joseph's* hands.

Paul stepped back in shock, and he looked round as his feet collided with something; he cried out in horror as he saw Lauren's body. He stumbled sideways and tripped over his own feet, fell onto his hands and knees, and used the opportunity to crawl away as fast as he could.

Joseph's got wings! his brain tried to shout at him, but he shook away the thought. *Now's not the time!*

Instead, he concentrated on the fact that Joseph was channelling some sort of angelic energy, and was managing to keep Metatron at bay.

He saved my life, Paul realised, and felt a sudden surge of gratitude towards him.

He knew this was what Joseph wanted – a chance to fight the angel responsible for his sister's death. Paul wondered how he'd react if it had been *his* sister who had died – his grief was pounding away at his chest, only kept at bay by concern for his best friend, and he couldn't begin to imagine the depths of anger and loss this angel / human must have been feeling.

"I'm surprised at you, Satan," Metatron said, her eyes focused entirely on the collision of energy half-way between them, "I didn't think you'd be able to stand up to me like this. You're still going to lose though."

A thin film of sweat had broken out on Joseph's forehead, while Metatron didn't even bat an eyelid. It was clear that, given enough time, Metatron would win, but Joseph didn't look overly concerned.

"Then you've underestimated me," he shot back. "Because I know something you don't."

"And that is ...?"

"He Knows That I Have Returned For My Throne."

Joseph smiled at the sudden panic in Metatron's eyes as the Almighty's voice rang across the Chamber. Paul's heart skipped a beat, but he didn't take his eyes off the battling duo.

For a split second, Metatron was distracted by the Almighty's arrival; she turned her head towards the massive double doors on the right of the Chamber, where the Almighty's voice had come from.

"No ..." she whispered, half to herself. She blinked, and began to turn back to Joseph but, by then, it was far, far too late.

Even after the event, Paul would have difficulty working out what happened in those quick final seconds; Joseph stepped forward and moved his hands, his blue-filled energy annihilating his opponent's golden light and *slamming* into Metatron's chest; it lifted her off her feet again and across the floor before she crashed into the first row of seating.

She was dead before her lifeless, crushed body hit the floor.

Every pair of eyes stared at the body.

"Joe," Paul whispered and, for once, Joseph didn't correct him. "Metatron – you just ..."

"Don't say it," Joseph replied in a croaky, stunned voice. "Just ... just don't."

The Almighty, closely guarded by Michael, walked slowly down onto the Floor.

I remember the first ... and last ... time he stepped down to this level, Paul thought. *No, that's not right, is it?* Lucifer *remembers. I just ... steal his memories from time to time.*

Michael walked straight over to Metatron and knelt down next to her. He didn't move to touch her, but Paul suspected that there was something deeper going on than he could see. He glanced at the Almighty; he had walked over to Joseph and was whispering something in his ear.

For a moment, Joseph didn't seem to register what was being said, but then suddenly – abruptly – he nodded. He then walked over to his sister's body. The human-angel hybrid knelt down, took her lifeless hand in his ... and began to sob.

You did it for her, Paul thought, as tears pricked at his own eyes. *For Lauren.*

He let his tears fall.

Paul's Flat:
Present Day

P aul groaned as his alarm clock began to buzz, loudly.

A quick glance at the LCD display confirmed the worst - 06:55. He had never been a morning person; even when he had been in the seminary, Adam and Rick often had to force him out of bed in time for morning prayers.

At least that's not something I'll ever have to do again, he thought in his half-asleep state.

He'd had a good night's sleep; his regular dream had been reducing in intensity over the last week – and he'd gone the whole of the previous night without it.

He knew he had no excuse not to get up; he was meeting a friend today, and didn't want to be late for that. He had absolutely no excuse.

A fist slammed down on the "OFF" button.

Just five more minutes, he thought. *That'll do. I'll feel alright after that.*

It was bizarre, after all this time, not to have his usual, angelic dreams invading his thoughts – instead, he found his semi-sleeping thoughts bringing up memories of his childhood, playing football with Joseph and having Lauren tell them off if they forgot to include her.

Lauren. Oh, Lauren.

Paul sat bolt upright, breathing heavily as a wave of grief washed over him.

"Idiot," he muttered, and rubbed his face to wipe away his tears ... but still they came.

He sat in silence for a few minutes, until he was could focus. He ran a hand through his hair, and shook his head. *I miss you, Lauren. That's never going to change.*

It was only then that he thought to check the time on his hated alarm clock. – his heart skipped a beat. *I had no excuse to be late! None whatsoever – now I'm going to be bloody late aga-*

07:00.

A smile crossed his face.

"Plenty of time," he whispered to himself.

Beaches Café:
The Same Morning

Paul leaned back in his chair and watched his companion chew carefully on a vegetarian sausage as he tried to process everything that Paul had just told him.

While he thought, Paul stole a quick glance around the cafe. He was thankful that it was so empty; in fact, only two other tables were occupied; although as it was 9.30am on a weekday, that wasn't too surprising. Paul caught the waiter's eye, and motioned for another round of strong coffee.

We both *need it, I think.*

He looked down at his plate; a Full English breakfast had disappeared fast, despite him having done most of the talking for the past 20 minutes.

"You know," he said, "even after all we've been through, I still don't know your first name."

DS Kirby laughed, but Paul noted he avoided eye contact – and his cheeks reddened in embarrassment.

"You can just call me Kirby," he replied. "Everyone does."

"Even your sister?"

"Even my sister."

Paul bit down on his toast. If Kirby was embarrassed about his given name, then he wasn't going to push it.

"It's ... incredible," Kirby said after a moment. "Absolutely incredible. I just ... I don't know what to say."

"You could say you believe me," Paul replied. "Unless you think I'm full of crap, of course. In which case, don't say anything."

Kirby laughed again, and Paul relaxed. He had been worried about Kirby's reaction, but he deserved to know everything; if Paul had held anything back, he felt he would have been dishonouring the memories of everyone who had died.

The detective shook his head. "No, I don't think you're full of crap. I'm the one with the dead sister who still talks to me, remember?"

"Yeah. I was going to ask about that – do you still hear from her, inside ... you know ..."

"Inside my head?" Kirby rolled his eyes. "Yeah. Yeah, I do. I can't shut her up."

He flinched for a moment, then rubbed his temple as his eyes unfocused ... and then refocused on Paul. "Luckily for me, I've got an off-switch."

Paul smiled in understanding, and Kirby hesitated, clearly dying to ask a question but unsure whether it would be polite.

"Go on," Paul said with an amused sigh. "Ask it. You know you want to."

Kirby's words came out in a rush. "What about Lucifer? Is he still in your head?"

"Yes, he's still there." Paul shrugged. "He's a part of who I am ... or I'm a part of who *he* is. I'm not really sure how the physics of it all work."

"Do physics actually apply in this situation?"

Paul hesitated. "Good point," he conceded. "I don't think I can answer that question. At least, not without some advanced degree of some kind." He smiled, and saw the naked curiosity still on Kirby's face. "I ... He's still in there, at the back of my mind. If I concentrate, I can hear a snippet of a thought or ... stream of consciousness, I guess."

"But I assumed, after all this, he'd wanted to get out, experience freedom – I mean, if Satan was able to do it with Joseph, then couldn't he do something similar? I mean, no offense, but I'm sure he'd be powerful enough to just take over."

"Yeah, he could do it if he wanted," Paul conceded. "I won't pretend it was easy, but we came to an agreement that works for both of us."

"Is that where you've been for the last four days?" Kirby asked. "Because I have to admit ... I started to fear the worse when I couldn't find you. It was as if you disappeared off the face of the -"

He stopped and grimaced at the awful pun he had been about to make. They ate in companionable silence for a moment, giving Paul a chance to think. He had been surprised to learn that four days had passed since his journey to heaven.

It didn't feel that long, Paul thought. *It just felt like hours. How could everything in my life change so much in just a matter of hours? I wish I had Joseph here to talk to about it.*

He looked up as a sudden change in the ambient noise level of the cafe registered in his brain; it had all stopped; everyone had frozen in place. The waiter was cleaning a glass, the customers were mid-conversation ... Kirby had a forkful of hash brown half-way to his mouth.

"Hello, mate. How's it going?"

Paul turned, and relaxed instantly. "I was just thinking about you," he said. He frowned. "Where are the wings?"

Joseph shrugged. "I just thought it would be less ... weird this way."

Paul looked at him closely; it was just like the old days. Joseph was dressed in exactly what he had been wearing – a blue v-neck shirt and black jeans, with no trace of Satan's angelic wings.

"I don't know," Paul replied, casually retaking his seat. "I got used to them."

Joseph ignored him, and quickly glanced round the cafe with a disappointed air.

"I never really liked it here," he confessed. "I always preferred the Belgium Bar."

With no warning they were sat outside the Belgium Bar, at their usual table, a cider in front of Joseph and a glass of red wine in front of Paul.

"Jesus Christ!" Paul unthinkingly exclaimed.

"No need to be quite so blasphemous," Joseph said lightly. He took a sip of his cider, and closed his eyes in a look approaching rapture. "Nothing quite like this upstairs."

Paul still hadn't recovered from Joseph's sudden trick. "A bit more notice next time would be appreciated, mate!"

"Sorry – just really fancied a cider. Try the wine."

"It's half nine in the morning."

Joseph shrugged. "Time's a different concept to me now, Paul ... and I don't like to be the only one with a drink."

Paul gave him a hard glare, but his best friend seemed immune to it – or was just deliberately ignoring him. Sighing, Paul gave up and tried the wine.

"Mmm," he said with a smack of his lips, "Bordeaux, south-lying regions. A 97 or 98, I reckon."

"How do you do that?" Joseph demanded. "I'm part-*angel*, for god's sakes, and I can't tell what it is."

Shrugging, Paul put down his wine glass and stared thoughtfully into it. "At least I know I'm still better than you at something."

He hadn't meant it to sound anything other than ironic, but it sounded hollow to his ears. With a sigh, he looked back up at his friend.

"Sorry," he said truthfully. "I guess I'm having a bit of trouble adjusting."

Joseph nodded. "I'd be more surprised if you were completely fine with it. The Joseph part of me is still having problems with it. I've spent almost all my life being a professional sceptic – now I'm a bloody angel!"

Paul chewed his lip for a moment, then caught Joseph's eye. They both began laughing in the same moment; at the very least, they still shared their ability to make each other laugh over things that really *weren't* that funny.

"What's it like up there?" Paul asked. "I can't imagine there's much of a frame of reference, is there?"

"You could say that," Joseph answered. "Yeah, it's ... weird. I've got all of Joseph's memories and all of Satan's in my head, and they're still settling down. I'm still Joseph, your friend ... and I'm still Satan, Lucifer's friend. It's difficult to explain. I ... yeah," he finished lamely.

Paul hesitated, then ploughed ahead with what he was going to say. "You could still come back, you know," he said. "I haven't called your boss or your family yet, I ... I haven't been able to face it," he added guiltily. "I was going to do it, I swear, but I just ... well ..."

Embarrassed, he couldn't quite finish his sentence. Joseph smiled, and it wasn't quite the smile his friend remembered; it had more wisdom behind it.

Satan's wisdom, he realised. Paul surprised himself by accepting it more readily than he had thought he would be able to. *You're still my friend, no matter what.*

Joseph sighed. "I wish I could, Paul ... but how can I? I've killed someone. Yeah, Metatron was evil, and she killed Lauren ... but ..."

He leaned forward, laying his hands flat out on the table. "I *killed* an angel, Paul. I've become half-angel myself, and found the power to *kill* Metatron! How can I come back to my life after that? I'm not that person any more, I'm ... different."

"Better?"

"No ... just different. I'll never be better ... I wouldn't allow myself to think like that. I just need to figure out what I am... now I've got this power, I need to learn how to use it."

Paul opened his mouth, and then stopped, a thoughtful expression on his face. He picked up his wine and took a sip. Joseph leaned back, picked up his cider, then put it down again, distracted.

Normally, they would watch the world go by; see the comings and goings of people and watch as they went about their lives. Of course, today was different. As it was in Beaches, people were frozen in position; at tables, in the street overlooking the harbour, frozen in mid-conversation.

Paul sighed. "It's not really the same."

"True." Joseph shrugged. "I'd just rather not be seen right now."

"Couldn't you put on a different face or something? You managed to hide your wings -"

Joseph lifted his eyebrows. "I'm not getting the wings out."

"Damn."

They were silent for a minute longer, then Paul glanced over at his friend.

"So ... there's something that's been bothering me," he said. "I've been trying to work it out, but I can't."

Joseph sat forward, intrigued. "What?"

Paul fiddled with his wine glass as he spoke.

"Metatron wanted to find me because she had this ... this desire to find out if her eldest son was somehow going to finally measure up to her expectations. But ... when she found me, she -" He sighed. "She didn't *do* anything. Just met me for breakfast with Rick, and then didn't follow it up. I don't get it, mate. What could she have learnt in just an hour?"

Joseph shrugged. "Enough," he replied.

"What do you mean?"

"Metatron felt let down by both her sons," Joseph said. "Gabriel kept his distance from her ... who could blame him after what she did? She systematically tortured him until he broke. Metatron knew that relationship could never be repaired." He sighed. "Metatron's biggest downfall was her own arrogance – I think that stems from her human upbringing."

Paul leaned forward. "So that was true?" he asked. "She *was* human?"

"Once, a long time ago," Joseph replied. "The Almighty ... well, he fell in love with her. When she died ... for the first and only time, he gave her spirit the opportunity to become an angel, and she grabbed it with both hands. The Almighty thought it would be the start of the union between the two realms, but Metatron resisted. As soon as she was an angel, she had no interest in revisiting her past."

Paul suddenly understood. "But she couldn't completely shed her human ... feelings?"

"She still wanted at least one of her children to stand by her side, and thought that, with you being in human form, you'd be more ... pliable." He smiled. "If I remember, your meeting with her didn't exactly go well?"

Paul shook his head. "Not exactly," he replied. "I ended up walking out."

Joseph spread his hands expansively, as if that proved his point.

"She really was evil, wasn't she?"

"Yep. Now can you see why I can't go back to being just human, after what I did to her?"

"... Yeah."

Paul bit his lip. He remembered, being there in Heaven and crying over Lauren's body. The Almighty's eyes were fully of sorrow; Gabriel, Lauren and Beelzebub were all dead, and he hadn't been able to help them. He had been briefly tempted to join Joseph in Heaven and explore the cosmos.

I can't, he thought. *There are still things I need to do on Earth. I still want to ... contribute something.*

He could still feel Lucifer's presence at the back of his mind, and he welcomed it. Lucifer was intrigued by humans, to try and understand what his Father had seen in them. When Paul eventually grew old ... well, that was a thought for then, not for now.

It had almost been a physical ache when Joseph, his best friend and staunchest ally, had chosen to stay. Paul understood why now, and respected it ... but it still hurt to know that he wouldn't be able to see his friend in the same way anymore.

"I have to go now, Paul."

Paul swallowed. "Now?" he asked.

"Yeah, now."

They stared at each other awkwardly for a moment, then hugged each other tight. Joseph couldn't help but laugh as he felt Paul's hands pat his shoulder blades, as if looking for the stumps of wings.

"Stop it!" he protested.

Their friendship had always been just understood, something that never needed to be expressed, and they weren't about to change the habit of a lifetime now. They didn't *need* to tell each other how much they meant to each other.

Paul thought of one last thing. "Mate ... what happened to Lauren?" he asked. "Her ... spirit, I mean? Will she live in the spirit world, like Kirby's sister?"

Joseph shrugged. "I'm still learning, I'll be honest with you," he confessed. "The spirit world is a closed book to me. I choose to ... believe she's there, or at least the part I thought of as my sister. The angelic part – Beelzebub ..." He sighed. "I just ... don't know."

Paul accepted his friend's explanation; he knew that there would be a sharp learning curve. His angelic side had been submerged for two millennia – it would take time for both halves to find a balance within themselves, and sort through all their memories.

Paul watched as a dot of pure, white light appear in mid-air and stretch itself down all the way to the ground. The light then widened to make an oval opening, much like an eye, but full of bright white light.

Joseph caught Paul's eye, and they nodded to each other. The half-angel, half-man turned and stepped through into the white light beyond.

Paul watched him go, with a knot of sadness deep inside his stomach; but also a sense of relief. He knew that was where Joseph now belonged, and needed to be, and here – on Earth – was where *Paul* needed to be.

He saw Joseph hesitate and turn his head ... and the part of shirt around his shoulders melted away. Two stubs grew rapidly from his shoulder blades and then quickly formed into full, angelic wings.

Paul was still laughing as the white light closed behind his best friend, and he found himself back in Beaches cafe, sat opposite Kirby. The detective bit down on his hash brown in surprise.

"What?" he asked. "What are you laughing at?"

Paul opened his mouth to explain – then closed it again and shook his head, knowing that Kirby wouldn't understand.

"Kirby, what's your first name?"

The detective swallowed his coffee and sighed; he seemed to know that there was no way out of it.

"I was named after my grandfather," he said. "He was French. My first name is Camille. In France," he added hurriedly, "it's a man's name."

Paul nodded. For some reason, he didn't find it as funny as he had expected.

"Want me to still call you Kirby?"

"God yes."

Paul sat back in his seat and smiled. Kirby watched him carefully, and turned his head thoughtfully to one side.

"What are you thinking about?"

Paul hesitated. There had been so much death over the past week; Adam Wild, Dr Tempest, Rick, Gabriel ... Lauren. They were his friends, and as near he would get to family. He would always grieve for them, but also knew that he couldn't let that grief stop him from living his life.

I owe them that, he thought. *They died for me. I won't allow their deaths to be in vain. I need to live my life for them.*

He knew, in his heart of hearts, that Joseph and the Almighty understood that, and that one day he would see them again ... in one form or another.

As an afterthought, he found himself thinking about Christina, the beautiful nurse from the hospital, and how he would very much like to see her again sometime.

"Paul?" Kirby asked again. "What are you thinking about?"

Paul smiled. "Life."

Biography

Matthew Munson lives in the south-east of England, a thirty second walk from the sea and not far from where he was born. After 30 years, he still hasn't left .

His life revolves around his friends, family and writing – oh, and Twitter, where he lurks as @mnwjm1981.

He is learning British Sign Language and will be starting Level Two at the same time this book is published. Matthew is a passionate advocate of deaf awareness and dyspraxia & autism studies - and often writes about these issues over at his blog, as well as more general musings about life, the universe and everything.

Now Fall From Grace is published, Matthew will be jumping feet-first into his second novel ... after having a few days off to consume his weight in chocolate to celebrate.

Author Website: http://www.matthewmunson.co.uk

Author Photo by Lucy Lindsell:
http://theartofindigo.com

Lightning Source UK Ltd.
Milton Keynes UK
UKOW050904120212

187155UK00001B/4/P